Jess Mey

GRACE & JO HAVE NEVER SOLVED A MURDER

DATURA

DATURA BOOKS
An imprint of Watkins Media Ltd

Unit 11, Shepperton House
89-93 Shepperton Road
London N1 3DF
UK

daturabooks.com
No Three Rules

A Datura Books paperback original, 2026

Edited by Ella Chappell
Cover by Eleri Stanton
Set in Meridien

ISBN 978 1 91741 530 9
Ebook ISBN 978 1 91741 531 6

Printed and bound in the United Kingdom by CPI Group (UK) Ltd, Croydon CR0 4YY

The manufacturer's authorised representative in the EU for product safety is eucomply OÜ – Pärnu mnt 139b-14, 11317 Tallinn, Estonia,
hello@eucompliancepartner.com; www.eucompliancepartner.com

9 8 7 6 5 4 3 2 1

FSC www.fsc.org MIX Paper | Supporting responsible forestry FSC® C013604

To Mike, Max, and Charlotte. The best pages in my story have you all over them.

And to every late-diagnosed woman with ADHD who wonders if she has enough focus to reach her dreams: You're holding mine in your hands. (Unless you're an audiobook girlie.)

Chapter 1

Everything Grace Anderson knew about murder, she learned against her will.

And like many uncomfortable truths, this knowledge tended to work its way into everyday life. While grocery shopping, she'd remember Alaska had one of the highest rates of serial killers per capita in the United States. In the middle of a massage, just as the therapist found that knot in her back, she remembered summer was the season when most murders occurred.

So it wasn't odd that when she saw a barista trip over the outstretched leg of a coworker while waiting for her coffee that morning, her brain went straight to death.

Workplace homicides account for a small number of murders. It's much more likely to be the spouse.

She couldn't have known it was foreshadowing.

Her cousin Maya's fascination with true crime started decades before she ever heard the phrase "true crime." Crimes of passion had a particular hold on her, so much that Maya's mom took her to a therapist once when she was worried the obsession was abnormal. She was assured, after being handed a bill for $300, that Maya was a mentally, emotionally, and physically healthy girl who happened to love a good horror story. Eventually, Maya's obsession paid off – she was a librarian now.

"Grace?" a woman called from behind the counter. Her hair was the same hot pink shade as her lipstick. Grace approached, giving the halfhearted smile of a person who hadn't yet had enough caffeine for human interaction.

The barista slid a cardboard carrier forward, two drinks inside. She held up a small pastry bag. "You want a raspberry scone? Someone ordered it by accident."

Not one to turn down free pastries, Grace nodded and thanked the neon-haired woman before slipping a few bills into the tip jar and grabbing her order. The scone was the latest in a string of events that led Grace to feel, intuitively, today would be a good day.

She'd woken up before her alarm. Her messy brown curls were somehow coaxed into a flattering position without her needing to rewash, apply dry shampoo, or throw her hair into a high bun, signaling she'd given up on it. The outfit she set out last night still looked good this morning, a floral blouse with a pair of yoga pants cosplaying as dress slacks. Grace felt there was something empowering about a pair of pants that looked office-appropriate but would allow you to do a split. You know, in an emergency.

Every light on her way to the studio was green, and when she put her playlist on shuffle, the first song to play was "Flavor of the Weak" by American Hi-Fi, a personal favorite. The last two months had been full of transitions, lasts and firsts, but she finally felt like her days were falling into a rhythm.

A downside to her job was that the studio space had no lot, so each day Grace had to battle it out for street parking or give up and park in a public lot a few blocks away. It wasn't a big deal in summer, but she wasn't looking forward to trudging through feet of snow for ten minutes in the bitter cold once winter hit. She would pick out a pair of cute snow boots to make the entire thing more bearable.

Philadelphia and its four distinct seasons were still new to Grace.

Miraculously, as she pulled onto the idyllic street that housed the studio, there was a spot right in front. It required her to begrudgingly parallel park, but the cars in front and behind her had graciously left enough space that she maneuvered it without much effort, only a short and shrill grinding sound as her wheel scraped the curb.

She straightened out, shifted into park, and hit the ignition. It was a relatively calm morning in the neighborhood. Several small tables were set up outside the cafe across the street, two occupied with pairs lazily sipping their drinks. In recent days, the air felt like summer and flower bushes were in full bloom, despite the threat of the impending autumn. Today was an exception, sunny with a chill in the air that required a light jacket. Something was mesmerizing about the way the light shone through the leaves on the trees, highlighting the veins fueling them. The trees themselves were spaced evenly down the street, an intricately planned pop of nature. The street looked like it could be on the cover of *Small Town Life* magazine.

On the right side were two-story stone buildings, several sporting plaques designating them historical sites. On the left side, where the studio was, it was more like a strip mall, with single stories attached five at a time. The stone facade was made to match the much older buildings across the street, and they'd done a pretty good job at making them seem like matching sets.

Grace glanced at the drinks in the carrier perched precariously in the passenger seat of her truck. She believed a coffee order could tell you a lot about someone. Garrett's macchiato said he was unfussy and straightforward. Her sweet cream cold brew said she was an agreeable people pleaser. It was September 6th and she'd been working for Garrett Baros for exactly a month, to the day. She was still getting a handle on him. She still had a note in her phone with his coffee order in it, in case she forgot.

Grace checked her makeup in her visor mirror, grabbed the coffee and her bag, slipping the scone in its wax paper into it as she climbed out of the truck. The front door was already unlocked, a sign Garrett was already here, as usual. He'd given her a key, but she hadn't had to use it yet. Inside, she set the cardboard drink carrier on her desk and hung up her jacket and bag on a hook behind her, turned on her laptop to take a look at the time, then slipped Garrett's drink from the carrier.

She'd expected to find him standing at his easel, staring at a blank canvas thoughtfully or focused so hard on capturing the exact curve of a man's nose that he didn't hear her come in. They'd recently gotten word that Garrett had been chosen as a featured artist at the Institute of Contemporary Art downtown. He'd been hard at work putting his spin on the portraits of Philadelphia-born artists who had paved his way.

But the studio was dark.

Each little stroke of luck before nine am had Grace feeling confident and secure in her decisions. She'd upturned her entire life to come here, with no real plan in place, but somehow she stuck the landing. She liked where she lived, what she did, and the independence that came with being thousands of miles from her parents. Life was good. She was *making* something of herself. It felt like she'd finally hacked the system.

Then at 9:02, she walked through Garrett's open office door and saw him slumped over his desk, his head resting in a pool of vomit.

She froze for a moment, blinking like it might undo what she was seeing, like the shake of an Etch-A-Sketch. Slowly, each muscle in her body started to tense as she took a few cautious steps along the side of his desk to get a good look at his face, which was slack, eyes open. She didn't need to check for a pulse to know he was already gone.

So much for trusting her intuition.

Chapter 2

The rapid flash of red and blue lights assaulted Grace's eyes as two blurry figures approached her.

I should have stayed in Florida, she thought.

She'd considered telling the first responders not to hurry, that there was nothing they could do to save him. But that sounded *insane*, right? *Please obey all traffic laws on your way to this emergency, it's already a lost cause.*

She'd looked for the comforting movement of breath at Garrett's back, the slow rise and fall of his shoulders. But it never came. His face was discolored, his skin cold to the touch when she placed her hand on his to be sure.

She didn't remember calling 911. Maybe she'd asked Siri to do it. One moment, she was staring at Garrett's body, unable to comprehend what was happening in front of her; then suddenly she had her phone in her hand, a woman's voice on the other end calm and even to balance the chaos sweeping through Grace's mind.

She'd remembered the office's address without looking it up, which would have been a great milestone out of context. Now there was no one to tell.

The 911 operator stayed on the phone while they waited for the police. Her proximity to the body made her skin crawl, so Grace had stepped outside, flinging the door open so briskly she'd had to check if the door handle had damaged the glass as they collided. No damage done. Not to the glass, at least. Grace's faith in the world, on the other hand, was fractured. She flopped down in a heap on a bench.

The operator's voice in her head sounded tinny, far away. "It's going to be OK, honey. Help is coming."

Easy for you to say. You didn't find your boss dead. Yours is probably sitting in his office, nursing a bagel and buying Bitcoin.

Garrett was a healthy forty-year-old man, and from Grace's understanding, it wasn't common for someone so young and fit to keel over and die. Based on the pile of vomit on the desk, common sense was telling her he'd either choked or... *could someone have poisoned him?* She couldn't remember what had been on his desk. Was there a cup? Any food? Drugs were a possibility, especially since you never knew what anyone did once they left the office. But Garrett was focused, alert, and friendly, never giving her the impression he was under the influence of anything beyond creativity and his go-to macchiato.

She left the office around 5:45 pm last night. Did he leave shortly after, go home to his wife? Or had he been there all night?

At some point, she'd heard the sirens; two police cars and an ambulance screeched to a halt in front of the studio, blocking traffic. Already, bystanders were gawking at the scene, someone even braving to snap a picture but not remembering to turn the flash off. *Have some tact, jerk,* Grace thought to herself.

The EMTs held back as the two police officers approached her. One was an older man with a stately handlebar mustache. The other seemed to be around Grace's age. He had kind eyes and brown hair shaved close to his head. He gave her a sweet smile as they approached.

"Hi there, are you Ms Anderson? I'm Officer Cordon."

Grace nodded, not bothering to get off the bench. The paint was peeling, and she'd found the perfect spot to chip away at it.

"OK, Ms Anderson. We got a report that you've found a body. Would you mind pointing my colleague and our friends here in the right direction so we can start to check things out?"

The second officer gave a polite nod as Grace turned her upper body to face the studio. She lifted a hand to point toward Garrett's office through the glass. "He's in there. He's sitting at his desk."

"Did you touch anything in the office? Since you found him, I mean?" asked Mustache.

"I touched his hand," Grace murmured, "to make sure he was… you know, gone."

Mustache seemed satisfied with this answer, and he motioned for the EMTs to follow him into the studio. Officer Cordon sat with Grace on the bench. She hadn't noticed the tablet in his hand, which he opened to an official-looking notes app. When he spoke, his tone was gentle but firm. He certainly looked like a cop, but he sounded like he should narrate children's books.

"You mind if I ask you a few questions, Ms Anderson?"

She glanced over at him, getting her first good look, and immediately regretted it. He was handsome. Maybe not a conventional Brad Pitt type, but he had a strong jaw, deep brown eyes, and a symmetrical face, which everyone knows is the cornerstone of attractiveness. It made her keenly aware of her blotchy complexion, the snot dripping at the bottom of her nose, and the strong chance her mascara was smeared from her forehead to chin like war paint.

"You can call me Grace. I'd prefer that." She sniffed, hoping to suck up some evidence of her breakdown.

"Grace then." That smile again. "What time did you arrive at the office this morning? And did you notice anything odd before finding the body? Any signs of a break-in?"

Grace reached for her phone to check the time. 9:22 am.

"I got here at 9:02 and the door was unlocked. I assumed Garrett had already arrived. I set my stuff down, took a quick look at my computer, and then I went to take Garrett his coffee and saw the body. I called right away. Well, as soon as I was calm enough for the operator to understand me. And yeah, then you showed up about fifteen minutes later. Now we're here. No signs of a break-in. Everything seems to be accounted for."

Officer Cordon took some notes, then continued.

"Did Mr Baros say anything about someone coming to the studio last night or this morning? Was he expecting anyone?"

Grace thought back to the night before. She'd been packing up her things and walked over to where Garrett was painting to ask if he needed anything before she left. He hadn't even looked at her but told her no thank you, he was almost done with this painting and had everything he needed. She offered to order him delivery, but he told her he had dinner in the mini fridge in his office. She relayed all this to Officer Cordon and finished with, "Nothing out of the ordinary, and no mention of having anyone coming to meet him."

Officer Cordon nodded. More notes.

"You said he was painting. I assume in the studio area?"

Grace nodded.

"And where would he have put the painting if he finished it?" Officer Cordon looked into the studio, shading his eyes from the sun. There was a clear view of Garrett's easel, which sat empty.

Grace tensed. Garrett would have left the painting there to dry overnight.

"He displays all his paintings right away. So if it wasn't on the easel, it should be on the wall. Occasionally, he'd take a piece home, but he was working on something for an exhibit. He wouldn't have taken it to the museum already. That was on my list of things to do."

Officer Cordon asked her to come inside with him. They walked through the lobby and into the studio, standing in front of the empty easel. He motioned to the room. "You see the painting he was working on?"

It had been a portrait of a man, with dark skin and piercing eyes. Garrett had been painting it in sepia tones, like an old photograph. She looked, expecting to notice it like a friend in a crowd.

"It's not here. I don't see it."

Officer Cordon added to his notes, then turned to Grace with a strained smile. To her right, she could hear Mustache shuffling around in the office. She assumed he was taking photos, looking for clues, dusting for fingerprints: all standard moves in the documentaries Maya forced her to watch. But she couldn't bring herself to look. Bile churned in her stomach – she never did get to eat her scone. It was still wrapped in wax paper in her bag behind her desk. She didn't want to be here anymore. She wanted to be anywhere else, eating baked goods.

"Would you mind taking a ride with me down to the station to answer a few more questions?"

Suddenly, staying here sounded pretty good.

* * *

The interrogation room (Grace assumed this was not the official title, but she forgot to read the plaque next to the door on her way in) looked exactly like police stations were portrayed on TV. White cinderblock walls with no windows. A two-way mirror. A metal table anchored to the floor, with two chairs and another placed in the corner in case the officer needed some backup, she supposed.

The ride had been a quick one, but Grace's anxiety pulsed in her throat every second she was in the back seat. She'd never so much as stolen candy from a convenience store; she never envisioned sitting in the back of a police car without her dad in the driver's seat, playing along in an elaborate game of cops and robbers.

Officer Cordon walked into the cinderblock room, sat across from Grace, and smiled. He set a plastic cup in front of her, filled with water, and then cleared his throat. In close quarters she could smell his cologne.

"So I have a few questions I need to ask you about Mr Baros. Shouldn't take too long, and then you can get on your way."

Grace nodded.

"Before we start though, I do want to let you know that, from what we've seen at the crime scene, we are investigating this as a suspicious death. We won't know for sure until we have all the details, including the autopsy, but it doesn't seem like an overdose."

Suspicious death was a family-friendly way to say murder. A shiver slid down her spine, boomeranging back up for special effect. A murderer had been in the studio last night, standing near her desk. Maybe they'd even seen her computer background, a screenshot of that viral Pedro Pascal meme where he was smiling at Nicolas Cage. And the only thing that kept her from crossing paths with a murderer was, what, a few hours? How long had she been gone when they showed up to kill Garrett?

"Any information you can give us could be a huge help," said Officer Cordon, his voice still soft despite the jarring change of scenery.

Grace cleared her throat. "So I'm not being arrested?"

Officer Cordon laughed. "Not unless you give some wild answers. Since you were the one who discovered the body, and since you've spent a fair amount of time with him over the last..." He paused to check some notes in a file in front of him. "...month... we want to make sure we get anything from you we can."

Grace nodded, her hands pulling at a loose thread on the hem of her cardigan. "You'd think I'd have a better understanding of how everything happens. My dad was a police officer."

Officer Cordon lit up a bit at this. "Oh yeah? He retired now?"

"For a few years, yeah. Now most of his interactions with the law are from old episodes of *Cops*. He likes to tell my mom what he would have done differently."

A sound somewhere between a wheeze and a snort (a whort?) came from Officer Cordon's nose and/or mouth. He cleared his throat as he pulled himself together. "It's a common pastime in this line of work. I've dabbled in my fair share of crime TV. But, uh, shall we get started?"

Grace nodded, relaxing slightly having seen the officer's awkward side.

"Great. So first off, do you have any idea who would want to harm Mr Baros?"

Grace thought she sensed movement on the other side of the two-way mirror.

"Honestly, no. Most of the time at the office, it was just us. I'd be in and out running his errands, but he spent a lot of time in his studio. The only guests we ever got were a friend of Garrett's who happened to be in town and the FedEx guy."

Officer Cordon nodded and jotted something down in his file.

"Did you ever meet Mr Baros's wife?"

Grace had seen photos of her. Once she knew Garrett's name and had the job offer, she went down the rabbit hole of finding out who he and his muse of a wife were. She'd found their Wikipedia pages but skipped over them in favor of an architectural magazine feature on their three-million-dollar mansion. It was more palatable to look at photos of the rich than to read their stories replete with trust funds and generational wealth. The main picture was Josephine lounging on a chair poolside as Garrett worked at an easel. She wondered if Jo, as Garrett called her, knew her husband was dead.

"No. I've spoken to her. A few times she called the office line if she couldn't get Garrett on his cell. But most of the time she called him directly."

"Did she call often?"

"Once, maybe twice a day, from what I overheard." Grace's breath caught in her throat. Did she just say she'd been listening in on a dead man's conversation? "Uh, I uh," she laughed nervously as she tucked a strand of hair behind her ear, "I didn't listen to his conversations on purpose. The studio has those big doors that open up into the lobby. Most of the time, Garrett worked with the doors open."

Maybe Grace was making it up, but Officer Cordon's gaze on her felt warm, friendly. He wasn't looking at her like a possible murderer, or even someone who had anything to hide. Still, Grace could feel her heart thundering from nerves, especially since she had no idea how many people were watching her on the other side of the glass.

"I'm sorry," she said. "This is my first interrogation."

Officer Cordon snorted softly and shook his head. "Not an interrogation. We call them interviews. It's you and me, talking." He paused, taking in the room. "In a very well-lit and slightly depressing setting."

Grace's turn to laugh.

"I'll be honest, I have no reason to suspect you of anything. We plan to confirm your location last night and this morning with video footage from the camera outside your apartment building, as well as the coffee shop you told us you visited. I have no reason to believe you're lying. And I'm sorry you're wrapped up in all this. It must have been terrible to find the body."

Grace wasn't sure she'd even begun to process it. Her own body was still buzzing from the shock of it all. But Officer Cordon was a police officer, not a therapist, so she simply said, "Thank you."

Officer Cordon cleared his throat again. Was he nervous, too? "Uh, a less fun question for you." None of the other questions felt *fun* to Grace, but sure. "Did you have any reason to believe Garrett was having an affair?"

Grace felt her face twist into something between confusion and discomfort. She understood why he was asking, of course. You always look at the spouse first, and there's often a big, scandalous motive. An affair, abuse, a chance to cash in on a life insurance policy – Maya had talked her ear off about all of them. She'd never met Jo in person and had no idea if she was capable of murder, but she'd also never seen anything that made her think Garrett was straying from his marriage.

"No." Grace tried to configure her face to look calm but could feel that she was failing. "He talked about Mrs Baros all the time. They sounded – stable? In love? No other woman ever came into the office and there were few times he left the office during the day. I don't even know when he would have time to have an affair, he was always working."

The corner of Cordon's mouth shot up at her answer, like he'd been hoping Garrett wasn't a cheater. Grace wondered if police officers took bets on cases in an attempt to make them more digestible; if they tried to guess the odds that someone was hooking up with the housekeeper or something along those lines. Cordon nodded as he added more details to his file.

"Did you notice anything off about Garrett in the past week or so? I know you haven't known him long enough to get a baseline, but anything that seemed like abnormal behavior?"

The days and weeks she'd spent with Garrett flashed through her mind.

"Not really. He seemed stressed a lot, but we've been trying to get him a spot in a temporary exhibit in the city. He said the placement would position him as a 'serious' artist. The pieces he was working on all day, every day, were for that. We got word last week that he got the spot, so the stress about getting it turned into stress about filling it."

"We had easy access to security cameras, so our guy has already started reviewing the tapes. From what he's seen so far – though there is a section where the video cuts out – it seems like Garrett may have spent the night at the office. Did he do this regularly?"

Grace was becoming hyper-aware of how little she knew the victim.

"It's hard for me to say. He always arrived before me and was still there when I left, except for one or two times when he left at the same time as me to head to dinners."

Cordon was nodding. "And who were these dinners with?"

"One was with his mother and brother. They were visiting and he wanted to take them somewhere nice. He had me book some Italian restaurant. And, uh, the other one was with another artist. I'd need to check the calendar for his name. It was one of my first days at the job, I don't remember all the details."

"Not necessary. We have your work computer, and Garrett's. We'll be looking at the calendar. But thanks for the tip, I'll want to talk with the three of them. Uh, let's see. Were you aware of anything unusual happening with Garrett's financial situation?"

Grace considered. "Garrett didn't say anything," she said. And in what was one of the most embarrassing moments of her life, her stomach grumbled so loud she was sure the sound could be heard through the cinderblock walls.

"Ohmygosh, I am so sorry," she said, cheeks bursting with color.

Cordon laughed, again. He sincerely seemed to be enjoying himself.

"I promise, it happens. You need a donut or something?"

"Wow, so the stereotype is true."

"You caught us."

Grace could feel her posture slip, her body's attempt at making her look as small as possible, shrinking until she could fit down a storm drain and start a new life in the sewer, putting all this behind her. "If it's not too much... I had this scone in my bag. I would have eaten it at my desk but, you know, I got to work and my boss was dead and I lost my appetite."

"Actually," Cordon said, standing up from the table, "I'm pretty much done for now. I'm sure I'll have more questions once we get the case together, but as of right now, I'd say you're free to go eat your scone." Grace felt a little flutter as Cordon smiled at her, which then prompted guilt to bubble up in her core. Her boss was dead, this was no time to be flirting with some cute cop.

Grace stood up as well, and Cordon handed her a business card. "Give me a call if you think of anything else. Texting is fine as well. Just remember, anything you say is part of our investigation."

She held the card in her hand briefly before putting it in her wallet. *Seriously, minus the dead body, this would have been such a good day.*

Chapter 3

Mustache's taste in music was as contentious as his taste in facial hair. During the short drive back to Grace's truck, his Spotify playlist served a blend of early 2000s Christian pop, Michael Bublé, and a band called Gatecreeper who apparently played a fusion of "death metal and metalcore" according to the quick search Grace did on some lyrics. He seemed like a good man and a competent cop, so she didn't feel the need to give an amateur psych evaluation based on one playlist. Maybe death metal helped him clear his head after a rough day at the office. Maybe Switchfoot brought back happy memories of his youth.

Oh, and his name was Officer Clark. *Mustache Clark,* Grace thought to herself.

He pulled up next to her truck, and she thanked him, especially for letting her sit in the front. It was a much calmer ride when she wasn't trying to google lawyers and death metal lyrics while avoiding car sickness. He left her with a warning to stay safe, and as she closed the door and rifled in her bag for her key fob, she could feel the familiar prickles of a panic attack. She'd had her first one when she was twelve and ended up passing out in the middle of a spring chorus concert. The theme was Broadway musical numbers, and she still felt woozy when she heard any song from *A Chorus Line*.

Her hand slid along smooth plastic, then distinctive buttons. She pressed the largest one and the truck beeped, headlights flashing. She climbed in, slammed and locked the door, then rested her head on the steering wheel.

She'd been waiting for this moment. She'd masked her panic all morning, trying to be helpful to the investigation, trying to seem like a woman who could stay in control when faced with danger. But now that she was alone with her thoughts, the same one was spinning around and around: a murderer had walked past her desk last night. She could feel the blood draining from her face.

How had she gone from free scones and perfect hair to being questioned about a murder? To top it off, the person who signed her paychecks was currently being autopsied, which meant she was unemployed.

She looked at the clock on her dash: two pm. Everything had fallen apart in a matter of hours.

As far as Tuesdays went, this one was total bullshit.

This was supposed to be a fresh start, a chance to finally make something of herself. This was going to be the place where she accomplished everything she'd been unable to do in Florida.

Grace had never considered herself beautiful, so it wasn't a shock to her that she didn't have all the things she felt came easily to beautiful people. A fresh thirty, her last serious relationship ended more than two years ago. Her social calendar was barren. Her last job, working as an administrator for her mother, a relatively successful accountant, was not even remotely luxurious. Back in Florida, she'd lived in her parents' small but detached guest house, paying no rent. An easy, empty life.

One she hadn't been able to accept any longer.

Within a week, Grace had let her parents know she would be moving out of state, picked a modest apartment in the suburbs of Philadelphia, sight unseen, and contacted a temp agency to secure a job before she made the move. Her contact at the temp agency, Hannah, had seemed flighty and distracted during their first phone call. She asked the same questions several times. At one point, she called Grace "Faith." So Grace was surprised at how fast she'd lined up a job. Grace had read the email from Hannah over and over again, making sure it was meant for her. She had no experience in the art world beyond a freshman art history class, and yet here was her name on an email saying she was going to be working as the assistant to portrait artist Garrett Baros.

The opinions on Grace's relocation were not mixed. Almost no one understood why you'd abandon your convenient living situation twenty minutes north of the happiest place on earth and relocate to… Pennsylvania. Did she know they got snow there? That its largest theme park didn't even have a castle, just a shit load of chocolate? Face after confused face contorted as they asked her, "Why there?"

Grace understood it was common for Northerners to flee to Florida's shores in order to *FEEL SOMETHING* in the dead of winter, but rarely did you hear of someone fleeing Florida for cheesesteaks and Southeastern Pennsylvania Transportation Authority, aka SEPTA, access. But what the doubters didn't know was that Florida had never felt like home, even though she'd been born there. Unrelenting sunshine gave her migraines. The beach was a sensory nightmare, involving her finding sand in crevices even after multiple showers. She wasn't a theme park person. She threw up on roller coasters. Heck, she threw up on children's rides. Touring a chocolate factory sounded downright delightful. To Grace, Florida had felt more like purgatory than paradise.

As much as Grace felt like the anti-Florida spokeswoman, her parents were perfectly suited for it. Her mother, Trish, was lizardlike, requiring hours of direct sunlight in addition to food and water to help her survive. Her dad, John, was a huge history buff. When they'd decided to settle down in Florida, he was determined to become an expert in both state facts and theme-park-related minutiae. He'd retired from the police force a few years ago, but still worked two days a week, MCing bar trivia. Florida was perfect for her parents, and they deserved to live on a permanent vacation, ocean dips and Bahama mamas a part of the weekly grind.

Grace felt guilty leaving her parents. Especially her mother, who relied on her for so many aspects of her business. She'd helped her mother find her replacement before she left and had even taken on her training. The new hire's name was Emma, and she was happy to tell everyone she met that she spent all her weekends at the park, updating her followers as a semi-popular influencer who focused on sweet treats and alcoholic drinks. She was no Grace, but she'd do.

When Grace decided she needed to leave home, she thought of New England first. She pictured sitting in front of a fire, watching the snow fall outside as she devoured a book, cracking open lobster shells while wearing a fisherman's sweater, or grabbing drinks with friends at a local pub. She did, for a moment, consider making a bigger jump and heading to Portland (Oregon, not Maine). She didn't know who could possibly feel out of place in a city filled with beer, food trucks, bookshops, and picturesque mountains.

But the trouble with each of these places was that she didn't feel any specific tie to them. Sure, they were calling her name, keeping her interest as she browsed videos on social media each night. *Don't you want your pictures to look like this? Don't you want your life to feel like this?*

She did. She *really* wanted it to feel like... more.

Specifically, she wanted it to feel different than whatever this feeling was, keeping her up at night.

And then one day her mother asked her to grab something from the attic, and she stumbled upon her dad's old yearbooks. By the time her mom called up to ask if she was OK, the wheels were turning in her head. Philadelphia had bustling food and art scenes, plenty of walkable neighborhoods to explore, a personal connection to her family, and, most importantly, it wasn't in Florida.

"Philly's nothing like Florida. It's tough there sometimes. But you know what? The people have a passion I haven't seen anywhere since," her dad gushed about his hometown over dinner, a pot roast her mom had taken from Martha Stewart's latest TikTok. "It's not sunshine and rainbows, but it's a good place filled with important history. And it made me who I am today."

While Grace's dad was excited for all the possibilities Philly held for her, her mother thought the move was a guarantee she'd end up the subject of one of those documentaries Maya was always talking about.

"It needs to have a state-of-the-art security system, Grace. You can't take any chances in a big city," her mother had demanded as she slapped a hand down on the dining room table, a small wave surging on the surface of her tea.

Once Grace checked that off the list, her mother ran out of excuses to stop her from uprooting her life.

So, Grace made the move. She'd sold her compact car and upgraded to a truck with four-wheel drive, which allowed her to tow a small storage container of all her belongings on a daylong trip up north. When she saw the final exit, she felt what she assumed anyone on the Oregon Trail felt when they finally reached the bountiful land of the west: *Take that, dysentery, we made it.*

Of course, there was nowhere to park.

She ended up finding a spot blocks away from the apartment and suddenly wished she'd taken her parents up on their offer to fly up to help her move. She could carry all her stuff up a flight of stairs, but she hadn't anticipated walking a mile between every trip.

She hopped out to survey her parking job and gave it a solid five out of ten. The trailer was sticking out enough that cars would have to maneuver around it, but it wasn't going to stop traffic, which she deemed good enough. She would wait until a space opened up closer to bring her stuff in, so for now she grabbed a backpack full of necessities and a sleeping bag and started walking toward her new home.

She'd texted the landlord, Pete, to let him know she was there. He lived in one of the five other units of the building, which was both convenient and a major anxiety trigger. She would probably get help with issues quickly but also have to keep her TV at a respectable volume. When she met him to get her key, he seemed nice enough. He had dark hair and a beard her dad would feel the need to compliment because of his deeply rooted beard envy.

While Grace opted for a one-bedroom apartment, Pete lived in one of the building's two-bedroom units with his wife and two daughters. He promised to introduce her to the rest of her neighbors, but she was glad to hear him add "another time, of course."

Grace's first thought after she slipped the key into the lock and pushed open the creaky door was that while the apartment had looked much bigger online, it was much nicer in person. Since the listing photos had been taken, it seemed like Pete had put in new cabinets and updated all the appliances. The parquet flooring she'd fallen in love with online was still there and well maintained. The room smelled like lemon and dust, which filled Grace with a sense of fresh hope this might all work out.

Pete told her an older woman had lived there for more than a decade, and she only left when she was unable to take the stairs anymore. Grace had been surprised Pete agreed to the month-to-month contract she requested after having a longtime resident, but when she didn't balk at the surcharge he suggested, they came to an easy deal.

Grace went through the checklist her dad had given her for the first few moments she was in the apartment. She turned the kitchen and bathroom faucets on and off, checked that the front door lock was functional and the chain slid easily, then made sure every window could be opened and locked again. Satisfied with this quick sweep, she went to the bathroom, dug in her backpack for hand sanitizer, and unrolled her sleeping bag.

She stared up at the ceiling fan for a while, its chain holding a steady, calming beat like a metronome. By thirty, her mother had established her business, her father was a well-respected member of the police force, and together, they had her. Grace, in comparison, had anxiety and a resume about as long as a fortune cookie. She wasn't just looking for a good life, she was looking for something to pass down, even if it was just a story worth telling.

Grace shook herself from her daydream. She was still sitting in her truck and Garrett was still dead. That morning, this street felt like a safe haven for her. Hours ago, she would have told you she was getting to know her new boss pretty well.

After all, the internet had given Grace a seemingly endless stream of information on Garrett. Though his main work was commissioned portraits, he'd done a series of murals in the city that went viral on social media. He married Jo in 2014 and purchased his studio space in 2019. Grace had his coffee order in her phone, texts asking if he wanted his suits starched, and these were proof she *knew* him, right? She went back to their last exchange. How long after pushing *send* did he die?

Grace: Forgot to call the museum back, but it's on my list first thing in the morning.

Garrett: Not a problem. Thanks for everything, Grace.

How naive she'd been, thinking this was what it meant to know someone. She had no idea what he thought about when he closed his eyes, no idea what traumas he carried from childhood into adulthood. She'd had no idea someone wanted him dead.

She tried to bring up the picture of his face. Though many would call him handsome, he wasn't a particularly notable man. His hair was dark, straight, and just long enough that it fell into his eyes a bit. His skin was olive. Greek, Grace had guessed. He wore glasses with a thick black rim and didn't seem to own any clothing items beyond jeans and plain T-shirts. With each new article she read on Garrett, mostly fluff pieces for art blogs and local news features, it became clearer that Garrett and Jo lived a life of opulence. Their cars were luxury, their clothes designer. They mentioned vacations in Greece and Japan, the Michelin-star restaurants they considered their favorites.

If Grace had worked for Garrett long-term, she planned on asking for a raise.

She'd just started toying with the idea that she might have a future in Philadelphia. She was nowhere near making any big plans, but she'd allowed herself to dream, to picture what it would look like if she still worked for Garrett in five years, or where she'd live once she grew sick of her apartment.

But now, quiet, maybe-Greek, T-shirt-clad Garrett was dead, and Grace could barely imagine the drive back to her apartment, let alone come up with a plan for the next few years of her life.

Her move had been the biggest risk Grace had ever made. She was often impulsive, but there was a difference between risk-taking and impulsivity. Impulsive decisions are those seat-of-your-pants choices you make in the heat of the moment, like grabbing a tub of ice cream not on your grocery list or drinking more than you planned because the bar had the right "vibes." Risk takes planning. Risks are things you know could end badly, but you need to try anyway. Grace was impulsive, but she didn't take risks.

She *needed* this new life in Philadelphia to work out, or she'd be returning to Florida a failure. How could she ever take another risk again?

Chapter 4

In 2022, the homicide rate was 6.3 per hundred thousand people in the United States, Grace thought as she tried to shower away her day. The first thing she'd done when she walked through the door of her apartment was drop her bag on the floor, shed her shoes and jacket next to it, and head toward the bathroom for the hottest shower of her life. She wasn't sure what temperature the water would need to be to remove the memory of a dead body, but she'd turned the shower valve to what she would describe as scalding. It still didn't feel like enough.

Hair wrapped in a towel, body strewn across her bed, the second thing she did was delete her recently created dating profile. It suddenly felt intimate to have any details available to strangers on the internet. Was this case going to make the news? Would her name be mentioned? Either she took a break from online dating or changed her profile to say, "Female, thirty, unemployed, and definitely not a murderer, despite what reports say."

She barely used social media anymore, so her dating profile felt like the only thing she needed to delete to go off the grid for a while. She shut her laptop after she finished and picked up her phone. How was it only four pm? She'd lived an entire CSI episode since she woke up this morning.

She grabbed a blanket off her bed and carried it out to the couch. Flipping on the TV, she wrapped the blanket around her like a cocoon she'd eventually emerge from as a new woman. This was an afternoon that could only be cured by binging old episodes of *Fixer Upper*. There wasn't anything Chip and Joanna couldn't repair.

By eight pm, Grace had barely moved. The past two hours could be summarized by her trail of Google searches:

- *Dead body vomit poison*
- *Dead body vomit choking*
- *What to do when you witness a crime*
- *Do they announce who finds a body*

There were dozens of them, since Grace had been armed with the time to collect information but no clear goal of what she was hoping to find.

There was no way she was going to gather the strength to cook dinner, so she went to the fridge and grabbed some leftovers. She didn't feel like waiting for the oven to preheat and tossed her chicken parm right into the microwave. She was waiting expectantly for a beep but instead heard a knock at her door.

Grace's entire body tensed. Was it the police? What if it was Garrett's murderer, thinking she knew more than she did? *I knew I shouldn't have quit taekwondo in third grade.* She tried to shake the worst of her intrusive thoughts as she walked slowly to the door, tiptoeing to not be heard in case she looked through the peephole and decided not to answer.

But when she looked, she saw a fish-eyed version of a familiar face.

Beep. Dinner was ready.

Jo Baros was even more striking in person. Grace had internally referred to her as Art Gallery Barbie, and as she opened the door and saw Jo in the flesh for the first time, she saw she fit the description exactly. Jo was wearing a long black jacket over white pants and a cream sweater, which felt like neutral overkill to Grace but looked painfully sophisticated. Her large bag was made from… well some sort of animal, Grace was sure. It couldn't be a Birkin? At her neck, Jo wore a brightly colored silk scarf to break up the understated simplicity of the rest of the outfit.

"Hi. Grace?" Jo raised an eyebrow, clearly unsure if she was in the right place. Her blonde hair landed at her shoulders, which looked hunched and stressed. A red tinge at the corners of her blue eyes made it clear she'd been crying.

"Yes. Hi. You're Jo. Oh, sorry, Mrs Baros. I – uh. God, I am so sorry." Word vomit, all over Jo's *probably dry-clean-only* sweater.

Jo nodded, not giving away her emotions in her facial expression. "You can call me Jo, that's fine." She paused. "Would you mind if I came in?"

Grace suddenly regretted not unpacking her apartment more. While she had a couch for them to sit on and a TV and bookcase for them to stare at, the living area was otherwise sparse. Nothing on the walls, no sense of who Grace was. Still, Grace moved aside and motioned for Jo to enter.

"Please," she said. "Go ahead and take a seat."

Jo walked slowly to the couch, looking left and right to take in the disappointing minimalist decor, if you could even call it that. She sat, crossing her legs and holding her purse on her lap.

"Uh, do you want something to drink? I have um. I have milk and water. Sorry, I haven't been to the store."

Jo smiled kindly. "No, thank you, I don't want to take up a bunch of your time." *Good,* Grace thought. *Because there are no tables in this room and it would have been mortifying to ask you to put your drink on a cardboard box from Home Depot.*

Grace sat down on the opposite end of the couch to Jo. "What can I help you with? Are you OK? I mean I – I don't even know how you could be OK." *I also don't know how I could possibly help if you aren't.*

Jo inhaled deeply and exhaled with the same gusto. "No, I don't think I am OK." She was still smiling. "I also don't think it's sunk in yet. Last night, I called Garrett to say goodnight, and he sounded great. He sounded exactly like himself, excited about work and life. I honestly don't have a clue who would want to hurt him."

Grace was stuck on the words "last night."

"Garrett didn't come home last night?"

"It wasn't weird for him to sleep at the office," Jo said, shaking her head. "He hated to stop working when he was on a roll and he told me he was feeling inspired last night. He kept an air mattress in his office so he could work until he was exhausted and then go right to sleep, wake up, and do it again in the morning."

This made sense. He was often so deep into his work, Grace had to repeat his name three or four times to get his acknowledgment that she was leaving. She'd just never assumed he was staying over.

An awkward half-minute passed as both women stared down at the floor before Jo broke the silence.

"You were the last person to see him alive."

Grace's head jerked up, her pulse speeding. Is this why Jo was here? There was nothing accusatory in her tone, but did Jo think Grace had something to do with Garrett's murder?

"Except for whoever killed him, I guess," Jo added. Somehow, this inclusion didn't make Grace feel much better.

"As of right now," Jo continued, eyes back to the floor, "you and I are the only people I know who have been questioned and released by the police. They tell me they're confident you were where you said you were last night and this morning."

Jo was sliding the zipper back and forth on her purse, which was admittedly annoying, but Grace felt like it would be both ill-timed and rude to tell her to cut it out.

"The police don't do much right, but I would assume they wouldn't let either of us go if they thought there was a chance we were murderers." Jo's lips tightened, her eyes shooting off to the left, as if it were physically painful for her to discuss this.

"I don't trust the police. I've had… well, there was a particular run-in with them I'd like to forget, and I don't feel confident they have the best of intentions. They don't even know anything about Garrett, yet here they are trying to, you know, find whatever justice they think is appropriate for his death."

Grace could feel herself frowning, her eyebrows leaning down to meet in the middle.

Apparently, Jo took the look as a question. *Where were you last night?*

"I run a nonprofit that helps support youth arts programs. I was at an event last night – a fundraiser to help build scholarship funds for children who can't afford lessons outside of their school curriculum."

"Oh, I believe you," Grace said. "You don't need to explain anything to me."

Jo took a deep breath, shuddering a bit at its peak. "Thank you."

Grace still didn't understand. "I'm sorry, Jo, I'm a little bit confused about why you're here. But if it's to have someone to talk to, I'm more than happy to listen."

Jo offered a warm smile. "I could use someone to talk to right now. And that's part of it. But I'd also like to offer you a job."

"A job?" Grace seemed to have missed something. How had Jo gone from giving her alibi to giving a job offer?

"I assume you didn't have a backup plan, if your job with Garrett didn't work out." Jo sat tight-lipped for a second as if holding back emotion brought on by Garrett's name. "And I could use someone I can trust. Someone who I know didn't do it."

She cleared her throat. "I want to offer you a job as my assistant."

Grace crossed her arms and set them on her knees. "Uh, I don't know if Garrett told you, but I don't have much, or any really, experience in art, let alone music."

Jo tilted her head, obviously confused by this. "He didn't tell me that. That's... odd. But..."

She pushed her purse off her lap and slid to the edge of the couch, leaning forward and bringing her hands together.

"Honestly, you don't need any experience for this job. Because the only thing I need assistance with right now is finding out who killed my husband."

* * *

The words hung between the two of them for a spell, Grace unsure of what to do with them. Once her thoughts found their footing again, words formed into her initial answer.

Absolutely fucking not.

She was neither a professional investigator nor was she interested in getting more wrapped up in Garrett's murder than she already was. Maybe this was the universe's way of telling her she did belong in Florida. If you couldn't spend a month in a place without finding a body, *maybe* it wasn't the place for you. It was time to return to the land of milk and mouse-shaped waffles.

Jo was staring at her, expectantly.

"I – uh. I mean, I'm not sure what to say. I'm not a... I mean, I don't think I'm qualified to do that. Do – do *you* feel qualified to do that?"

Jo uncrossed her legs just to cross them again.

"I've never thought about it before. But desperate times, as they say."

The silence screamed as the women sized one another up. With little in the room to distract her, Grace kept her eyes on Jo, who kept her eyes down.

"It doesn't sound very safe, I mean. There's a reason we have professionals to do the job, and–"

"And I don't trust the professionals, like I said." Jo met Grace's eyes. "I'll be doing this no matter what your answer is." She swallowed hard. "But if you'd come to work for me, there would be a significant raise in it for you."

Grace had spent enough time reading through her mother's emails to know the word "significant" was subjective in the world of finance.

"What percent is *significant*?" she asked Jo.

Jo sat up straight. Her face transformed from nervous to confident. This wasn't her first negotiation.

"Thirty percent."

Grace hadn't noticed she'd been scraping her nails along the arm of the couch, but at hearing the number, she dug in. Thirty percent was *certainly* significant. Grace had saved a decent amount of money when living with her parents, but she was no millionaire. If she had to go back to Florida, going back with a well-padded bank account would soften the blow. It beat the narrative that she was returning home having gained nothing but the trauma of finding a dead body.

"Garrett was a great boss, but I can't volunteer to put myself in danger to solve his murder." This felt like a reasonable boundary, and setting a reasonable boundary felt like something a real adult would do.

Jo adjusted the silk scarf tied around her neck, loosening it slightly.

"I'd never ask you to put yourself in danger. I plan on being discreet about the whole thing. And you'd have the option to stop at any point."

Grace crossed her arms and leaned back. She could smell her dinner, growing mushy and cold in the microwave. Would it be crazy to consider this offer? She barely knew Jo, had just come to terms with the fact that she barely knew Garrett.

But then there was the money. And the promise she'd never be in danger.

"What's your plan?" she asked Jo.

"Well." Jo slid her palms back and forth along her slacks uneasily. "I'm not sure where to start." She bit her lip.

"Garrett's body isn't even cold yet. I haven't had time to think."

A wave of nausea rolled over Grace as she remembered touching Garrett's soft – and yes, cold – hand.

"And any suspects we come up with... don't you think the police will have already questioned them?"

Jo shrugged. "There's no harm in checking their work, right? Besides, the police have rules. There are regulations they need to follow, lines they can't cross. We can be creative with our investigation."

Grace wasn't sure she wanted to cross any lines.

Jo stood up, perhaps propelled by anxiety as she sputtered, "P–please let me know by the end of the weekend. I have to get going." She pulled her bag onto her shoulder and gave a weak smile as she held her hand out, a business card perched between her pointer finger and thumb.

She gave a little nod. "Thanks for seeing me. I'll be waiting for your answer."

She turned toward the door, took a few long, hurried strides, and she was gone.

Grace's face was illuminated by the glow of her laptop screen. It had been a long day, she needed sleep. But first, she needed to know more about Jo Baros. She was still shocked that Jo had shown up at her door. How bold did you have to be to knock on the door of a relative stranger and ask for help? Grace felt a pang of jealousy over the self-assured way Jo seemed to move through the world as she typed Jo's name in her browser. The first hit was her Wikipedia page.

"Josephine Wallis Baros (née Smith; born July 18, 1987) is an American philanthropist and socialite as well as the heiress to a real estate fortune. Daughter of Malcolm Smith, famed real estate developer, and Molly Wright-Smith, Baros resides in Philadelphia."

Oh. Heiress?

Grace scanned the page. Jo hadn't gone to college. In an interview, she'd said she'd skipped it at the insistence of her father. "He wanted me to take over the family business, but neither Sam nor I was interested." Sam was Jo's little brother. Comments led Grace to believe that not only did Sam not want to inherit the family business – he wasn't on speaking terms with his father at all.

Jo had a brief period in her twenties where she was known as a barfly and troublemaker – a mention of an arrest for public drunkenness linked to a local news article. Grace scrolled down until she saw Garrett's name. Jo met him when she was twenty-five and he was credited with turning her life around. They got married when Jo was twenty-seven and Garrett was thirty. There was another link to look at their wedding pictures, which Grace would check out later. She saw Garrett's Wikipedia page, but skipped over it again to view Malcolm's.

His was the great American story of hard work and perseverance. As it turns out, the Philadelphia skyline had his fingerprints all over it, and it was clear that thanks to his career, Jo and her brother had never wanted for anything. Grace thought about her own middle-class upbringing. Most of the time, it felt like she had everything she needed. She couldn't even wrap her head around the amount of wealth Jo had grown up with. Then again, Grace could admit she had relatively simple needs. Too simple, probably.

Grace clicked on Garrett's page but didn't make it past the first line, the line listing his birth date but not his date of death. She knew something the internet didn't yet. She slammed her laptop shut.

Taking Jo up on her offer would mean financial security, a reason to stay in Philly, and the chance to meet people in Jo's circle. A great opportunity, because she didn't know anyone else in the area, but also a possible death wish. Someone in Jo's circle probably murdered Garrett.

But there was another reason to stay. She may not have known him long, but Garrett had been a good boss. He was, based on all her interactions with him, a good man who worked hard and loved his wife. She thought back to the day she met him, when he showed her the desk she'd be sitting at each day. He'd gotten her a bouquet of wildflowers to celebrate her arrival, asked her about the move, and wrote out a list of some of his favorite local spots.

Garrett was good. She hoped he'd get justice. It would be nice to be here to see it happen.

After midnight, Grace's head swirling with pros and cons, she'd dug to the bottom of a box labeled "junk drawer" and found a notepad and pen. She drew a vertical line down the page and started writing the list out.

After ten minutes, she attempted to review the chicken scratch she'd scribbled onto the page. The "pro" side was twice the length of the "con" side. Still, Grace was feeling uneasy.

She needed a second opinion. An expert's opinion.

But since she didn't know any *real* experts, she decided she needed Maya's opinion.

Chapter 5

Growing up, Grace and Maya had shared everything: clothes, secrets, makeup, and during one unfortunate and short-lived moment in high school, a boyfriend. When they figured it out, Maya punched him in the middle of the cafeteria, his Salisbury steak hitting the ground a few seconds before he did. Once she was caught up to speed, the principal let Maya off with a warning, then gave Maya a high five once she was sure no one else was around.

Maya was loud, loyal, and opinionated, often Grace's key to parties, friends, and new experiences. She was also one of the most intelligent people Grace had ever met, and Grace was in one of the rare situations where Maya's knowledge of true crime could actually help.

Grace grabbed her phone.

It was nine am on a Saturday and there was a good chance Maya wouldn't even answer. Ever since Maya had her son, Miles, two months ago, it had been understandably harder for her to slip away for a video chat. Motherhood was central to who Maya was now, and that was something she and Grace *didn't* share.

To Grace's surprise, the call was picked up, the screen showing… a ceiling?

"HEY GIRL!" Maya seemed to be in a good mood, not that Grace could see a happy face to go along with the cheerful tone.

"Uh, hey. Did I catch you at a bad time or…?"

"No! This is perfect. The baby is napping and Xavier is at work and I decided to cook a real breakfast for myself." Grace could hear pots and pans clinking against one another over the sound of liquid being poured. "I've been keeping the Greek yogurt industry in business. But you're going to have to stare at my popcorn ceiling while I do this."

It felt good to hear Maya's voice, even without her face.

"Well, that's great, because I had an insane day yesterday. I need to talk to someone."

"I'm all ear – SHIT! Shit! It's fine, I burned myself on bacon grease. Continue."

Grace cleared her throat. Where to start? "I woke up yesterday morning and I had this feeling it was going to be amazing. I looked good. I felt good! I got a free scone."

Maya snorted. "I mean how could a day including a free scone go bad?"

"Yeah, that's what I thought. And then I walked into my office, and my boss was there. But he… he had died. He was dead. Like *murder* dead."

From what Grace could figure, Maya had tried to grab the phone and dropped it, as the screen seemed to show it tumbling before it went dark. Then it quickly changed to Maya's face. "Way to bury the FREAKING LEDE, Grace. Are you serious right now?" Grace fought back the desire to respond, "Dead serious."

"Uh, turn off your burner. But yes, I'm completely serious. Someone poisoned my boss. Or choked my boss?

I haven't gotten any updates lately. But he's dead, that part is confirmed."

A look Grace couldn't place spread across Maya's face. Something at the intersection of disgust and insatiable curiosity. She opened her mouth like she was going to speak, closed it, opened it.

"Well. I have questions. My first one is, are you OK?"

There hadn't been enough time for Grace to consider that. Physically, she was fine. She'd been in the room when their grandmother passed away, so this wasn't the first body she'd seen. But there was something unnerving about seeing Garrett slumped over his desk. She'd been laughing with him the day before about a dog walking past the studio. Grace had named him Puddles, because every time his owner had tried to get him to walk, he'd melted into the sidewalk like a puddle. She had whiplash from how fast it had happened, laughing at Puddles in one moment, finding Garrett in a puddle of his vomit the next.

So mentally, it was complicated. And Jo's job offer somehow made it all feel more complicated.

"I think I'm OK. I also don't know if it will hit me for a while. He was fine and then he wasn't. It was a good reminder of how finite everything is. I think I need to process it. And another detail to add to the craziness: my boss's widow asked me to work for her. Which is good, it means I don't need to hunt for a new job and–"

"Wait, you're STAYING? In Philadelphia? And you're working for the wife?! G, that's crazy, what if she killed him?! Believe me, statistically, you always look to the spouse!"

"Exactly!" Grace was pacing in her kitchen, taking laps around the small island at the center. She stared at a single rotting banana in a bowl on her counter. "People always think it's the spouse, which means she got questioned right after me. She was at a fundraiser Thursday night. The police verified my movements via security camera and I'm sure they did the same with her. The officer in charge seems capable." *And fit, humble, like he calls his mom regularly,* Grace thought to herself.

Maya's face turned pensive. "You said this Garrett guy was rich, right? What kind of people are we dealing with? Are they in the Mob?"

"I can't say it with one hundred percent certainty; however, I don't think they are in the Mob."

Maya threw her hands in the air. Based on the angle, Grace assumed her phone was on her kitchen counter, propped up on something. "OK, well, Mob or no Mob, what if she hired someone else to do it?!"

There had been a moment when Jo was sitting in her apartment that Grace had considered this. Maybe Jo was the woman who called the shot, not the one who took it (not that there were any literal shots involved).

"I don't think she did it."

"Based on? Based on what? Had you even met her before?"

"No," Grace shrugged. "Still, he talked about her so reverently. I never heard them fight. Plus, she wants me to help her find out who did it."

"I'm sorry, say that again?"

"She said she wants me to help her find the killer. Obviously, the police will find the killer, but I figured I could go and sit with her, listen to her theories, get her tea and, I don't know, paint her nails. More of an emotional support system. She doesn't trust the police, so I think she just wants to make sure no angle is missed." There was a scrape on the wall, maybe from when Grace had moved her dining room table in. She'd need to get some magic erasers.

"Why doesn't she trust the police?"

Grace hadn't wanted to ask. If someone told you they didn't trust the police, she assumed they had a deeply personal reason for their views. As the daughter of a police officer, Grace had immense respect for anyone in uniform. She was also a straight, white woman from a middle-class family. Not that Jo fit the profile of "marginalized."

"She didn't say. But she made it clear."

Maya looked at Grace skeptically.

"And why you? If she's so loaded, why not hire a private detective? They aren't cops, but they know what they're doing." Maya leaned into the camera, tilting her head slightly. "No offense, but you have no idea what you're doing."

"I'm acutely aware of that, actually," Grace said, dragging a hand down her face in exasperation. But that was a good question. Why *didn't* Jo hire a PI? Whatever the fee was, Jo could pay it. Even the most novice investigator was more suited for this work than Grace.

Maya seemed to relax at Grace's frustration. She knew her well enough to know when to stop pushing. She turned toward her breakfast on the stove.

"Have you told your parents?"

"Absolutely not. I have an unopened text from my mom this morning reminding me to carry the pepper spray she bought me. She scheduled this text to go out EVERY MORNING. So I haven't broken the news to her that I identified a dead body before I even got the chance to check my email yesterday."

Maya nodded, then leaned into her kitchen counter. "Listen, G. I don't like the idea of you staying and not having anyone to support you nearby. You need someone who can get to you in an emergency. Have you made any friends there? Not counting the probably-not-in-the-Mob wife?"

"Can I count her dead husband?"

"No, Grace. They need to be alive."

That felt like a low bar, and yet...

Since Grace's arrival in Pennsylvania, she hadn't made a big attempt to form friendships. However, there were people she saw regularly as part of her routine. There were two baristas who were typically at the drive-thru window of the coffee shop in the morning. She didn't remember their names. And then there was the woman at the post office she chatted with when she needed to drop off Garrett's deliveries. Her name was definitely Sharon and she had two sons in college. Plus, there was a nice woman who worked at the sandwich shop where Grace liked to go on her lunch break. They'd got to talking and realized they were both from Florida. They'd each gotten food poisoning from the same Margaritaville.

These kinds of acquaintances weren't what Maya was talking about, though.

Grace had a core group of friends back in Florida. They met in elementary school and their friendship had outlasted puberty, college in different states, first jobs, engagements, and even outlandish bachelorette parties and black-tie weddings. She still felt the kinship as she sat around the table with her friends and their husbands and wives, listening to them spout off good qualities in whatever guy they were trying to set her up with that week.

But when the pregnancy announcements came, it started to feel different. It wasn't even just that they were busier now. Grace didn't expect anyone to focus on their friend over their child, no matter how far the relationship went back. It was that she realized they had crossed over into a world you didn't understand until you were in it.

It began to feel so trivial, discussing what book Grace was reading or the weekend trip she was taking later in the month, when her friends were trying to keep actual humans alive. She wholeheartedly felt that having children was not required to live a full, beautiful life, but Grace could feel an inner pressure growing to define her goals, her dreams. She knew she wanted to travel and make a positive impact on the world at large. And God, did she *ever* want to get out of Florida.

The week Miles was born was the week Grace started looking up new cities to move to.

She was still in a group chat with her old friends. A few times a week, her phone lit up with a new video of a child walking, questions about rashes, and excited yet exhausted date night selfies. She realized she never told them she moved. None of them had the time to ask about her life, either. The thought made her feel a new level of loneliness. Maya was right. She needed to make a friend.

"Maybe I'll join a bowling league or something," Grace said lightheartedly.

Maya's face was a mix of entertainment and worry, a look Grace was used to getting from almost every person in her life at this point. "You gotta do something, alright? Meet the neighbors. Join a book club. Ooh, a murder mystery book club!"

Grace shuddered. "Let me figure out one murder before I dive into a full series, OK?"

Maya looked guilty.

"Is it terrible that I'm excited you're wound up in a real-life mystery?"

"Yes, Maya, it's kind of terrible."

She groaned. "You know I can't help it! It's my lifelong passion! Hey, maybe I can help you solve it. I've seen every trick in the book at this point. And my skills are fresh; I've been listening to crime podcasts while I pump and do laundry and the trillion other things that need to be done around here."

The bags under Maya's eyes were deep and dark in the blue light from her phone. Grace wished she could hug her.

"Well, like I said, I'm hoping the police take care of the actual investigation. However, if I run into any murder-related questions I can't answer myself, you'll be the first person I call."

Maya sighed contentedly. "Maya Morgan: mother, investigator, librarian, general badass."

That she was.

"So what do you think? You think I should take the job?"

Maya contemplated. "What's the money like?"

Grace leaned in close to the screen so her face encompassed it. "Like Mob money."

Maya laughed. "You're a big girl. I know you felt trapped here, but I want you to stay safe. Make sure you're not *actually* trying to do any police work."

"I swear I will not participate in any stakeouts."

Maya sighed in response.

"I need to get going to finish my breakfast. Miles is scheduled to start screaming in about fifteen minutes and once I pick him up, he's not going to let me put him back down. Are you sure you're OK?"

"I'm good." *As good as it's going to get right now.*

"Let's talk next week. I can schedule you in between a pumping session and my hour of doomscrolling before bed."

"Sounds like a plan."

The rest of the weekend passed without any remarkable events happening. On Sunday, Grace attempted to unpack the apartment some more, but after she got her closet put together, she felt too tired to do anything else. Instead, she lay on the couch and looked up therapists. It felt like this was the next step for a full-grown adult who had been thrust into a murder investigation. She browsed, not filling out any contact forms.

When she got hungry, she went for a walk and looked for a restaurant that seemed like it could be a contender for her new favorite place. She chose Thai, ordered tofu rad prik, and decided she would come back. She knew she should be cooking at home, especially since technically she was unemployed, at least for today. She was tired of breaking down recipes for one person. Tired of being in charge of the cooking, and then the dishes… it was easier to leave.

That night, she called Cordon, telling him Jo Baros had offered her a job. She asked if there was any conflict of interest there, if he thought it was safe.

"Please, call me Sean," he'd said, and Grace swore she could hear his smile. It probably wasn't something to brag about, being on a first name basis with a police officer;

however, she felt important nonetheless, like she'd passed some sort of test, allowing her to stand in the doorway of Sean's life.

"I don't see any issue with you working for Mrs Baros, though... I have to admit it's out of the ordinary. If you don't feel like it would be traumatic to either of you, I just ask that you both stay on high alert until our investigation is wrapped up." His kind voice had taken a stern tone, like a preschool teacher who is tired of telling four-year-olds to stop licking the glitter off their craft projects. "Someone dangerous is still out there. However, I have no reason to believe either of you have anything to hide."

She didn't tell him what this new job consisted of.

Ten minutes later, Grace texted Jo to accept her job offer.

Chapter 6

Grace had to be at the wrong house.

She'd spent an embarrassing amount of time studying the article featuring Garrett and Jo's sprawling estate. Painted white with black shutters, it was a modern twist on classic Southern luxury. Wisteria climbed a trellis near the front door, the photographer even managing to capture several butterflies using it as a place to rest. The yard was a love song to local greenery, but Jo had been quick to point out in the magazine article that neither she nor Garrett had anything to do with the vegetation.

"I've got a black thumb," the interviewer quoted Jo as saying. "Actually, I'm probably closer to completely thumbless."

Grace had saved the article in her bookmarks and came back to it several times, considering it one of the most beautiful things her internet stalking had unearthed. *I cannot use the word "stalking" in front of the police.*

But the house in front of her was not the one she'd dreamed of one day seeing. Instead of white siding, the house was constructed of beige bricks. These shutters had the appearance of aged copper, their pale green catching the light with a metallic sheen. She slowly released her foot on the brake, taking in what she saw as she inched forward.

The entire property was bordered with thick shrubs and trees. It wasn't a gated community or an island oasis, but it was certainly private enough.

Grace parked, grabbed her bag, and slid her sunglasses onto the top of her head. She could expect high temperatures through the end of this month, the internet told her. Summer would sometimes hold on until mid-October, finally letting go as children shivered their way through trick-or-treating. Grace had been looking forward to experiencing her first "true" fall and winter. But since Garrett's death, the idea of longer, darker days seemed depressing. Every day was a day of the dead when you had a murder hanging over you.

Grace rang the *Ring* doorbell and waited for someone to answer. She'd assumed the house was filled with hired help. That a stranger would greet her at the door and walk her to a library where Jo sat drinking Prosecco as someone fanned her and fed her grapes. Jo or Garrett's parents may even be here. Grace hadn't been given details about a funeral, but it had to be coming up. Or was the normal timeline thrown out the window, considering his death was part of a police investigation?

Grace was startled when she saw a blurry figure appear and draw closer through the glass, opening the door to reveal Jo herself.

Even more startling was that the Jo standing in front of her seemed to be a different Jo from the one who had stood in her apartment. Her eyes were puffy, deep purple crescents showing beneath them. She wasn't sleeping. She wore makeup; however, her lipstick was faded, and her mascara smeared, which probably meant it hadn't been applied today. She wore a lounge set under a silk robe with no jewelry or accessories. The outfit probably cost more than

Grace's rent and utilities, but this seemed to be a dressed-down look for Jo. Had she forgotten Grace was supposed to start working for her today?

Jo smiled at Grace and took a step forward. Grace stiffened as Jo wrapped her arms around her in a hug. She could smell alcohol. Not Prosecco; something much harder. Jo stepped back, seemingly unaware of how unexpected the physical touch had been. "Please don't mind the mess," she said. "Our household manager, or housekeeper, Gloria, has the week off. She's a friend of Garrett's mother. Knew Garrett his entire life. She's taking it hard." She let out a long sigh. "Please, come in."

Grace stepped inside to a bright foyer smelling of freshly cut flowers. To her right was a formal dining room with beautiful open built-in shelving. To the left was a recessed living area with a large fireplace and chunky leather couches. The foyer was two stories with a staircase trimmed with a wrought-iron art-deco-style banister. Beneath her feet, the floors were light wood placed into a chevron design; they seemed new, the banister old, and Grace wondered which of these touches had been done by Jo and Garrett.

The white walls of the foyer displayed plenty of art, but none of it appeared to be the same style she now attributed to Garrett. Directly across from Grace was a grand piano, sheet music opened to the middle of a song, several bouquets of flowers placed on top of it, explaining the smell. News of Garrett's murder had broken late Sunday night. Obviously, Jo had people in her life who moved quickly,

"Let's start with a tour, yeah?" said Jo, already heading toward the living area. "This is the secondary family room. I let Garrett decorate this one because I knew we'd never be in here." She gave a wistful smile and scanned the room.

Before Grace had taken it all in, Jo turned and was headed in the opposite direction.

"This is the dining room! We also rarely ate here."

And Jo was off again, heading away from the front door into the main living area, her movements manic. A white clay fireplace stretched to the ceiling and luxurious velvet couches sat in front of large arched windows. Between the windows and two skylights in the ceiling, the room had the natural light Grace understood to be a real estate agent's dream.

Next was a modern kitchen.

"This is my favorite room in the house," said Jo. "Because I like eating." She patted her flat stomach as if there were some physical proof of her culinary indulgences. "And also, we looked for months for the right marble." She sounded nervous, like she wanted Grace to like the room as much as she did. The room could have been plucked from a magazine, a masterclass in design, lighting, and feng shui. The sleek cabinets were painted navy blue, and all the hardware was gold to match the large farmhouse sink, knobs on all the white appliances, and the trim of the massive oven hood. The refrigerator blended in with the cabinets. She could see not one but two wine fridges. If nothing else told her that this room came with an exuberant price tag, Grace could have guessed solely based on the pot filler above the stove; a true luxury for anyone who loves pasta.

Everyone loves pasta.

"I've never seen a house like this before," Grace said, mouth hanging slack, sounding like a child the first time they see a big city.

Jo stared around the room proudly. "Garrett wanted a big kitchen to host in. He came from a large extended family, and he wanted to share the things we were fortunate enough to have with them, and our friends." Her face fell. "I think we hosted them once." She let out a dark laugh. "What a waste."

She sighed again. Grace tried not to keep count of them.

"Anyway," and Jo was off again.

She was headed in the direction of the stairs when she pointed down a hallway. "There's a bar, powder room, laundry room, and Garrett's office down there. I'll finish the tour with that. We'll head upstairs first."

The first bedroom turned out to be the master, which took Grace by surprise. This felt too intimate a space to have access to. Centered on the wall opposite of the door was a large wooden sleigh bed. Grace assumed the disheveled side was Jo's. Garrett's side was tucked neatly, like it was waiting for him to come home and fall into bed after a long night at the studio. She felt a weight land in her gut. Their wedding picture was framed above the bed, Garrett dipping Jo back gracefully as he placed a gentle kiss on her mouth. Her dress was more casual than Grace expected, more of a cocktail dress than a wedding dress. Behind them seemed to be some sort of restaurant, a neon sign peeking out of the top left corner.

Jo finished the tour of the upstairs, showing off the ensuite, massive walk-in closet, as well as two more beds and baths before heading to the basement.

The basement floor was covered in a dated jade tile. Jo breezed through a theater, game room, her office, and an additional bedroom before they went back to the main floor, and she led Grace out onto a large deck. Jo walked to the railing to survey the yard, a steep hill sloping down into a wooded area. Grace noticed that Jo was slightly out of breath after practically running through the house to give the tour. She seemed so nervous.

Jo pointed back toward the house. "On the other side, there's a small guest house. We have a few regular employees and at times when they're working late, they'll stay there."

Grace nodded. Her mind was still on the pot filler in the kitchen, barely registering the rest of the lavish house. She was trying to keep up but also stuck on the fact that the house wasn't at all what she expected.

"I read an article about you and Garrett," she started, carefully leaving out the word "stalking" this time. "It was a tour of your house... it wasn't this house, right? When did you move here?"

Jo laughed and shook her head. Birds chirped sweetly in a nearby tree and Grace immediately understood the appeal of the back yard, a cozy oasis away from the busy lives Garrett and Jo lived once they left home. "*That* house was a wedding gift from my dad. It was twice the size and four times the cost of this one. It made no sense to have money tied up there and a bunch of empty rooms we didn't care to fill, so we moved about a year after that article was printed. My dad loves extravagant things. Me, not so much."

Jo bent over, leaning her elbows on the railing.

"I assume you saw the photo of me next to the pool?"

Grace nodded. Jo had the aura of a Hollywood starlet in the photos. If you squinted, she looked like Marilyn Monroe, which Grace felt probably sounded more complimentary in her head, so she left it there.

A sharp "ha" escaped from Jo's mouth. "We *never* used that pool. Not once. The photographer was insistent we take advantage of such a beautiful backdrop." She laid her forehead on her arms, face turned down. "It was a beautiful pool."

It seemed like Jo needed a moment to herself, but it also felt rude to walk away and explore the house on her own, so Grace stood there, hoping she was the only person who felt awkward.

After a minute or so, Jo's head popped up, a smile on her face. "I want to show you Garrett's office," she said.

The women passed through a single door and into a wood-paneled room. At the center of the room was a sturdy wooden desk, and behind it stood row after row of bookcases. Like the rest of the house, this room had plenty of light, thanks to glass-paneled double doors leading outside.

The wall opposite the door was familiar to Grace. She knew this art was Garrett's.

There were landscape paintings of places he'd traveled, sketches of what Grace assumed were friends and family, and everywhere, in paint, in charcoal, in pencil… was Jo.

She'd clearly been his muse. And in all the ways this house represented them both, they'd clearly been quite the team. If there had been any question before, Grace was now sure Jo had nothing to do with Garrett's murder. And the anxiety of that possibility was immediately replaced with the crushing weight of Jo's loss.

Many of the books on the shelves were art books, but a surprising number were fiction. Classics, mysteries, fantasies. How did he ever have time to read these when he was always working? Grace pulled out a copy of *Fahrenheit 451* and was skimming through when she heard Jo sniffle behind her.

She turned to see Jo was crying. Not gently crying, either. A full-blown Kim Kardashian ugly cry. Jo placed her hand down on the armrest of the chair across from Garrett's desk and then fell into it with a thud. Grace ran over and kneeled next to her. "Are you OK? Do you need something? Do you need me to get someone?"

She had seemed excited to show Grace this room, but maybe being here, surrounded by all of Garrett's things, was too much.

Jo wailed at Grace's last question. "There is no one to *get*. There is no one to make this better. There are people to feed me, clean for me, and make me beautiful; however, there is no one who can fix this."

She slumped over, folding herself in half and placing her face in her hands. "Sorry. I had no intention of falling apart like this. I've been trying not to fall apart in front of anyone else. And it's not even a pride thing, it's that I'm honestly terrified. I have no idea who could have killed Garrett. I probably seemed cold when I showed up at your apartment. I'm terrified to show a moment of weakness, even when I'm alone. Because whoever killed him is still out there."

Jo sat up, face red and streaked with tears, and said, "How do I know if I'm next?"

Grace hadn't seen Jo as cold during her visit. She'd seemed like someone who was understandably shaken by tragedy. She didn't consider Jo was scared that whoever killed Garrett would come after Jo as well. She'd assumed the person who killed Garrett had a personal vendetta against him. That the crime had already taken place and now came the solving. Jo was worried there was more to come. No wonder she was in a rush to get answers.

Grace couldn't think of something to say in response. She had no idea if Jo should be worried or not. And it wouldn't be a comfort to Jo if she insisted the police had it under control.

"Garrett has gotten a decent amount of attention in recent years. He's a new, trendy artist. I started to get worried when reports would come out about what his paintings were selling for. I think that has to be who is to blame for all this. Someone who saw those sales on the news and decided to get him out of the way so they could cash in on his success."

The killer might have been after money, but how would killing Garrett give them any access to his finances? Grace thought about the missing painting. Maybe they'd stolen it and hoped to sell it for a big profit. However, they didn't seem to take anything else, and no reputable art buyer was going to pay for a piece that was evidence in a murder case.

Or maybe that was part of the appeal.

Grace decided now wasn't the right time to bring up the painting. Jo was scared and venting, and her adding to her conspiracy theories would make everything worse.

Jo wasn't in a state to listen anyway. She was clearly stuck on something in her head, and then she blurted out, "Garrett doesn't even have money! That's the most ridiculous part of all this!"

Grace felt her mouth fall open. How did Garrett have no money? She'd seen those exact reports of what his art was selling for. He'd been featured in local and national media, and his schedule was always full.

"I come from money," Jo said. Grace already knew this, but she tried to offer up the face of someone who was learning new information in the moment. "A lot of money. Money I invested to make more money. And while Garrett is an amazing artist, it also costs money to get your name out there. I've been bankrolling him since before we were married because I believed in what he was doing."

Jo turned her chair toward the double doors, looking out at the horizon. "When we were dating, we went to museums together. I mean, until a few days ago, that was still our favorite thing to do. He would stare at all the paintings, walk ten feet to his left and stare at them again over there. He would soak up every stroke, every color choice. And I, in turn, would soak *him* up. Watch him be passionate about something so deeply it felt intimate."

Profound love and profound sadness tangled together in Jo's voice.

"Once, we were visiting this castle in Austria, and the entire ceiling was one massive painting – you probably know the kind I'm talking about."

Grace had only left the country to go to the Canadian side of Niagara Falls and on a Caribbean cruise, where she'd puked off the deck not once, but twice. But she nodded along like she'd seen her fair share of ceiling art.

"And he said, 'Look at this, Jojo. This was someone's *life*. His entire *life* was spent recognizing beauty and trying to replicate it in a way that would outlive him.'"

Jo let out a shuddered breath. "I knew two things after our first museum trip: I was going to spend the rest of *my* life with this man, and I was going to do whatever I needed to do to make sure he spent *his* life making the world more beautiful. And until last week… that's what I did."

As Jo spoke, her eyes focused out the window, Grace made her way back around the desk, but paused when her eyes fell on the leather office chair. This had all been Garrett's. Every item in this room had been chosen and arranged by him. And he'd never see any of it again. Grace felt nervous, like she was about to break some priceless artifact at a museum. She looked to Jo with apprehension, but Jo nodded toward the chair, urging Grace to sit. Grace nearly declined, but then thought better of it. The last thing Jo needed right now was an argument.

It felt so surreal to be in Garrett's chair, in his home, all the formalities of boss and employee thrown out the window now that he was gone. Grace had known him for such a short time and now she was getting a tour of his house, sitting on the expensive furniture he picked out, and standing in the kitchen he didn't get to host enough parties in.

Jo took a deep breath. "I wanted you to see his office because this was his favorite spot in the house. It reflects who he was, what he loved." She laughed, which caught Grace off guard. "You know, it's funny... I've realized I feel bad for you. That you met Garrett but didn't really get to *experience* him." She wiped at the corner of her eye. "He was someone worth experiencing."

Jo spun her chair back around to face Grace. She was no longer crying or laughing but rather had a fierce look of determination on her face. "I don't know how to move forward with my life until I find out what happened to Garrett. I refuse to live in fear, waiting for other people to figure it out. I need you to sign some paperwork today, your contract and whatever else my lawyer drafted up for us, but tomorrow we get to work. I'm not stopping until I have the name of the person who killed my husband."

Grace swallowed the lump forming in her throat.

There was no employee handbook for a job like this.

Once Grace had signed everything, Jo walked her to the door. Grace stepped out onto the landing, but Jo stopped short, glancing at Grace and clicking her tongue, seemingly contemplating what she wanted to say next.

"You're a size medium."

It was somehow a question and also not a question.

"Around there, yes." Grace didn't understand where this was going.

Jo nodded, satisfied, then pulled out her phone. She scrolled for a few minutes, not sharing what she was up to.

"Are you ordering me a tweed jacket and a pipe?" Grace asked, trying to make everything feel lighter.

Jo let out a little snort but continued browsing. "Close. Leggings and a sports bra." She looked up, her head surrounded by bobbing moths drawn in by the porch light, which buzzed quietly.

"Do you lift weights, by chance?"

Chapter 7

If you'd ever happened to be at Costco at the same time as Grace, you wouldn't need to ask if she lifted weights. She'd stopped buying rice in bulk because she wasn't able to carry it by herself and was too stubborn to bother anyone and ask for help. She now ate rice from normal-sized boxes, the slight price increase worth avoiding embarrassment.

She knew she *should* lift weights, and was exceedingly aware of its benefits. She was at an age where the women in the osteoporosis commercial looked more like her mother than her grandmother, and she knew her time was coming.

But no, Grace did not lift weights.

However, there were only so many things Jo knew about her first suspect, Kelly Dewitt, and one of them was that she never missed the 9:45 am class at Liberty Bootcamp. Each forty-five-minute class focused on either strength, cardio, or endurance, and promised to push members' bodies to their limits.

Another thing Jo knew about Kelly was that she harbored years' worth of resentments toward Garrett. And it was all thanks to a gift shop.

Before Garrett owned the studio space, it was a gift shop owned by Kelly's family for three generations: Wishlist Gifts. They sold exactly what you expected, mainly the items you'd find at your average hospital gift shop and cheap clothes from China that were labeled "high end" because they could only be found in small boutiques, but should have been labeled "highly flammable" due to their questionable fabric makeup.

When Jo had brought up a photo of Kelly, Grace almost laughed in her face. She looked to be in her late sixties, still rocking the feathered bangs that fell out of style forty years ago. Her face was plump and wrinkled, her expression friendly. "She looks like my Aunt Anne. You think she could kill Garrett?"

Jo had put her phone away and crossed her arms. "Oh, I've seen what she can do. When her family fell on some hard times and were forced to put the store up for sale after Kelly's mom died, she absolutely lost it."

They'd been standing in Jo's kitchen, a tea kettle starting to whistle as Jo told the story. "Kelly's mother and grandmother were saints, always donating money to charity and their time to the children's hospital. But at the end of the day… you still need to be able to pay your bills. Kelly didn't think they should have to sell, thought someone would come bail them out and keep the store open. But then Garrett saw the space and fell in love with it."

Jo had paused to remove the kettle from the burner and pour a cup of English breakfast tea for each of them.

"I guess Kelly thought she would carry on the family legacy, but it didn't happen, and she ended up trying to contest the sale. When that didn't work, she made it her priority to ruin Garrett's reputation. She had picketers outside of the studio, badmouthed him to everyone she knew through the Chamber of Commerce, and after one overindulgent happy hour, vandalized the front of the studio. Cameras caught everything, and Garrett called the police but ultimately didn't press charges."

Jo had looked at Grace with an eyebrow raised, letting the literal and figurative tea steam between them.

"Rumor has it, she still isn't over it."

So here Grace was, five days into her job with Jo, breathing in the humid, sweat-laced air of Liberty Bootcamp, surrounded by a sea of Lululemon, to find out if the rumors were true.

"Are you ready to change your life?" Tanner, the trainer, asked Grace.

He looked all of twelve years old, which probably meant he was fresh out of college. He certainly looked the part of an athletic trainer in his branded gym shorts and tank, muscles front and center, jutting each time he moved as he showed Grace around the gym.

I'm ready to change my mind about being here, Grace thought. "Yes!" she said aloud.

Around her, women of all shapes and sizes (but mostly small and toned) stretched, downward dogs leading to upward dogs, and moves Grace didn't think were any kind of dog but which she didn't have the correct terminology for.

Tanner gave her a basic rundown of the class. They'd start with three easy warm-up exercises, then split into pairs and rotate through two other lists of moves, switching off with their partner when the designated counter finished. Tanner pointed toward the weight rack and encouraged Grace to test out the dumbbells to see which ones she might want to use at each station, then turned his attention to an absolutely jacked woman who, without counting, Grace assumed was on her 458th pushup.

Grace walked away from him, scanning the crowd for a glimpse of red hair. If she didn't spot Kelly and make sure they were paired together, the time she took shoving her body into that spandex prison would be wasted. It was a good questioning she was after, not a good workout.

A noise pinged from Grace's phone. She hadn't realized she'd left it in her pocket. She headed toward the cubbies at the entrance to the gym, to set her phone down with her water and jacket, but first she stole a glance at the screen. The notification was for an email from Jo, subject line "Research." She'd read it later.

Grace went back to the floor and studied the weight rack. Ten pounds seemed like nothing. Twenty seemed more appropriate, but while she was here, she may as well push herself. She grabbed for the thirty-pound weights, pulled them toward her, and was immediately humbled at their mass. Her shoulders were hoisted down with the weight, and she struggled for a moment as she attempted to get them back on the rack. *Hopefully, no one saw that.*

"First time?"

Grace whipped around, embarrassed someone had clearly witnessed her obvious lack of strength, and was both startled and relieved to have Kelly Dewitt's eyes staring back at her.

"I just didn't recognize you. So if you're new here, welcome!" Kelly gave a kind smile, her fluffy bangs pulled back with a Nike headband, the rest of her hair in a tight bun. She held out her hand and Grace noticed her firm bicep squeeze at the movement. She could have strangled Garrett with her bare hands if she wanted to.

"I'm Kelly," she said, and Grace mirrored the motion.

"Hi! Grace! Yes, it's my first time. I'm a little bit nervous." *Shit, should I have used my real name?*

"No need to be nervous," Kelly said, her elbow bent above her head, her other hand pulling it for a good stretch. "But my first suggestion is to go with less weight than you think you're going to want." She lowered her arms and pointed at the ten-pound weights. "They might feel light right now, but you get two reps into side raises, you'll be grateful you started small."

Grace gave a nod and a smile, and grabbed the weights. She looked over her shoulder at Kelly, who had at least twenty, maybe thirty years on Grace but looked like she could run circles around her. "Would you want to partner up?"

Kelly gave another smile. "Sure, sweetie. As long as you don't mind the front row."

Grace *did* mind, but she was knee-deep into this now, no turning back. She knew she wouldn't get to phone this one in. Kelly's social media profiles had a distinctive theme, and that theme was GYM. For the past year, Kelly had focused on protein and PRs after a health scare led her to "reevaluate what I was doing to my body." You could see how seriously she was taking it from the way her leggings fit her muscular legs and her arms bulged under an athletic tee. If Grace were going to keep up with Kelly, she needed to muster every bit of confidence she had failed to gather each time at Costco.

Grace followed Kelly to the front of the room and placed her weights down where Kelly stopped. She tried to copy the stretches everyone else was doing, but it was clear their bodies moved in ways she hadn't yet unlocked, so she eventually decided to do squats over and over again until she was given specific instructions. She thought about trying to engage Kelly in conversation, but when she went to ask what Kelly did for work, the trainer's voice came over a loudspeaker, filling the room.

"GOOD AFTERNOON, LADIES! WHO'S READY TO SWEAT?!"

Grace pulled up her leggings nervously. The outfit Jo had picked fit like a glove; the kind of glove that could stand to be a little bit looser and had the fingers removed, showing off some skin. Since she didn't pay for it, Grace didn't feel right giving her opinion on the style and print of the outfit, which is how she ended up in leopard print leggings and a matching sports bra, a mesh tank top tossed over it just because. She looked like a Mob wife in her cardio era.

Tanner instructed the class to stretch while he did a demonstration of each exercise, a remix of a Britney Spears song pumping in the background, making it impossible to hear.

Each exercise was written on a whiteboard at the front of the room, but Grace didn't understand what any of it meant. *Burpees? Dragonflies?* Tanner could have made these things up right before she got there and she'd have no idea. She looked over at Kelly, who was positioned like a soldier ready for battle. She watched Tanner closely, miming his movements as he demonstrated.

He made it to the burpees and Grace watched in horror as he explained (she thought, she still couldn't hear) that these involved crouching, shooting your legs out into a plank position, doing a pushup, pulling your knees back in, and jumping up in the air. Surely she'd signed up for an advanced class. They wanted her to do ten of these? The odds of her projectile vomiting after five was high.

"To modify down," Tanner yelled, "just take out the pushup!"

He started to give instructions on how to modify up, but Grace stopped listening because who the hell wanted this to be *harder*?

Kelly did, apparently.

They started out with Kelly on burpees and Grace on deadlifts, dragging her ten-pound weights up and down her shins, impressed she was keeping up but horrified by her own form. Tanner came over and told her to straighten her back, asking if she was feeling the move in her glutes. She nodded even though she had no idea where she was feeling it. Her bones? Her soul? They all felt pretty fatigued.

Kelly modified up, then up again, adding a "star jack" to the end of each burpee, and finishing so quickly that Grace only got seven deadlifts in. Kelly tapped her on the shoulder to signify they needed to switch, and Grace took her place on the floor, nervous about doing a burpee wrong and having the whole gym acknowledge her mediocre physical abilities. But as she took a moment to collect herself, she realized everyone was so into what they were doing, they weren't paying attention to anyone else, unless it was to shout compliments in their direction.

"YOU'RE SO STRONG!" one woman shouted to her partner in the middle of a chest press.

"Is that a PR?!" someone squealed from behind Grace.

There must be something behind the science of endorphins, because these women were downright *delightful*. She looked across to Kelly, who was (wo)manhandling eighty-pound barbells, and had to catch herself as her jaw hung open in awe.

Grace could do this. She could do twelve burpees. Hell, this moment had her feeling like she could finish this class, get her answers from Kelly, solve Garrett's murder, run a marathon, and climb Mount Everest.

And this confidence lasted for about four burpees, until the contents of Grace's stomach started to make themselves more known and her breathing went from quick and light intakes to the way Grace assumed she'd breathe with two collapsed lungs during an asthma attack.

At the end of the forty-five minutes, Grace collapsed in a pile on the floor, her heart slamming against her chest like a rabid animal in a cage. Tanner was telling everyone what stretch to do based on what hurt, but she hurt everywhere. Somewhere in the back of her throat, she felt the metallic taste of blood, and she briefly wondered if anyone had ever exercised to death.

A shadow fell over her face and she looked up to see Kelly backlit by the gym's fluorescent lights. She reached out her hand to help Grace up.

"Great job, newbie!" Kelly said as she hoisted Grace to vertical, supporting her a bit as she wobbled dizzily.

"Oh, thanks. I think I might have coughed up a chunk of my lung."

Kelly giggled. "It gets a little bit easier every time. But don't tell them that. Tanner is always looking to make his members more miserable."

Grace smiled and followed Kelly toward the lockers where gym members kept their things. No time for recovery, Grace's real work was starting.

"So, Kelly..." Grace said, grabbing a small towel off a table to wipe her soaked face. She scrunched it into a ball and threw it toward a laundry basket, missing completely.

I'll come back for that.

"...what do you do when you're not here, training for the American Gladiators?"

Kelly clapped her hands and squealed. *"Ooh,* I wish. I loved that show!" She opened a locker and pulled out a black leather purse. "My job is not gladiator-level exciting, unfortunately. I run the local chapter of our historical society."

"Oh, I am such a history buff!" Grace lied.

"Oh yeah!? That's wonderful! Are you into Philadelphia's history in particular?"

"Actually, I'm from Florida. I was very involved in the... you know, with... any history stuff. Anything I could find."

Please don't ask me to name a single fact about Florida.

"I love to see it! It's so rare to find someone your age who is passionate about history." Kelly was turning to head back out into the lobby of the gym. Grace needed more time to speak to her, preferably when she wasn't so aware of the smell of her own body. She took a few strides to try to keep in step with Kelly.

"I am *so* passionate. I'd love to possibly get a look at your office. See what the setup is like. I'd love to get involved with... that scene... here."

Kelly stopped walking and looked toward Grace. She bit the corner of her bottom lip and seemed to be considering something. She started to root around in her bag for something and pulled out a glossy pamphlet. She held it out for Grace to take.

"By chance, are you free tomorrow?"

TO: grac3and3rson@gmail.com
FROM: Josephine.Baros@gmail.com
SUBJECT: Research

Hi Grace!
Wanted to send a quick email so we're on the same page! Clearly, we're no experts when it comes to investigation. But every expert was an amateur once, and I'm sure that with our combined brainpower and the internet, we'll be Poirots in no time.

But we will need some help, so I've started a list of tips that might help us out. Here's what I have so far. They're all about how to question suspects:

1. When interviewing a suspect, allow them to sit by a door so they feel more comfortable and like they can leave.
2. Speak low and slow to help keep them calm.
3. Ask them questions about positive things in their lives.
4. Expect simple answers from simple questions if someone isn't lying.

Planning on adding these to a shared document for both of us to add to as we go along. I'll send the link when I get a chance, but I thought if you read this before you met up with Kelly, it might help! Good luck!

xo,
Jo

Chapter 8

"So uhhh… what exactly does this have to do with history?"

Grace could barely see through the eye holes of the costume, and breathing was even harder. She'd placed the head on a mere thirty seconds ago and already she could feel the sweat drip down her forehead. *This day was a waste of makeup.*

She felt a hand, presumably Kelly's, on her arm, pulling her to the right. She went along with it, mostly because whoever it was *had* to have a better look at where she was stepping than she did. The arm slid up to her shoulder, then she felt another hand on the other side. The hands rooted her firmly in front of a mirror where, if she squinted, she could see her body, green and bulbous, covered head-to-toe in the Philly Phanatic costume.

"Well, it's less about history and more about pride in our city," Kelly said, smiling. At least, Grace assumed she was smiling. Her voice sounded amused, possibly relieved it was Grace suffocating in this lime nightmare and not her.

When Kelly recruited Grace for the "Philly Heritage Festival" this was not what she'd had in mind. She'd mentally prepped to hand out educational fliers or man a table of "FLY, EAGLES, FLY" T-shirts, not to be Dutch-ovened in a temple of other people's sweat.

Kelly grabbed Grace again, turning her so they faced each other.

"Thank you *so* much for doing this. The usual mascot broke his ankle and they told me they were sending backup, but I didn't believe them. And it's a good thing I didn't, because he's nowhere to be found." She patted Grace's shoulders, her eyes narrowing. "If they hadn't sent the costume ahead of time, I'd be knocking down their door right now. I may look sweet, but when someone wrongs me, I don't let them forget it."

The muscles in Grace's stomach constricted as she thought of all the ways Kelly could make someone *remember*. Poison, for one.

Kelly's features grew softer. "Don't you worry, alright? I'll be acting as your handler today, so I'll be here to answer all your questions."

Even the ones about Garrett's death, Grace added in her head.

Kelly grabbed onto Grace's furry green hand and started to lead her toward the door of her office. The festival was mercifully outdoors, just outside Kelly's building. When Grace turned her head at the right moment, she could feel a faint, refreshing breeze. Kelly led her through two doorways, down four stairs, then out into the crowd, standing shoulder to shoulder with no clear paths. They made it about ten feet before something collided with Grace's right leg. She couldn't look down to see what it was, and when she heard a low growl, she panicked that a dog was attacking her. She couldn't blame it, really. She looked like an oversized chew toy.

But then Kelly spoke to it. "Hi there, sweetie! You want to give our buddy here a hug?"

A human child, then, Grace thought. She almost greeted the little guy or girl before she realized that in her esteemed role, she had no speaking parts.

She felt a little squeeze on her leg, and her heart melted a bit. Maybe she could get used to this.

And then, like clockwork, she felt a heavy arm fall over her shoulders. She turned to face what she assumed was the father of the child, who asked, eyebrows wagging, "Is there a boy birdie or a girl birdie hiding in there?"

Nevermind. There was no getting used to it.

The Northwest Philadelphia Heritage festival was in its fourth year under Kelly. For two days every September, the four blocks outside of Kelly's office were closed to traffic and lined with local vendors, artists, and entertainers.

Garrett had never gotten an invitation to show off his art, Jo had pointed out.

Like any other outdoor event, the air around the festival smelled like freshly roasted nuts and porta-potties, with an occasional whiff of cotton candy or hot sausage depending on where you were standing. While Kelly and Grace would be roaming, meeting adoring fans, their base camp was under a large balloon arch in front of a Phillies-themed backdrop.

"People love a good selfie," Kelly yelled in Grace's ear.

"Renegade" by Styx played over the crowd, and Grace wondered how she was ever going to put this into a resume.

Grace nearly cried tears of joy when, about an hour later, Kelly announced, "Our furry friend needs something to eat right now, so we're going to take a quick break and be back soon!"

She felt Kelly's sturdy grip again, and they headed in the direction of the office. Grace was going to milk this break as much as possible. First, she was going to hydrate heavily, and then she was going to try one of the gyros being sold next to their designated photo spot. The wafting scent of lamb and tzatziki had been making her mouth water. She was pretty sure some drool had fallen into the costume. Maybe she'd grab a funnel cake when she was done. Surely she deserved it.

But then Grace's foot touched something, and all her plans for a gluttonous lunch break went out the window. Grace had no idea what she had tripped over. She worried it was another small child coming in for a hug, or maybe a large dog, caught up and terrified between her furry green legs. All she knew was that she was falling, and hard.

No one thinks of holding their head on as they fall, because 1) it's typically attached, and 2) you're more focused on putting your arms out to cushion the blow and protect your face. And that's what Grace did as she slammed into the ground, the padded mittens of the Philly Phanatic a welcome blessing as they slammed the pavement instead of Grace's skin. But just as she felt the relief wash over her as she realized she was unharmed, she heard the screams. To her left, three small children watched everything unfold. They saw her trip, her journey to the ground, and the shock that sent her mascot head flying through the crowd.

Minutes ago, these kids had been hyping themselves up to meet a beloved baseball icon, and now they were staring at him on the ground, his head removed and replaced with the head of a woman who needed to start applying retinol more regularly. Grace thought about the therapy bills, all the sessions they'd need to sit through to watch a baseball game without wondering whether their favorite mascot would leave with his or her head attached.

An overstimulating cacophony rose over the crowd; the children's screams, the shocked and amused murmur of spectators, and then a man's voice, booming over it all: "THIS IS COMPLETELY AGAINST PROTOCOL!"

Much like her knowledge of murder, Grace now knew more about the best practices of working as a professional mascot than she ever wanted to know.

For instance, it was imperative that as a mascot, you were never caught headless or pantless. While Grace felt like a mascot missing its pants was much more problematic than it missing its head, Phillies contractor and local actor Brett Martin assured her they were equally as damning. The other cardinal rules of being a mascot were to never walk around without your handler, and to never pick up a child. Brett seemed unimpressed that Grace hadn't committed these infractions as well.

"When you fail to follow protocol, you disrespect the suit and the organization it represents." Brett's arms were crossed, the veins in his neck protruding like bright purple worms.

He took this very seriously.

Grace looked toward Kelly, unsure of the appropriate reaction, and was relieved to see Kelly come undone in a fit of laughter. This disgusted Brett, who stormed out of the building, nearly getting a Phanatic foot stuck between the double doors.

"I bet he's fun at parties," Kelly gasped, holding her stomach.

Grace let herself laugh, too. She was probably on some sort of blacklist now. Every costume rental company for ten miles in any direction would have a copy of her picture with a red X over it.

"I'm sorry, Kelly. I did my best." Grace wiped under her eyes, looking at her hands afterward and cringing at the residue from her cheap mascara.

Kelly was shaking her head and walking toward her desk chair. "It's alright, sweetie. Not your fault. That piñata came out of nowhere."

"Wha– I tripped on a *piñata*?"

Kelly was laughing again, tears forming in the corners of her eyes. "Yes! They were trying to get it ready for the kids when the wind took it, I guess." She pulled a tissue from her desk and gently patted at her eyes. "Don't worry, the kids who saw you headless were given the first spots in line to whack it. They've probably forgotten all about it by now, halfway to a sugar coma."

Grace walked over to the seat across from Kelly, face plastered with a smile. "Is this a normal day at the historical society?"

Kelly smiled contentedly, the wrinkles on her face deepening. She clearly loved her job. "Luckily, there are no normal days here. But it's never boring, if that's what you mean."

As Grace relaxed, she remembered she was here for a reason. She couldn't leave today without Kelly's alibi or confession. She needed to steer the conversation toward the gift shop.

Ask them questions about positive things in their lives.

"How did you end up in this position anyway?" she prodded. "What did you do before this?"

Kelly's posture stiffened, a hint that Grace was poking close to a bruise. She thought about what Kelly had said earlier about revenge.

"Well, you could say it was my own embarrassing slip-up that led me here."

Grace tried not to react. She wanted the conversation to happen organically.

"My family owned a gift store for decades. It was the cutest little shop on the cutest little street, and generations of families would come in to find the perfect gift. I grew up there, I have so many beautiful memories with community members." She smiled sadly.

"And then my grandmother died, and my mom took over the store. I was next in line, but my mother got sick. I'm an only child and there was no one else to care for her after my dad died, so I had to shut the store down until she recuperated." Kelly was picking at one of her cuticles, unable to look up.

Behind her was a temple to her successes. Photos of her at community events, even a photo of her shaking hands with the mayor as he presented an award, the same trophy sitting next to the photo on the shelf. Kelly was obviously well regarded by the people around her. Did that make it easier to get away with murder, or was it evidence that she'd never do anything to tarnish that reputation?

"But she didn't recuperate. She spent a few long, expensive months in the hospital, where she died." Kelly let out a sniff. "And thanks to the hospital bills and the months the store was closed, I didn't have the money to keep paying the mortgage. I was forced to put the store on the market."

Tears slowly poured down Kelly's face, and Grace's heart tingled at her pain. "I'm so sorry, Kelly. That sounds awful."

Kelly grabbed her tissue again and wiped at the fresh tears. "Yeah, it was. It was really awful, but then I went and made it even more awful." She laughed at herself. "A man ended up buying the building, and I was furious. It wasn't his fault, I know, and it's not like I expected some handout would save me from selling, but..."

She trailed off, wiped her nose with the back of her hand, forgetting the tissue.

"The store was everything to my mother and grandmother, and then it was just gone. And I was so, so angry. So angry that I showed up at the art studio that used to be my store and spraypainted the sidewalk to deter visitors." She placed her head in her hands. "So, far more embarrassing than tripping on a piñata, I'm afraid."

There are bad people and then there are good people who do bad things, and it seemed like Kelly was the latter.

"Did you – I mean, have you apologized? To the man?"

Kelly leaned forward and placed her elbows on her desk. "I meant to. But..." She tilted her chin down, staring at a large desk calendar covered in red and blue scribbles. "...he passed away, unfortunately. Recently. Just last week."

Grace tried to keep her voice from quaking. She was so close to the information she needed. "Oh my gosh, that's terrible. What happened?"

Expect simple answers from simple questions if someone isn't lying.

When Kelly spoke, she looked right at Grace, her answer clear.

"They think he was murdered."

Grace held eye contact.

"Do they have any idea who did it?"

Kelly finally broke the stare, looking back at her desk. "I don't know, but I haven't heard anything about a lead." She stood now and walked over to the window. "I wish I'd said sorry sooner. I wish I'd been in town, maybe the universe would have sent me a sign to go over there, say what I've wanted to say, before it was too late."

Grace's spine stiffened. She stood too, but didn't move closer to Kelly.

"You weren't around? When he died?"

Kelly shook her head. "No, the board took a trip into the city to get a behind-the-scenes tour of a historic hotel under restoration. Here, look."

Kelly pulled out her phone and started to search for something. She let out a few "oops" and "darn its" and Grace considered asking her if she needed help before Kelly seemed to find what she was looking for.

She turned her phone around to reveal a picture of her in front of the "LOVE" statue. "Can you believe I'd never visited this before? My New Year's resolution was to be a better tourist in my own city."

She turned the phone back to look at the screen again, smiling down at herself posing for the camera.

Kelly Dewitt was most definitely not a murderer. She'd made a mistake, had an embarrassing little slip. But she didn't kill Garrett. Even without the alibi, Grace was sure.

Kelly seemed to remember herself, and she looked up at Grace, eyes misty. "Another resolution is going to be to apologize to the artist's wife. It's the closest I'll get to saying it to him, I suppose."

She slipped the phone back into her pocket and wiped at her face with both hands. "Oh, look at me, blubbering. I need to get back out there." She offered Grace a smile. "If you sign up on our website, you'll get emails about all our events. I'd be happy to have you volunteer again. I send the emails out myself, so you can reply to them directly. I promise, none will require a costume."

When Grace got home that night, she called Jo to update her. Jo had been just as surprised as Grace that Kelly was so torn up over Garrett's death, but it would have been a shame if she'd turned out to be the killer. It wouldn't feel as satisfying if finding Garrett's murderer also meant destroying the reputation of a local family.

"I hope she reaches out to me," Jo said, a hissing noise rising from the background. "Sorry, I'm having a late dinner."

Like it heard the mention of food, Grace's stomach growled. She didn't feel like cooking and decided to grab a Hot Pocket from her freezer on her way to bed. But before she hung up, she wanted to ask a question that had been nagging at her.

"Hey, Jo?"

"Yeah?"

"Why didn't you hire a private investigator to help you solve this? I mean, I understand you don't trust the police, but a PI would work for you directly."

Grace heard the clanging of a pan on the other end of the line, then what may have been a plate placed on the counter. For a moment, she considered asking again. Maybe Jo hadn't heard. But finally, she answered.

"Maybe it's silly of me to be so untrusting of a world where I've most often gotten the benefit of the doubt, but paying a total stranger to help solve a crime didn't appeal to me. If I can buy them, it means they're for sale. You never know what someone is willing to do to make a buck."

Grace took a seat at her dining table. "But you're paying me. And you didn't know me, either."

Jo was quiet for a moment, and Grace wondered if she'd accidentally led Jo to an epiphany. *"OH MY GOSH, YOU'RE RIGHT."*

But there was no shocked realization in Jo's voice. Just the hint of a smile. "I don't know how to explain it, Grace, but even when you were a stranger, I knew you were someone I could trust."

Chapter 9

Grace learned more about Jo and Garrett's relationship every day.

For instance, she learned Jo and Garrett had met at a small gallery opening downtown, and for Garrett, it was love at first sight.

"I don't even know why he noticed me. I was still a mess at twenty-five. I was plastered. The gallery opening started at six pm, so it was not an appropriate time and place to be drunk." Jo had smiled while telling the story, but her eyes imparted the deep sadness she was working through. "He was twenty-eight, and he'd wanted to settle down for a while at this point. I figured I had a few more years to be wild and crazy. I guess he saw my potential." Jo stared at her wine glass, swirling the dry red like some great truth would be revealed at the bottom of her glass. "He moved in a week later."

Jo reached up to pick at a patch of skin on her arm. A nervous tic, Grace assumed. "At first, I didn't even think we'd get married. I was happy enough to live in sin, traveling the world and tackling one adventure after the next. But when Garrett proposed in Iceland – oh, it was stunning. We were floating in this hot spring, and I looked over at him, steam rising off his shoulders, and the most beautiful piece of jewelry I'd ever seen in my life… and realized it felt right. I wanted to be Mrs Baros, for better or worse. The next year, we got married." Jo dropped her arm now, still smiling but shaking her head. "My dad was furious the prenup wasn't more punishing in the event of a split, but from day one, I knew I could trust Garrett. I believed in him. I believed in us."

Jo's smile strained. Grace wondered what scene from their lives Jo pictured when she thought of Garrett.

"And how did your dad react when you sold the house?" Grace asked as she repositioned herself on the couch, pulling a leg up beneath her. Her untouched wine glass sat on the coffee table. Normally, Grace would never drink on the job. However, most jobs didn't involve solving a murder with a wealthy, depressed widow.

"Oh," Jo scoffed, "he wasn't pleased, but he didn't put up much of a fight when I told him I'd be investing the money from the sale. What use did we have for all that room?"

Grace looked around at the six-bed, seven-bath home that Jo downsized to. How different her and Jo's lives had been.

"We did use a small portion of the sale to purchase Garrett's studio space as well. At first, he just used it as an office, a place for him to go and paint undisturbed. Eventually, as word about him started to spread, he realized he needed help and hired Vivian."

Jo's tone changed as she said Vivian's name, her nose scrunching as if she'd smelled something rotten.

"And… what was Vivian like?" Grace asked, finally reaching for her drink. It was risky business to ask about someone you'd replaced, whether it was an employee, an ex-girlfriend, or a friend. Comparison is the thief of joy.

Jo considered the question for a moment, then turned to Grace. "You know how there are some women… you just know they're a girl's girl? Well, Vivian wasn't like that. She was a hard worker, and she clearly didn't feel we had that in common. I admit, I've had a lot of lucky breaks in my life, but I've also worked hard to build things." She grabbed a throw pillow and hugged it against her body. "I never felt like she was cheering for me. I was always cheering for her. I was the one who pushed for her last raise." She sighed, then reached for Grace's hand, which she gave hesitantly.

"To be honest, I'm glad Vivian wasn't the one who was working for Garrett when he died. I wouldn't have offered her a job. She never felt trustworthy to me." She pulled her hand away.

"Was she so untrustworthy that you think she may have been involved in Garrett's death?" Grace said before taking a sip. Very dry. She preferred sweet.

"Oh, no," Jo replied, rolling her eyes. "Honestly, she doesn't have it in her. She's far too prim and proper to get her hands dirty. And she's far too smart to bite… or kill… the hand that feeds her. Her professional reputation is everything to her. If she were going to break the law, she'd do it somewhere else."

Jo set her glass down on the coffee table and reached both hands into the air to stretch, a high-pitched yawn escaping as she did so.

"Still," she continued, "I was surprised when she put in her notice. I'd encouraged Garrett to get her to spill more details, but he insisted Vivian's career moves were her business, and he'd start looking for a replacement right away. Garrett was awful at any part of a business that wasn't creative, so I was excited when he said he'd hired a new assistant two weeks later. For some reason, he didn't give many details about you either. He didn't mention that you didn't have the same art history experience Vivian had."

A wave of imposter syndrome hit Grace square in the chest.

"What made you think you could trust me?" she said, unconsciously pushing for Jo to boost her confidence. Their conversation about why Jo didn't hire a private eye had lingered in Grace's mind.

"Well, there was the whole police aspect. The fact that they didn't see any glaring red flags in you."

Grace nodded. *But you don't trust the police,* she thought.

"And then I took the chance and showed up at your apartment. I figured I'd be able to judge if you were someone I wanted to be around."

Jo stopped to take a sip of her drink, then gently placed the stemless glass back on the table.

"If I'm being honest, when I first walked into the apartment, I was pretty sure you were a sociopath. Nothing on the walls, everything in boxes." She chuckled. "But you were kind and you asked about me and... I don't know. You looked like a deer in headlights, and that's how I was feeling. I knew I was about to spend a lot of time alone, that I'd now be coming home to an empty house. If I was going to find out what happened to Garrett, I would need to have someone to hold my hand through it all." She shrugged. "You didn't have a coffee table, but you seemed to have a heart."

A week passed with some semblance of normalcy. In certain moments, you'd never believe Jo was a grieving widow.

Others, it was hard to imagine her getting out of bed. She continued to show signs of grief, depression, and a possible drinking problem. More than one night ended with Jo passing out on the couch and Grace rinsing out an armful of wine bottles in the sink. Jo was prone to crying fits followed by long periods where she stared out the window. Grace didn't mind this caregiver position. She'd taken care of her mother after her grandmother passed in a similar way. However long this period of mourning lasted for Jo, Grace could support her through it.

At the start of the last week in September, Jo sent Grace on a field trip.

Jo led her down to the basement and opened a storage closet Grace hadn't noticed before. Once Jo had turned on a dim light, Grace realized she was looking at dozens of Garrett's original paintings, including the ones intended for the Institute of Contemporary Art.

Jo crossed her arms and stared into the closet. "The museum called. They still want to feature Garrett's art, minus the stolen painting, of course."

Grace's stomach clenched at the mention of the missing painting. It had to be a clue. Why else would someone take it with them?

Jo wasn't even looking at Grace, which was good, because Grace could feel perspiration building at her hairline.

"I thought about telling them no. It would be easy to keep these last paintings for myself, even if they are portraits of a bunch of old dead men." She shivered after saying "dead men." "These were created with a purpose, and I'd like for them to be seen."

She looked at Grace. "I need you to take them to the museum before I change my mind."

The Institute of Contemporary Art is nestled into the Ivy League UPenn campus within walking distance of a Wawa, both of which are big deals if you're familiar with Philadelphia culture. The building itself is not memorable, square panels of sheet metal resembling a wedding dance floor, large windows tossed in for function. But Grace knew once she was inside, she'd get a peek at some of the more impressive art experiences in the city.

She parked at a garage a block away and grabbed the oversized Ikea bag containing Garrett's last pieces from her passenger seat. She made quick work of the walk, pulling her coat up to shield her face from the bitter wind, but by the time she stepped through the glass double doors of the museum, she couldn't feel any of her exposed skin. As she rubbed her hands together, a man at the welcome desk called out.

"Hello, ma'am! Welcome to the Institute of Contemporary Art! How can I help you?"

Grace looked up and realized that *man* was probably the wrong word. The *boy* in front of her had perfectly smooth dark skin, a strong hairline, and braces. She cringed at his use of the word *ma'am*. How old did he think she was?

"Hi! Um, my name is Grace Anderson. I'm looking for Hilda Thompson. She should be expecting me, I'm here on behalf of Jo Baros."

The boy looked eager to help, displaying the kind of joy in his job usually reserved for CEOs and Chick-fil-A workers.

"Absolutely, ma'am." He unclipped a walkie-talkie from his belt and pointed to the corner of the room at something resembling a rock. "You can take a seat over there, and I'll call Hilda down. Shouldn't be long."

Grace thanked him and walked to the designated seating area. The rock was some sort of large ottoman upholstered in a canvas-like cloth, but she was absolutely not going to sit on it. This whole place felt like she was six years old standing at the threshold of a friend's parents' formal living room. Everything was too breakable to touch.

Grace was in the museum for less time than it had taken her to drive there. Hilda, an elegant Asian woman who appeared to be in her mid-fifties, did not like to beat around the bush. She thanked Grace for transporting the art and then bluntly asked, "Did they find Garrett's killer yet?"

Grace hadn't discussed the murder with anyone other than Jo and Sean, and she felt a stab of discomfort in her stomach. Garrett's death had probably been a fruitful event for Hilda; the most revered artists were the ones struck down in their prime. Art is still business, at the end of the day.

Grace forced her face into what she hoped was a soft smile. "No. Not yet," she said, before excusing herself and hurrying back out into the cold.

She took a few moments to collect herself. Hilda's unexpected question had Grace's nervous system on high alert. She took stock of everything around her. Since she was already in the city, she figured it wouldn't hurt to do some exploring. She felt guilty playing tourist on the clock, but a quick spin around the UPenn campus wasn't really sightseeing, it was just a different route back to her truck, right? A detour.

A college campus would be the perfect spot to get a good cup of coffee, she hoped. She started off down the street, taking in the bustle of the city. A delivery man was dropping off produce at a bodega. Two doors down, a vape shop owner was lifting the metal gate that protected his storefront. It was the third vape shop she'd passed that morning. Maybe she'd missed her calling as an entrepreneur.

Just as she got close to the sage green facade of College Hall, her phone rang. She worried it was Jo, upset that she hadn't immediately reported back to the house once she finished at the museum. What if Hilda called her? But when she slipped the phone from her pocket and saw her mom's name, she let her body calm.

She answered with a sweet, "Hello, mama!"

And was responded to with a sharp, "Grace Anderson, when the hell were you going to tell your dad and me that you discovered your boss's dead body?"

Shit. The anxious feeling returned as quickly as it had retreated.

Grace didn't get a chance to respond before her mother launched into a lecture.

"I *knew* it was a bad idea to let you go up there. Your father was *so* excited for you to 'get back to your roots.' Bullshit. You can't have roots in a place you've never been! He was excited for you to check out *his* roots, and now it's clear his roots are *in a danger zone.*"

"Mom. Mom. MOM!" Grace attempted several failed interjections.

"Since when do you not tell us things like this? I've been asking you how you've been doing and you've been LYING to me, telling me you're fine, and you're not!"

"I AM FINE," Grace yelled, suddenly regretting her short trek to the university. The lawn was still a vibrant green, though the semi-mature trees that lined the brick walkways were starting to lose their leaves. Onlookers were probably wondering why she'd chosen such a peaceful slice of nature to scream into her phone.

She started walking again, back in the direction she came.

"I am fine, Mom. I live in a safe apartment building you vetted yourself. I never came into contact with anyone dangerous, and I already have a new job."

"How in the world do you have a new job?! It's been, what? Two weeks? Were you updating your resume at the crime scene?"

"Well, I got lucky. Something came up, and it was a good opportunity."

"You're being vague here, Grace, and I can't help but think it's on purpose. You'd better start giving me some details before I book a plane ticket and make you explain it to me in person."

Trish Anderson did not share her daughter's meekness. She meant every word of this.

"OK, OK, I am working for my old boss's wife."

A pause.

"You're working for the dead man's wife?"

"Yes."

She was back to yelling again. "Are you *kidding me*, Grace? Who's to say she's not the killer's next victim?! Or hell, that she didn't kill him herself?!"

"She's been cleared, Mother. She has a strong alibi, and she's dedicated to helping the police solve the murder." Well, she was dedicated to *solving* the murder, but Grace didn't feel the need to give her mom an aneurysm by filling her in.

"Wait," said Grace, thinking through the conversation. "How do you even know the details of what happened?"

Maya wasn't usually a snitch, but it would be easy for her to blame the postpartum hormones.

"When you got the job, Dad added your boss's name to his Google Alerts. He's been spending time in his garden, which helps with his stress, so he hasn't been on the computer much. He logged on about an hour ago and read one of the news articles."

There was silence for a moment.

"Honey, are you alright? The article said his assistant found the body. That's you, right? That had to be tough."

Grace sighed. Her mom meant well.

"Honestly, Mom, the new job is already helping. Supporting the widow through this helps to keep my mind busy. My fingers are crossed that the police will figure all this out soon, so I can figure out my next steps. For right now, this feels like the right thing for me to do."

She held her breath, hoping her mom's next words would not be, *"I booked a flight."* She was almost back to the parking garage now, and too worked up to stay in the city a minute longer. She'd get her coffee from a Starbucks drive-thru like all the other suburbanites.

Trish sighed. "I don't know, honey, I don't like this. It's not like you to put yourself in a dangerous situation, but I also trust you know what you're doing."

She could be dramatic, but Grace could say this much about her mother: she was supportive. Even of the stupid shit.

"I promise, I know what I'm doing. I miss you. However, I am doing well here. Tell Daddy I love and miss him, too. If anyone knows the police have it under control, it's him."

If things continued the same way they were, the police would have Garrett's murder solved before Jo even mentioned her investigation again.

Chapter 10

"I made a crime board!"

Jo was waiting at the door when Grace arrived on Tuesday. She still looked tired and melancholic, but she was wearing jeans and a silk blouse, her makeup light and fresh. As Grace grew closer, she didn't smell the scent of booze she'd been starting to associate with Jo. Instead, she caught a hint of Jo's light and citrusy perfume.

Jo grabbed Grace's hand and started to pull her toward the door leading to the basement. Grace let her bag slip off her shoulder onto the floor and tried to slide her shoes off, to no avail. They rushed down the stairs and turned toward a spare bedroom. "I worked all weekend," Jo huffed, out of breath. They walked into the room, where a large whiteboard-turned-crime-board was waiting for them, ominously. "I got everything finalized while you went to the museum for me yesterday."

Jo was elated, beaming as though she were showing off her life's work.

"I found YouTube videos on how to set everything up," she said, gesturing to the whiteboard taking up the bulk of the room. "There were even videos on how to *solve* crimes. Give the internet a few more years and it will render the police useless."

Grace didn't even respond to this, especially since she was still hoping the police would call at any minute to tell them they had it all figured out. She looked at the whiteboard. It seemed a little bit silly that Jo had set this whole thing up, because from the looks of it, she only had two suspects, one of whom they'd already ruled out. Still, she should have expected that Jo had something in the works. She'd taken a peek at the research document at midnight and saw that Jo was adding details in real time.

"Why is Kelly on here?" Grace asked. Surely Jo didn't have any suspicions of Kelly now. Grace was *not* climbing back into that costume to get any more answers. Besides, Brett would never let her.

"Oh!" Jo trilled. She took a marker and drew an X over Kelly's face.

"You know when you're writing a to-do list and you start with something you've already done so you can feel more accomplished?"

Grace nodded, and Jo nodded back as an answer.

"So, who is the guy?"

In a photo next to Kelly's was a thirtysomething man with blond hair and a five o'clock shadow who looked faintly familiar.

Jo cleared her throat, obviously ready to present the case. She signaled for Grace to sit on the edge of the guest bed, then took her place next to the whiteboard.

"This is Wyatt Randall." Jo suddenly had a pointer in her hand that she smacked hard against Wyatt's photo on the board.

That name. Grace had heard it before. "Where do I know him from?"

"If you've been handling Garrett's calendar, you probably added their dinner to it."

Ah. The artist Garrett was up against for the exhibit in the city.

"They were both on the shortlist for the Institute of Contemporary Art's exhibit," Jo confirmed. "As you know, Garrett was ultimately picked for the show, but when they met for dinner, a few weeks before it was announced, Wyatt begged Garrett to drop out of the competition. He said the exhibit was exactly what he needed to get his career off the ground. It's not a secret in the area or in the art world that I come from money, though I don't think anyone knew I was funding Garrett's work. Wyatt told Garrett not everyone had a rich wife to fall back on. He promised him that if he dropped out, he'd talk him up in interviews about the exhibit. Garrett let him know in simple terms that it wasn't going to happen. He told Wyatt he was hoping to get his name out there more on a national scale."

"You think Wyatt would kill Garrett over one exhibit?"

"Ask anyone in the local art scene and they'll tell you Wyatt is a loose cannon. It's why he's still looking for that huge break. He's a talented guy, but his temper has cost him opportunities." Jo turned to Grace with a serious face. "Based on what some women in the industry have hinted to me, he's an all-around bad guy."

"OK, that's a motive, I guess."

Grace went to ask who had leaked this information to Jo, but her phone rang. Grace apologized and pulled the phone out of her pocket to see the caller was "HANNAH TEMP."

"Ahh, I've got to take this."

Jo was already waving Grace away with a hand. "Go ahead and take it in the theater."

The way Jo said it made it seem normal. Like sending someone to the theater was akin to giving them directions to a bathroom or another essential room in the house.

Grace ran down the hall, kicking herself for not updating Hannah before this. As part of her contract, she had a quick call with the agency every two weeks to give updates. The last one had fallen just after Grace started working for Jo, but with so many changes happening, Grace had cancelled, not feeling up to giving the full explanation.

Grace shut the door of the theater as she pressed the green button on her phone. "Hello?"

"Grace! Hi, there! It's Hannah. You OK to talk right now?"

"Hi, Hannah. And yes, I can take a few minutes."

"Just wanted to see how everything was going with Mr Baros!"

Grace took a deep breath and stared up at the ceiling.

"Um. Mr Baros is dead."

There was silence at the other end of the line for what felt like too long of a beat.

"I'm sorry, can you repeat that?"

"Mr Baros, my boss, died. Just over two weeks ago. I found his body. The police think he was murdered."

"Holy shit," said Hannah quietly. She obviously panicked when she realized this had come out and followed that up with, "I'm so sorry, that was unprofessional of me. I'm sorry to hear this. Are you OK?"

"I guess I'm better than him."

Oh my god, that was so inappropriate.

Hannah didn't seem to know how to respond. "Well," she said before clearing her throat, "I guess it's back to the beginning to find you a new placement."

"I have another job."

"Oh. Well. What are you doing?"

I've joined a novice detective agency run by a thirty-seven-year-old possible alcoholic who is processing immense trauma, Grace thought.

"Mr Baros's wife offered to hire me as her assistant. It has been... uh... therapeutic for both of us to have someone to lean on."

Hannah seemed to consider this, and Grace had to admit when she said it out loud, she and Jo were an odd pair.

"Well, that, uh, I mean that's a wonderful thing to come out of such a tragedy," Hannah said, unconvincingly. "Do you know how long you'll be working with Mrs Baros?"

Much like many other things in Jo's life, Grace's contract was loose and open to interpretation. During her first (and only) read over, Grace questioned whether it was even legally binding, but she took Jo's lawyer's signature to mean she had nothing to worry about.

"I'm not sure. To be honest, I'm taking it day by day."

"Oh, yes, I'm sure," said Hannah. "That's to be expected. But um," Grace could hear the shuffling of papers on the other end of the call, "how about I keep our next scheduled call, to check in? And in the meantime, I'll talk with my team to make sure you get all the payments you're owed from the agency. We want to make sure the contract is wrapped up smoothly from every angle."

"That sounds great, Hannah. Thanks."

"Sure, Grace. We'll chat soon."

Grace imagined Hannah hanging up and running to the breakroom to tell everyone about the client who found her boss's body. If anything, at least it made for an interesting story.

Grace made her way back to the guest-bedroom-turned-detective-agency and sat back down on the bed. "Sorry, that was the temp agency," she told Jo.

Jo had been writing something on the corner of the whiteboard, but turned when she realized Grace was back. "What temp agency?"

"You know, the one Garrett hired me through."

Jo looked at Grace quizzically. She capped the marker, set it on the tray of the board, and turned back to Grace with her arms crossed.

"Why would Garrett use a temp agency to hire you?"

"No idea. He wanted someone quickly?"

Jo wasn't looking in Grace's direction; instead, she was tapping her foot on the carpet and staring at a blank wall.

"You can get a quick hire on social media nowadays. You use a temp agency when you aren't sure if the position is going to be available for long," Jo mumbled. Grace wasn't even sure if she was meant to hear it.

Jo looked at her. "You said you didn't have any art experience, right?"

"No, I have a business degree. I barely made it through one gen-ed art class in college."

Jo was pacing now, her elbows pushed back and her hands at the base of her back, giving her the posture and composure of a confused Forrest Gump.

"I remember when Garrett was hiring Vivian. He was adamant he needed someone with some art experience so they could work smoothly with the galleries. It took him months before he found her, and he turned down a ton of candidates who I think would have done a great job." Jo stopped and looked at Grace again. "So why was he not picky whatsoever when it came to you?"

Grace tried to pretend this was not the biggest burn someone had ever uttered directly to her face.

"I have no idea. I can ask Hannah. She's my contact at the agency. Maybe she'd have a better idea of what Garrett was looking for?"

Jo was chewing on her bottom lip as she thought about it. "Bring it up the next time you talk to her, I guess. It might not be important, but it's not making sense to me."

At this, Jo seemed to shake herself from that train of thought.

She smacked the pointer into her palm. "We know a few facts related to Garrett's murder. First, all the security cameras on the street went offline from ten pm to twelve am. They're all part of the same system that can be monitored from a security office, but they don't have a security officer on call 24/7, so no one local noticed an issue. The cameras came back on at 12:04 am. The police said they did their best at knocking on doors and questioning neighbors, but no one had seen anything, and it's possible they missed a few people who weren't home at the time."

Grace was astounded at the detail in Jo's story. "How do you know all this?"

"I've been calling the police station every few days."

Grace's face crumpled at this.

"What? Just because I don't trust them, it doesn't mean I can't use their intel."

Grace shrugged, and Jo continued.

"The medical examiner agrees that the ten to twelve window is most likely when Garrett died. They also believe poisoning was the cause of death, though the tests aren't back, and they said no bottles or glasses were found anywhere."

Jo was now pacing and staring down at the floor, clearly concentrating on getting the facts straight.

"This means whoever killed Garrett, he trusted. At least enough to sit down and have a drink with them."

"And you think he trusted Wyatt enough for that?"

Jo pointed in Grace's direction and seemed pleased she was engaged enough to ask questions.

"Yes, I do. It was only a few weeks ago that he met him for dinner. What difference does a change in scenery make? Despite his issues with Wyatt, I don't think Garrett held anything against him. He wasn't one to hold a grudge."

Clearly his wife doesn't share this personality trait, Grace thought. "OK, what else?"

Jo let out an exasperated sigh. "I mean, unfortunately, not much. The only fingerprints found were either Garrett's, yours, or belonged to the cleaning staff. Besides the missing painting he'd been working on, everything else seemed to be in place, including his laptop, which the police still have. And like I said, they haven't shared the results of the toxicology report."

"What about any eyewitnesses?"

"Most of the businesses on the street close at five pm, including the cafe, because they don't do dinner. And while I'd normally say there would be business owners hanging around to get some work done, there was a Chamber of Commerce meeting that night from six to nine pm. I'd assume most of them were home by ten."

"No people out for walks? No runners? That's weird, isn't it?"

Jo shrugged. "None that reported anything out of the ordinary. People walk around without looking up from their phones now, so it doesn't surprise me."

This didn't feel like an entry-level crime. In every mystery novel or whodunit movie, the killer leaves some clues behind. There was a witness, even if their story didn't line up. Or there was a wet footprint that was tracked to a specific type of shoe. This felt like a situation that should be handled by professionals, which was almost comforting to Grace. Surely, they would reach a dead end pretty quickly and have to let the police do what they needed to do.

She had been listening intently, but when Jo seemed finished laying out the facts, something popped into her head. "You told the police all of this, right? I mean, you gave them the names of the people you suspect?"

Jo crossed her arms and looked to her left, avoiding Grace's gaze. "Basically."

"What does that mean, basically? Did you tell the police exactly what you told me?"

"Not exactly. They are the 'professionals.'" She made air quotes around the word "professionals." "Surely they'll piece everything together enough to know who they need to talk to. And if they don't, it's fine. We'll handle it."

Grace was dumbfounded. "Jo! They are trying to help solve this! You can't keep information like this from them!"

"Listen," Jo said, taking a seat at the end of the bed next to Grace. "I led them in the right direction. I told them Garrett had a few tense moments with another artist who was hoping to land a spot in the exhibit, and I told them to check the local paper for an issue with the previous owners of the space. I did everything but give the names."

Grace couldn't understand Jo's motivation behind not giving the police every little detail. Even if she didn't trust them, their chances of finding out who killed Garrett would only improve with the precinct's help.

"OK, I promise I'll give them names afterward."

"After what?"

"After we find out what Wyatt was doing the night Garrett was murdered."

When Grace and Jo emerged from "the board room," as Jo was calling the spare bedroom, Grace almost screamed as she collided with someone. She backed up to see a petite older woman, maybe in her early seventies, wearing sweatpants and a faded black Beatles tee. The woman didn't seem too shaken up despite being nearly trampled, as if this was a normal part of her day.

"Oh God, I'm an *idiot,*" Jo said, taking the woman by the arm. "Grace, this is Gloria. Gloria, Grace. Today is her first day back since… everything happened with Garrett. But I was so excited about our… project… that I totally forgot to mention it."

If Jo was calling her investigation a "project," then Gloria didn't know about it. Knowing Gloria was good friends with Garrett's family, maybe she was worried about anyone finding out what they were up to. Grace didn't particularly want anyone to know she was sticking her nose where it didn't belong, so she was fine with Gloria being in the dark.

She reached out her hand to shake Gloria's. "It's nice to meet you. I know you were close to Garrett and the Baros family. I'm so sorry for your loss." She cleared her throat. "And for practically hip-checking you."

Gloria smiled warmly. "Not a problem, dear. These hips are in surprisingly good order." She looked at Jo and winked. "Just ask Andre."

Jo shook her head and gave Grace a look that said *can you believe her?* "Gloria is married to my driver, Andre. They were friends before they were employees." Jo wrapped the woman in a side hug, laughing as she said, "And Gloria, I love you, but that's disgusting."

Gloria hugged Jo back tightly. It was the kind of hug that revealed a matronly sort of affection. One that told you Gloria loved Jo and would protect her at any cost.

When the women broke their embrace, Jo turned to Grace again. "I'm going to run to the bathroom, and then I want to go over a few things that I added to… that document… with you. Meet me in Garrett's office?"

Grace gave a nod and Jo passed her, disappearing up the stairs.

Gloria seemed to be taking Grace in. Grace struggled to find a topic to make small talk, but the silence was interrupted by Gloria instead.

"I'm glad she has help, you know. Poor girl has gone through enough." Gloria grabbed a rag from her back pocket and swung it up over her shoulder. "I'm just going to ask that you keep a close eye on her. I've tossed more liquor bottles in the last few weeks than I have in my life." She let out a little choke.

"Anyway, I know she wants to find answers. We all want answers. I just hope she doesn't lose her mind in the process."

RESEARCH

How to lie effectively to suspects to get them to talk:

1. ***Base your "character" on something true.***
2. ***Know the story so you can almost believe your own lie.***
3. ***Only lie when necessary.***
4. ***Act detached or aloof so you don't panic if you mess up.***
5. ***Don't do any over-the-top gestures.***

Chapter 11

At home that evening, Grace couldn't tamp down her anxiety. She'd done the dishes (by hand, even though the apartment had a dishwasher), attempted to start a new smutty romance novel, then resigned herself to staring at the ceiling.

It seemed like a good idea at the moment, but knowing Jo was keeping their investigation from Gloria was making Grace nervous. When the police were investigating, they always had backup; people knew their locations and their intentions, and there was a plan B. She was going to do everything she could to make sure she and Jo didn't put themselves in any actual danger, but shouldn't *someone* know what they were up to?

She grabbed for her phone.

Sean was saved under "Officer Cordon," but when she brought up his contact information, she realized Jo might see it, and she would probably be angry that Grace was conspiring with the police. She cleared his name and simply wrote "Sean." She felt the same little spark here as when Sean asked her to use his first name, and she realized she was doing a bad job at tempering her expectations when it came to him. He was just really good at his job. Her reading into his every move made her no better than the men who thought they and the stripper made a profound connection. She pressed the call button.

It was 6:30 pm and she didn't quite understand what kind of schedule police officers kept. He could be home binge-watching documentaries, or he could be working undercover, posing as an investment banker, for all she knew. She hoped, if it was the latter, that his phone was on silent.

"Hey. Hi, Grace. What's up?"

He sounded out of breath, like she'd interrupted him mid-workout or like he'd run to answer the phone in time.

"Hi, uh, Officer... Sean." *Smooth.*

"Is everything OK?" He sounded concerned, and all of a sudden she felt silly for calling. He probably gave her this number in case she got a death threat or found another body. Not because she was feeling anxious. But she'd felt guilty about not giving him all the details of her employment with Jo. And now that the details were mapped out on a whiteboard in Jo's basement, she wanted someone else to be aware of what they might be getting themselves into.

"I think it is," she said, too quickly. "But I need to tell you something about Jo and the work I'm doing for her."

The line was quiet for a moment before Sean said, "Do I need to grab a notebook?"

He was thorough, Grace thought. "Yes, I think so. I don't have a lot of information or anything, but... Jo is trying to find out as much as she can on her own."

Sean let out a low "hmm" noise. "You mean like her own separate investigation? Is that why she was calling the station so much?"

"Yes, exactly," Grace said.

More silence. Grace thought the confession would take some weight off her shoulders, but now she felt even more stupid than she did when he first answered. *I know you've dedicated your life to serving and protecting, but we, two unarmed and inexperienced millennial women, have decided to handle it on our own.*

"Grace, are you telling me Jo wants you to help her solve Garrett's murder on her own?"

"Yes." She was scared to say too much and decided she was just going to answer whatever questions he threw her way.

"Pardon my French here, but why the hell are the two of you doing that?"

Only lie when necessary.

"Because Jo doesn't trust the police. I don't know her reason, it felt wrong to pry it out of her. I trust she has one. I–I absolutely do. Trust the police, I mean. And I'm hoping you guys solve this. In fact, I was hoping you'd answer and tell me we got our guy."

A sigh went through the line. "We haven't got our guy. But I also don't want the two of you doing anything dangerous to *get* our guy. Or gal."

Grace instinctively wanted to tease Sean for his use of "gal." *Give me a Werther's Original and tell me more about prohibition, old man.* She identified that this was not the time.

"Well, I wanted you to know. And also… I know the names of the people she suspects. She didn't tell you because she wanted you to do your job and find them on your own."

"You understand how counterproductive that is?"

"I know, I know. But I'm not the boss here. She'd probably be upset if she knew I was even speaking with you."

She heard shuffling noises and assumed Sean was rearranging, preparing to take notes.

"If you could give me their names and whatever motive she thinks they have, I'd appreciate it."

"Please don't relay to Jo that you got this from me. Her job offer was the only thing that allowed me to stay in Philly. I can't get fired."

"Yeah, no." Sean cleared his throat. "I won't give away that we spoke. We want you to stay here."

We?

Grace sighed deeply, then opened her notes app where she'd written down the details. She told Sean about Wyatt and Kelly, about the situations that landed them on Jo's board, and how they'd already ruled Kelly out. She left out the part where she dressed up like a giant bird and then fell on her face. His pacing between responses told Grace he was taking detailed notes.

She finished rattling off everything she knew, then said, "That's it. For now."

"Weeelllll," Sean said slowly, "I'm not sure if this is good or bad news to you, but both of these people are already on our list."

It was good news to Grace, but if Jo were to find out, she might see it differently.

"When we interviewed Jo on the day of the murder," he continued, "she mentioned the art exhibit and told me to search news archives for Garrett's name, so they were pretty easy to find."

See? Grace imagined a conversation with Jo in which Jo would let go of the idea of solving this on their own. *They are fully capable. They want to help.*

"She told me she led you in the right direction but left out the names. I know that sounds dumb."

Grace braced herself for a talking-to. For strict instructions not to go any further with their investigation. To hear that Jo was interfering with official police business.

Instead, Sean's tone was sympathetic. "People grieve in different ways," he said, his voice softer than before. "I can't know what's going on in her mind. She's probably in pain, and I can't fault her for the way she deals with something unthinkable."

Wow. Grace had grown up with a police officer for a father. He was a sweet guy, and he loved her and her mother, but she'd never heard him express this much empathy for anyone he encountered on the job. He'd dealt with cases ending with still-missing children, multiple casualties, and had even held the hands of a few people during their last breaths. You could never get him to talk about it. Somewhere in him was a container for all the grief, anger, and sadness he collected from his years of service.

She wondered if this little peek at Sean's humanity was a sign of a different generation, or just an example of what kind of guy he was.

"I think trying to find out who did this is the only thing she can do to not... fall apart," Grace said.

"Yeah. Yeah, I get that." Sean sounded somber. Then his tone changed quickly. "*But,* I have no interest in getting calls about the two of you injured or being held hostage somewhere."

This was Grace's fear, too. It was why she'd called.

"You're grown women, and I can't tell you what to do with your time, as long as it doesn't interfere with the official investigation. But it's naive to act like there isn't a murderer on the loose out there, and I'm not going to have any more blood on my hands."

Grace nodded, realized he couldn't see her, then said a quick, "Yes, right," into the phone.

"Here's what I'm going to ask of you. The two of you should *never* be around any of the suspects in a private place. Better yet, I'd like you to never come face to face with any of them, but again, I can't keep you on house arrest."

House arrest didn't sound so bad to Grace right now, especially at Jo's house, where she had access to a sauna and theater-quality speakers.

"I can do that."

"I'm going to need you to check in with me, OK? If Jo offers any other information about who she thinks is responsible, or if the two of you come across anything as you hunt for information, I need to know about it."

"Yeah, that uh, that makes sense."

"Maybe we can talk at Garrett's funeral. Does Jo have a date yet?"

Grace hadn't realized that Sean would be at the funeral. She wondered if he was attending on or off duty. "Friday. We're picking up his ashes this Thursday, and Jo was telling me about all the arrangements she needs to handle this week. I think the announcement goes out today."

Jo and her lawyer had already met to go over the will. Not surprisingly, all of Garrett's assets were left to Jo. Grace hoped the investigation would slow down a bit as they prepared for the funeral.

"I'll see you then. And in the meantime, I'll move this Wyatt guy to the top of our list."

An awkward silence. Or maybe a normal one, misread by an awkward woman.

"We're going to solve this, Grace. Pretty soon we'll all have the answers, and Jo will be able to breathe again."

Chapter 12

"What do we *do*?"

Grace and Jo stood in the doorway separating the church's entrance from the sanctuary, their eyes trained on a pile of gray dust.

It all happened so fast. One moment, Jo was juggling all the pieces of Garrett's memorial for the funeral, the urn situated on a box filled with picture frames. Grace was reaching for the sanctuary door when Jo tripped on a pile of hymnals sitting on the ground and jolted forward, the picture frames landing with a clunk, and the urn catapulted five feet ahead. The lid bounced away as the contents spread across the low pile carpet.

"Go get Gloria," Jo whispered. "And ask her how we get Garrett out of the carpet."

Grace returned with Gloria ten minutes later, Andre trailing them. Jo was kneeling next to the pile on the ground. She looked up, panic-stricken. "We can't throw him away!"

"No worries, my dear. I keep this in each of our cars for reasons like this." Gloria held out her cordless travel vacuum for Jo to examine.

Grace wasn't sure "like this" was the right phrasing. *You keep a vacuum in your car in case you need to sweep up the remains of your friend's son?*

Gloria grabbed an offering plate off a pew sitting outside the sanctuary. She turned to Andre. "Go make yourself useful and fill this with some soapy water. Find a rag or some towels or something for us to scrub the carpet with." She switched her focus to Grace. "You keep an eye out and make sure we do this without being seen."

There were a few extra people at the church today, including a technician there to look at the air conditioning, which had inexplicably stopped working overnight. The day was unfortunately balmy, and Grace's dress was already clinging to her lower back. She stood back to let Gloria assess the damage, keeping an ear out for interlopers.

Gloria got down onto the floor with Jo. "We'll suck him up in this and dump him back into the urn. Easy peasy."

Jo was visibly sweating, either from her hysteria or the temperature that crept up minute by minute. "We're going to lose some pieces of him."

"Oh, sweetie, those were probably the bad pieces anyway." She smiled and switched on the vacuum, Garrett's ashes slowly flowing into the clear canister at the end. Grace jumped when she heard someone approaching and headed toward the sound, but it was Andre returning with the water bowl. He set it next to Gloria, and when she had sucked as much of Garrett off the carpet as she could, she handed the vacuum to Jo so she could return him to the urn. Then she took the rag Andre hunted down and gave the carpet a good scrub.

She climbed off the floor slowly, knees cracking and audibly groaning. She dusted off her hands. "OK, everyone. Let's keep this between us and God."

* * *

Grace wasn't sure if funerals could be categorized as good or bad, but Garrett's, held exactly three weeks following his death, wasn't off to a great start.

The technician needed to order a part to fix the air conditioning, so the church staff set up box fans around the sanctuary. It would have been loud enough in there with the polite chatter of funeralgoers, but now it was accompanied by the *whoooooosh* of a dozen fans.

The spot where *Ashgate* went down was nearly dry and impossible to see if you weren't looking for it, but the residual trauma of the whole thing was buzzing beneath Grace's skin. She could tell it was gnawing at Jo, too, who insisted Grace not leave her side. Grace always planned to go to Garrett's funeral, of course, but she'd also planned on finding a seat near the back and slipping out once the service ended and the socializing began.

However, each time she strayed even a short distance from Jo, she felt her strong grip on her arm. It made her uncomfortable to be so close to the woman of the hour. She imagined the priest announcing the family, the way they do at weddings: "In the front row, we have Garrett's loving parents, his devoted wife, and the stranger who found his body!"

As a stream of people sorry for Jo's loss took turns approaching her, Jo clasped her hands behind her back and smiled politely. She put on a brave face, hiding the stress of the day and the last three weeks well. Grace thought about Jo's fear of appearing weak and making her an easy target for whoever killed Garrett.

It was hard for Grace to believe she'd only officially known Jo for a few weeks. They'd fallen quickly into the intimacy of two old friends, and Grace wasn't quite sure how it had happened. Sure, once you were invited into Jo's world, she was an open book. And they had the shared trauma of Garrett's death to bond over. However, it typically took Grace a while to warm to other people. Jo felt as familiar as Maya now. Maybe more, now that Maya was a mom. Motherhood felt lifetimes away from where Grace was.

Grace started to look around the large cathedral. It was a traditional church with tall ceilings, statues of Christ, and stained-glass windows. At the front of the church was a massive organ that seemed to be carved out of one large piece of wood. Grace had been surprised a church service would be held. She got the impression Jo and Garrett were atheists, maybe agnostic. But it was a beautiful space, and Garrett's appreciation of beauty was one of the most obvious of his traits.

Grace's eyes shifted from the room to the people standing in it. While Grace felt like it would be risky for the murderer to show up at the funeral and slip up in conversation, Jo was insistent that people always returned to the scene of the crime. With the studio now closed, that wasn't possible. Maybe this was the closest thing.

The guests seemed to fall within four neat groups: the friends, the family, the artists, and the money managers. Grace chalked the high percentage of finance bros up to Jo's father's business. Mortgage brokers, accountants, personal finance consultants: they all lined up to pay their respects to Jo. Grace's mother was an accountant, and a pretty successful one, but she wouldn't survive in this elite world of wealth. Grace knew luxury labels and fancy gadgets weren't a true sign of wealth, but each man's wrist seemed to be graced by a Rolex, his suit fit for an awards show.

Grace felt a sudden warmth for her mother, who did her best work in an oversized Mickey Mouse sweatshirt and Hanes drawstring shorts.

Grace hadn't spent much of her life thinking about money, which she knew meant she grew up in immense privilege. She'd figured the worst money-related burden would be not having enough of it. But her presence in Jo's world was starting to make her feel differently. Jo seemed to think about money constantly. How it should be distributed within her nonprofit, and how she didn't have enough to fit the needs of every student she worked with. How it could be best used to help family members and friends. How to invest it to make the most of what was given to her by her father. Grace didn't feel bad for Jo and her abundance of blessings; however, she was starting to see that not enough and too much each had their dark sides.

After all, someone might have killed Garrett for the money, yet money wasn't going to bring him back.

There were hundreds of people, and it was starting to make the hulking room feel tiny. Grace wondered if there were enough pews to hold them all. It might be standing room only. This was a benefit of dying young, Grace supposed. There were plenty of people still alive to miss you.

Grace's eyes scanned the crowd again and caught a man and a woman speaking at the center of the church aisle. They looked like they fit the profile of some of Garrett's industry friends. Was Wyatt Randall here? Grace realized she should have studied the pictures on Jo's crime board better. She remembered Wyatt was a relatively good-looking man with light hair. Three men in the group of artists fit this description.

Grace was about to walk away and stand closer to them when she felt Jo's hand on her arm again. When Grace turned, she saw Kelly Dewitt approaching them. When she clocked who Grace was, she stopped, then continued slowly and carefully. "You ladies know each other?"

Grace couldn't let on that she had been Garrett's assistant. "Kelly! Hi! We met recently, actually, but became quick friends." She reached an arm behind Jo's back and gave her a squeeze. Then she looked back at Kelly and feigned artificial shock. "Oh, Kelly. Was Garrett the artist you..." She let her voice trail off.

Kelly looked down nervously. "Yes. Yes, he was. Small world." She looked up. "It was actually my conversation with you that inspired me to come here today. To pay my respects, but also," she looked at Jo, "to apologize for the way I acted after Garrett bought the gift shop."

"It's all in the–" Jo started to say, but Kelly cut in.

"It's not all in the past. Heck, I got questioned by the police because I'd had such a public outburst. It's the biggest regret I have, the way I treated him. And I wish I could have told him how sorry I am." She heaved a sigh. "But I can tell you. So that's why I'm here. I'm so sorry, Jo."

Kelly's eyes were tearing as Jo grabbed her hands. "I appreciate that, Kelly. A quick Google search will show you how many embarrassing public outbursts I've had. Garrett never held it against you, so you know. And as far as I'm concerned, you're completely forgiven."

Kelly began to cry. "I appreciate that, Jo. So much. I know I can be a little bit... *petty* is probably the best word. But I'm working on it." She pulled her hands away and wiped at her eyes. "I'm going to get out of your way. There are a lot of people here who want to talk to you. But maybe we," she gestured to both Grace and Jo, "could get together for a coffee sometime?"

Jo smiled. "We'd love that."

As Kelly disappeared into the crowd, Jo spotted someone and began frantically waving them over. A plump old man in an expensive-looking suit approached, serving Jo a full-teeth smile.

"Grace, this is Daddy! Daddy, Grace."

Jo's father looked so much the way Grace had pictured him, she momentarily wondered if she'd met him before. Then she realized he just looked like every other older, rich, white guy (and also eerily like the Monopoly man). His hair was white and Grace assumed at one point a hair transplant had taken place, because it was unnaturally thick with a defined hairline. His middle was especially round, and when he reached out and shook Grace's hand, his grip was strong.

"Grace, nice to meet you," Jo's father said as he continued to shake her hand. "Actual name is Malcolm. And my Jo has told me you've been a great comfort to her during this hard time. Sorry you had to be the one to find Garrett."

Malcolm moved aside to reveal a man close to his age but much shorter, hair appropriately thinning. "This is my financial adviser, Jack. More than that, a good friend."

Jack flashed a bright smile. "Good to meet you." Then he turned to Jo. "I'm so sorry, my girl. Garrett was a real talent."

Jo grabbed Jack's hand and gave it a squeeze.

Malcolm looked at Jo proudly – how could he not? She was successful yet humble. She'd been thrown into this terrible situation and was handling it with grace (and also Grace). As a father, it must hurt to see his little girl go through such an experience. Her own father had been so torn up over Grace's first heartbreak, he'd told her he wished he could take on all the pain for her. Obviously, pain is how people grow, and Grace was better off for having experienced it. And one day, Jo would be able to look back on this moment in time and be proud of how she survived it. Still, there was something beautiful about a parent's love, the way they would carry all of life's burdens if it meant their child didn't have to feel the weight.

"It's nice to meet you. Both of you," Grace said. "And honestly, working with Jo is probably the best job I've ever had. Other than working for Garrett." Grace left out that she'd only ever had one previous job, at which she had reported to her mother. It felt pathetic to say something like that to two men who looked like powerful oil barons from an old-timey cartoon.

Malcolm nodded. "He was a good man. He will be missed."

Just then, Jo noticed her mother in the crowd.

"Mama! Perfect timing. Come meet Grace!"

The crowd parted a bit and a stunning woman approached them. She had Jo's golden hair, which obviously came from a box and not Mother Nature. Jo had a few gray hairs, so there was no way this woman twenty years her senior was magically gray-free. Grace's mother had large brown eyes and wore a bright-red lipstick. And while normally Grace would assume a tweed jacket and skirt were *Chanel-inspired,* she knew enough details of Jo's parents' financial status to know this was probably *very real* Chanel.

Grace heard Malcolm grunt disapprovingly to her left.

"This is my cue," he said with a nod as he started to walk away. He brushed shoulders with Jo's mom and simply said, "Molly," without looking at her.

Molly seemed amused by this, though her neutral expression stuck. She reached Jo and Grace and said, "I cannot believe that man is allowed in here. I would have assumed God would strike him down at the threshold."

Jo's brow wrinkled. "Mama, be good. You need to make a good impression on Grace here."

"Nice to meet you, ma'am," Grace said to Molly. Unlike Malcolm, Molly didn't reach out her hand. Instead, she kept both hands on her clutch and gave a simple nod. She also didn't seem to feel the need to move the conversation forward.

"I wish Sam were here," Jo blurted out. "Obviously, I understand why he couldn't be."

Sam, Jo's younger brother, lived in London. His wife was heavily pregnant with their first baby, meaning she couldn't fly, and he was too afraid to leave her so close to her due date. Jo had also confirmed what Grace had read online – Malcolm and Sam hadn't spoken in years.

Molly kept her rigid posture as she showed the first signs of emotion, tilting her head and frowning a bit in Jo's direction. "I know, my dear. But as soon as I get word about the baby, I'll be headed his way. I'll give him a giant hug for you."

She did not offer a giant hug for Jo, who was probably in need of a very, very big hug.

Jo started to say something, but at that point, the priest asked everyone to take a seat. Grace nodded back to Molly as Jo grabbed her wrist and pulled her toward the front of the church.

"Do you think it's appropriate? For me to sit with you?" Grace asked.

"The widow makes the rules," Jo replied.

* * *

The service was touching and pleasantly short. Jo got up to say a few words. She described feeling like a traveler without a home now that Garrett was gone; that she felt thankful to have him as long as she did, and maybe the cost of having someone so wonderful was that she was never supposed to have him for long.

Garrett's mother attempted to speak, but she was crying too hard to get out anything more than, "My boy." Garrett's stepfather had to go to the altar to help her back to her seat. Grace thought it had to be the cruelest fate imaginable to have to bury your child.

Garrett's father didn't get up. He held his wife's hand and kept a stoic face. Garrett took after him, she realized. He was the one with the olive skin, the dark hair. His was graying now, in a way Garrett's never would.

As Garrett's best friend stood to speak, Grace surveyed the pews and realized Sean was sitting near the back. He noticed her looking right away and gave a little wave. She smiled and waved back. He wasn't in uniform, but wore a simple gray suit without a tie, the top two buttons of his shirt undone. She shifted her attention back to the front of the church. She felt hot, and she wasn't sure it was because of the broken air conditioning.

Following the service, the priest announced the family would host a luncheon at a restaurant up the street. It was walkable, and the day was beautiful, though scorching. Grace winced as she stepped out into the sun, the shift from dark to light straining her eyes.

A man cleared his throat behind her, and she turned to face Sean.

"I guess the job is working out, then?" he said.

Grace moved out of the doorway and motioned for him to follow her. "Yes. Many job perks. VIP funeral seating." She laughed, then stopped. *Probably not something to laugh about.* "But yes, Jo is a good boss."

Sean looked side to side nervously, dropping his voice to a near whisper. "And is, uh, finding Garrett's murderer still part of the job description?"

Grace loudly let a gush of air out of her mouth. "Yes, it is. But to be honest, I'm really hoping it's you who solves this."

Sean chuckled. "Me too. It would look bad if I didn't find the killer and instead the murder was solved by a woman off the street."

"Officer Cordon, did you call me a woman of the streets?" Grace showed fake shock.

Sean's cheeks blushed, his head shaking ferociously, "*Off*, not *of*. I absolutely did not mean–"

Grace laughed. "Calm down! A joke!" It was cute, the way he'd been nervous to offend her.

He eventually laughed too, and the two of them stood silently, staring down at their feet for a moment. Grace wasn't sure of the protocol. Was she supposed to talk to him as an officer of the law, or a painfully handsome and totally normal fellow adult?

He looked up at Grace. "You going to the lunch thing?"

"Oh yes! I'm starving!" He hadn't asked Grace if she was hungry, but she put it out there and couldn't take it back now.

Sean laughed. "I'll walk you."

* * *

Grace had been to a handful of funerals in her lifetime, but none as swanky as this one. It was typical after a service to end up in a church basement, eating bland food cooked by Good Samaritans who weren't aware that spices existed beyond salt and pepper.

Garrett's memorial lunch, on the other hand, was full of flavor. There were French dip sandwiches, small bowls of pasta with vodka sauce, seasonal salads featuring ingredients like beets, walnuts, and pears. The balsamic reduction on the lightly breaded chicken was so heavenly, Grace almost asked to talk to the chef.

Grace had her first break of the day from Jo, since Jo's parents insisted on sitting with her and bringing their friends along. Instead, Grace sat in the corner with a few of Garrett's acquaintances… and Sean. Grace wasn't sure if her stomach was in knots because of the funeral, or because Sean's leg regularly grazed hers. Either way, she found herself unable to eat more than a few bites of her food.

She could feel Sean watching her.

"So," he asked, pausing to swallow the last of his sandwich. "How did you end up working for Garrett anyway. Did you study art?"

Grace wondered, for a moment, if Sean might be impressed with her if she were an artist.

Only lie when necessary.

"Absolutely not." Grace chuckled as she wiped a drop of condensation from her water glass. "I'm a terrible artist. I've even tried those paint-by-number kits and still end up messing everything up."

Sean smiled, a small dimple popping on his left cheek. "OK, how did you end up here, then?"

Grace told him about her identity crisis, and her decision to move to Philadelphia because her father grew up there. She gave the shortest version possible, sure that Sean was going to be disappointed over how boring she actually was, but his response surprised her.

"That was really brave of you, to move like that."

Grace's fork made a screeching sound as it slid along her ceramic plate. She'd been sliding the same piece of chicken around for a few minutes. She didn't look at Sean when she replied. "I don't think I've ever been called brave in my life."

Sean's leg touched hers again, and she looked up at him to see if it seemed like an accident. He was looking right at her. "I'm happy to be the first. I certainly won't be the last."

Grace looked back at her chicken because she didn't want Sean to see how deeply she was blushing. "Well, speaking of bravery… why did you decide to be a police officer?"

Sean had gone back to his meal and was in the middle of chewing. He wiped some pasta sauce off his face. "I actually wanted to be a chef, but as it turns out, you have to make food that people consider edible." He shrugged, his head tilting in such an adorable way, Grace wished she could take a photo to remember the moment, frame it on her bedside table.

She chuckled. "Well, I'm sure the community is grateful that you were such a bad cook."

"You'd be surprised how much of my job requires little to no bravery. On a really good day, it doesn't require any at all. There is nothing better than a twenty-four-hour period where the hardest thing I have to do is help save a kitten from a tree." Sean placed his napkin down on his now empty plate, and Grace tried to pretend that the idea of Sean holding a kitten wouldn't melt her insides like lava.

A strange look spread across Sean's face. "And then you have cases like Garrett's, where you stress over each day that passes where you haven't caught the bad guy."

Grace shot a look at Jo's table, where Molly and Malcolm were arguing with one another across the table. Jo's mother held a fist in the air while her father pointed aggressively. Jo was rolling her eyes, and seemed to be looking around for a waiter.

"Yeah," Grace said to Sean, still looking in Jo's direction. For a beat, she forgot what they were talking about, then she snapped her attention back.

"Do you think it will last much longer?" she asked. "The case, I mean?"

Sean inhaled nervously, then let his shoulders fall on the exhale.

"I'll be honest with you. There was no physical evidence at the scene. All our suspects so far have alibis that can be corroborated by other people. The tips we've gotten haven't led anywhere. I'll never give up if I feel like there is even a sliver of a chance, but in this specific case… I'd prepare for the chance that we don't catch whoever did this."

Chapter 13

Most funerals don't have an after-party, but most funerals weren't hosted by Jo Baros.

Grace rode to the house with Jo, Andre, and Gloria again. Sean left to go back to the station. He gave Grace a polite handshake when he said goodbye, squeezing before he let go. It was the sort of exchange that would occupy Grace's brain for days even though it could have meant nothing.

Jo couldn't stop fussing with her hair in the back seat. Unsurprisingly, she looked on edge.

"I hope my dad can manage to keep the conversation off the subject of money. Twice he's started to mention a great investment opportunity to me, when typically money is an off-limits topic for us." Jo rolled her eyes. "He's made money the center of his being. It's his career, it's his hobby, it's his passion. Sometimes I think he judges me, because money is none of those things to me. I know it's his way of supporting me and keeping me safe, but sometimes people need the kind of support that can't be bought."

Jo pulled a tube of lipstick out of her bag and applied it lightly without checking it in a mirror. "It's why he and Sam don't speak anymore. My dad thought Sam was being reckless with his inheritance, and Sam thought he should mind his own business. He's never been into the trust fund baby thing. He's rebelled against it even more than I have. It's probably what prompted him to move as far away from here as possible. And since the move, he's cut off communication with Daddy completely."

Jo turned to look out the window, lost in thought, and Grace felt a pang of gratitude that she'd never had so much money that her very existence was defined by it.

A few people beat them to the house and stood in the driveway, idly chatting as they leaned on their luxury cars.

Jo hopped out of the car as soon as Andre parked to welcome her guests, giving them instructions on where to place their coats as they entered the house. She'd hired waitstaff to serve hors d'oeuvres. "Just some bacon-wrapped oysters. Plus some fig flatbread and pear and brie tarts. Nothing fancy."

Grace felt like Jo would have an aneurism if she ever attended a party at her parents' house and had to eat buffalo chicken dip.

Jo was busy greeting everyone, so Grace helped herself to a fig flatbread before meandering over to the self-serve bar. She poured herself some vodka and threw in a splash of orange juice before she surveyed the crowd.

She recognized Jo's friend and financial adviser, Ava, from social media posts. It was one of those cases where she knew an uncomfortable amount of information about a woman she'd never met. Ava, who Grace thought could be a dead ringer for Kerri Washington, was a fellow transplant, originally from New York (though not the city). She was a self-made woman with mainly female clients with portfolios over five million dollars.

Ava's head jerked in Grace's direction and she felt panic spread through her. Had her staring been so obvious?! As

Ava walked toward her, she wished she could somehow disappear.

"Are you Grace?" Ava said as she approached.

Grace took a quick swig of her drink. "Oh, yes! Hello!"

Ava presented her hand and the women shook, Ava's hands much steadier than Grace's. She wore her hair naturally, her clothes were bold and bright. As they spoke, Grace was struck by how brilliantly articulate Ava was. In contrast to Grace, Ava had seemed to take every risk possible in her life, and they all seemed to pay off. She had that same *cool* factor that Jo did, and Grace found herself wishing she could be part of their little club. What would it take? More confidence? More money?

Ava was telling Grace about a play she and her partner had recently seen when a hand tapped Ava on the shoulder.

Ava turned, and for just a moment, her mouth fell. She recovered quickly, putting on a broad smile. "Malcolm! How are you?"

"Oh, doing well my dear!" He gave a nod of acknowledgment to Grace. "Just wondering how business is going."

Ava bit at her lip and then let out a little laugh. "I'm glad you asked, Malcolm! We're set to blow last year's numbers out of the water." Ava stood tall and proud as Malcolm surveyed her.

Malcolm seemed politely unimpressed. "Well, be sure to let me know if you ever want Jack to give you any pointers. He's around here somewhere."

Ava's eyes narrowed, but she kept her smile. "I'll do that."

"See you girls later," Malcolm said with another nod, and he disappeared into the crowd.

When he was out of earshot, Ava groaned. She tilted her head toward Grace, her cheekbones even more perfect at this angle. "That man doesn't think I'm capable of doing my job, when, according to the rumor mill, he hasn't made a decent investment in the last decade."

Grace almost asked for more details, but Jo showed up on her right, looking exhausted.

"Whose idea was this again?" she huffed.

Ava clinked her glass against Jo's. "Yours, my friend. It was your idea."

Jo looked between Ava and Grace with a content smile. "The two of you have met! I'm glad, I wanted to make an introduction. I think you–"

Jo was interrupted by the loud clang of piano keys, followed by an off-key soprano.

"Oh, God, not again!" Jo mumbled as she ran out of the room.

Grace followed, and when they made it to the front room, a crowd had already formed around Molly, who was hitting the keys almost as hard as she'd hit the bottle.

"Mama, do you need to go to bed?" Jo asked in a hushed tone.

"The party has just *started*, my darling! To Garrett!" Molly mashed the keys with abandon, sending Jo into publicity mode.

"How about we all head to a different room, yeah? Have you tried the oysters?" she said, leading the spectators away from Molly's circus act.

Something shoved into Grace's arm, and when she turned, she saw it was Malcolm's shoulder. He was heading right for Molly.

"Molls, how about you head home, alright? I'll call you a car."

Molly hiccupped, then burst into acidic laughter. "How about you pay your alimony?" Her head was rolling back and forth as if she were struggling to keep her balance while sitting. "We all know you've got the cash!"

A frustrated Malcolm gave up, shaking his head as he turned and headed back to the living room.

Molly started to sing "My Heart Will Go On" from *Titanic* when Grace decided it might be best to head home.

She turned toward Ava. "It was so nice to meet you, but I'm going to leave before the ship, and this very sinkable-looking Molly, both crash."

Chapter 14

A week later, the sun shone through the slats in Grace's bedroom blinds, illuminating the dust and dead skin floating in the air. As a kid, she'd always found it beautiful to watch these little specs, slow-moving fireflies that never came out at night. Such a pure thing, the way childhood never forces you to look at something for the ugly thing it is.

She had no plans for the day, and with the calendar freshly turned to October, it might be the last beautiful weekend she'd see in months.

She hadn't been to the local library yet, and it was on her list. She also wanted to try a coffee shop a few blocks away that Jo recommended, a local chain. But first on her agenda was mindlessly scrolling on her phone until she was fully caught up on celebrity gossip and whatever Pinterest thought should rent space in her mind that day.

Then she saw a text from Maya.

Check your email. 🔍

She'd sent it the night before at 11:39 pm. At that point, Grace had been asleep for at least an hour. The anxiety around Garrett's death popped up often and unexpectedly, so she needed to take advantage of sleep when it came easily.

She went to her inbox and scrolled through her latest emails until she saw Maya's. The subject line said, *Have you seen this?*

In the body was a link, and when Grace clicked it, it took her to a subreddit called r/TrueCrime. It was a post about Garrett. And it had hundreds of comments.

Maya talked about true crime Reddit often. Social media had truly changed the game when it came to active and cold case investigations, she'd said, putting cases in front of thousands, even millions of eyes instead of only blasting it in the local papers. That meant brains all over the world could analyze data, look for clues in videos, or search through records.

Maybe these internet sleuths had already solved the murder.

Like a true millennial, Grace crawled out of bed to get her laptop because this was not a small screen task.

She brought the laptop into bed and went to the feed, searching for Garrett's name. There was so much information here, it could take her all day. She started to read through the top comments, and when she saw the theme most of them followed, she felt goosebumps ripple down her arm.

[dude it was the wife. Your welcome i solved it.]

[have you seen pics of the wife? Total bitch. If it wasn't her, then she bought someone with Daddy's money.]

And then she saw one that hit way too close to home.

[Did you see that his secretary found him? Bet she was with him all night and killed him when she was done with him.]

It may have been an uneducated stranger on the internet, but it was still jarring to see someone accuse her of murder. She should have been able to brush it off, but she was no good at that. She still sometimes thought about the time she'd been excited about a new haircut only to show up to school and have Hailey Claussen tell her she had a mullet. *That bitch.* She was a third-grade teacher now. Anyway,

Grace didn't let things go easily. She and Kelly had that in common.

She realized the comments were filtered based on relevance, so she hoped something fresh would show up if she switched to most recent.

The second comment caught her eye: Garrett Baros's last painting listed for sale on the dark web.

The concept of the dark web was sort of like the rules of cricket to Grace – she didn't have the skill or interest to make heads or tails of it. But the name alone told her it was bad news. She took a picture of the post on her computer screen and texted it to Maya.

What does this mean?!

Omg. Another text from Maya came through a second later. *Do you think we're dealing with some sort of art trafficker?*

I could pretend to know what that is; however, I think it would be easier to ask you.

Traffickers sell stolen art pieces. It has ties to organized crime and often happens to lesser-known artists because their work isn't as recognizable. People could display it, and no one would know it was stolen. Grace was constantly in awe of how much Maya knew about things that had nothing to do with her.

It always comes back to the Mob with you.

I mean, yeah, occasionally it does.

This felt like something for the police. Jo would probably want to know about it too, but… was she going to send Jo a link to a massive discussion about whether or not she killed her husband?

For now, she would tell Sean. Actually, there were some things she wanted to ask Sean. Jo had gotten so wrapped up in her investigation, she hadn't called the precinct recently for updates. In fact, Grace had noticed several changes in Jo over the past week. She looked a little more put together each day, for instance. She'd also stopped drinking, which Grace was grateful for.

She picked up her phone off her bed, went to Sean's contact information, and let her finger hover over the call button. Was this weird? To call a police officer to chat about a case? In the back of her mind, she knew if she had to convince herself something wasn't weird, it was probably weird. She pressed the button anyway.

It took three rings for Sean to pick up. "Grace! Happy to hear from you. What do you need?"

He's happy to hear from me. Grace could feel her cheeks flush.

"Hey! I wanted to talk about something I found online. It uh-h-has to do with the case." She could hear how nervous she sounded and silently cursed herself and her lack of seduction skills.

"Oh, well it's my day off and I'm running some errands right now, but–"

"Gosh, I'm so sorry," Grace said as she slapped herself on the forehead. "I didn't mean to bother you on your day off, it's not that important."

Sean laughed at the other end of the phone. "You didn't let me finish. I was going to suggest we meet up? I'm not too far from Garrett's studio, actually. We could meet at that little cafe across the street from it in, say, an hour?"

Grace froze. She started to breathe like she was hiking a mountain, and covered the bottom of her phone in the hope that Sean wouldn't hear. *This is not a date,* she told herself.

"Uh, Grace?" he asked when she didn't answer.

Grace hadn't seen the studio since she found Garrett, but surely she'd be fine just seeing it in the distance. "Sure, we can meet there." Her voice toed the line between a croak and a squeak, to her horror.

Sean didn't seem to notice. "In an hour? Does that work for your schedule?"

Yes, that worked with her serious schedule of watching Netflix and assembling furniture without reading the instructions. She could pencil him in. "That works! See you then," she said, hanging up and already jumping up to pick her outfit.

She'd already tossed three options on the floor when her phone started ringing.

At first she worried it was Sean, canceling their casual work meeting/not date, but it was "HANNAH TEMP."

Weird. Their call wasn't until Tuesday. She picked it up, knowing it would probably be short.

"Hey, Hannah!"

Hannah spoke quickly, nearly cutting Grace off. "Hey, I know this isn't the time we agreed to, but I wanted to get something off my chest. I wasn't totally honest with you."

Grace tensed. Jo had wanted her to ask Hannah about why Garrett had gone through a temp agency, but maybe Hannah had something to confess on her own.

"Uh, OK," she said. "What is it?"

Hannah took a deep breath. "I lied to you."

Despite being alone, Grace tilted her head to the side, confused.

"What?"

"I can see on my end you've gotten all the payments from us, someone reached out and let us know Mr Baros was done using our services. Everything is all wrapped up between us.

I should have just sent you an email and cancelled this call, but… I still kept it because I *need* to know what happened to him. It's a wild story."

"You didn't know him, then? Garrett?"

"No. I mean, I emailed back and forth with him, but I never met him."

Grace smiled. "You're just nosy then?"

Someone older, more professional, may have been mortified by this interaction, but Hannah let out a laugh. "Yeah, that's terrible, huh?"

This was the first time Grace realized how young Hannah sounded. Maybe this was her first job out of school. Maybe she hadn't even graduated yet. "Wait, Hannah, did you say someone emailed to break Garrett's contract?"

"Oh, yeah," Hannah said. "It came from the same weird Gmail account he always used."

Grace was biting down on her tongue. The only email she had for Garrett used his web address: hello@garrettbaros.com.

"Wait, what email are you talking about, Hannah?"

Hannah inhaled sharply. "It was garrettbaros123@gmail.com, which I thought was *super* weird. I remember because those are the same numbers my grandpa included in his email address. He couldn't think of anything else and panicked. But I'm not sure Garrett ever gave me a reason for using a temp agency other than just wanting someone fast. His email said his old assistant quit and he didn't have someone lined up to replace her."

Why would Garrett have two email addresses? Grace thought. *Not to mention, Garrett cared a lot about his reputation. Surely he wasn't emailing people regularly from an email address that looked like it was created by a third grader?*

"And you didn't think it was weird that an artist who has sold his work for tens of thousands of dollars was using a free email account?"

"Different strokes for different folks, ya know?" Hannah replied.

The retort rendered Grace temporarily speechless.

"Anyway, I have to go. But I'm glad we talked." Hannah heaved a dramatic sigh. "I'm going to keep up with this story in the news, because I'm completely invested now."

She laughed. "This will probably not come as a surprise, but working at a temp agency isn't exactly the most thrilling job on earth. The most exciting thing to ever happen at the office was a small fire in a trash can. But anyway…"

She trailed off, and Grace felt empathy for this young woman who'd clearly found herself in a job that wasn't what she'd imagined. She could relate to that.

"How about when it's all over, I call you to give you one last update?"

Hannah squealed. "Sweet."

Unprofessional, but not unhelpful, Grace thought.

Grace was wearing an amount of makeup she hoped conveyed, *I tried, just not too hard.*

She'd gone with a casual look, pairing a plain grey tee with wide-leg jeans. She didn't exactly feel comfortable in wide-leg jeans, but the internet told her they were the only forgivable silhouette of the moment, so she'd been trying to make them work. Knowing how cyclical fashion was, she'd shoved her skinny jeans in the back of her closet instead of donating them.

She was five minutes early to her lunch with Sean and asked for a seat outside while the weather was still cooperating. She sat and looked over the menu for a few minutes. While technically they had already shared a meal, Grace had only taken a few bites at the funeral luncheon. This would be the first time she *consumed* an entire meal in front of Sean, which brought up that age-old debacle anyone faces when they grab lunch with someone they may be interested in. Not that Grace was interested *in* Sean, though he certainly interested her. These were different things… right?

Anyway, there were a few dishes you didn't want to order if you were worried about how you looked to the person across from you. You couldn't order a burger with a lot of toppings and run the risk they end up on your shirt. You couldn't get wings, because then you'd end up licking your fingers, and the only two ways to interpret this were that you were either sloppy or attempting to be seductive. On the other hand, Grace didn't want to order a salad. Not only could they be messy too, but they gave the impression you were scared to eat a hearty meal in front of the other person, and she loved food too much to give someone the expectation that they would never see her take down a two-thousand-calorie meal in a single sitting. *Moderation,* she told herself.

A car pulled up and she could see Sean through the driver-side window. Right on time.

He climbed out of his sedan and flashed his award-winning smile (this was an assumption on Grace's part, she'd never seen a trophy or anything) in her direction. He had his police-issued tablet with him, she noticed, but he looked every bit the relaxed citizen in jeans and a white polo with teal stripes. Though he'd worn a suit to the funeral, it still felt weird to see him out of his uniform, like running into a teacher at a grocery store. This was a much better kind of run-in. One she hoped might happen again, if she was honest with herself.

Grace sat up straight and smiled as he sauntered up to the table.

"Thanks for grabbing us a seat! I meant to get here earlier," he said, picking up his glass of water and taking a sip as soon as he was seated.

"No problem, it gave me time to look over the menu. Have you been here before?" A first-timer, she was eyeing the Italian hoagie and wondering if Sean would grab a beer so she felt less awkward getting a cocktail. *And if he does get a drink, surely that means he doesn't consider this a work meeting.*

"I have. Everything is pretty good, in my opinion." He leaned forward and took his voice to a whisper. "Except for the cheesesteak. It's an embarrassment to the city of Philadelphia."

Both of them laughed, and as Grace spotted the waitress out of the corner of her eye, she wondered what they looked like to her. A couple? A nice police officer giving face time to some woman who thought she was helping him with his case?

The waitress asked for their drink order, and when Sean requested a Guinness, Grace took it as an opportunity to order a peach Bellini. A twinge of excitement went through her; Sean considered himself off the clock. Since they were ready, they put in their lunch orders as well. Sean went with wings. Apparently he wasn't worried about the sloppy/seductive debacle.

Once they were alone again, Grace clicked the link to the subreddit and slid her phone across the table to Sean.

"This is what I wanted to tell you about."

Sean brought the phone to his face and started to read the post. It was short and didn't provide many details, just that a Reddit user had found the listing for the painting, attempted to find the IP address, and failed. They said the poster, username diamondplateau239, wrote that the painting was the last work of a "recently slain" Philadelphia artist.

Sean let out a little groan and brought a hand up to one of his temples. He seemed to be reading the post again, then looked up at Grace.

"We knew about the listing for the painting. We also know about the subreddit. I didn't know the latter had discovered the former."

It wasn't that Grace thought she'd uncovered something vital to the case, or Maya had, more specifically. Still, she was slightly disappointed Sean already knew about it. This meeting could have been an email after all.

"So you've been reading the posts on there?" she questioned. Because if he had, he'd have seen everything being written about her and Jo.

He put the phone down, his face serious. "Yeah, most of them at least. Are you specifically asking me about the posts that mention Jo? Or you?"

Grace leaned onto the back of her chair and looked down at her lap. "I may be asking about them, yes."

"You understand those are only internet trolls, right? Social media has been a great tool for helping us collect information on our cases, but for every one good piece of information there are fifty pieces of insults, lies, and libel." The corners of his mouth lifted to a slight smile. "And the occasional cat meme, of course."

"Of course."

And Grace *did* know that. This was not her first encounter with a self-righteous keyboard warrior looking for their next victim. But Garrett's case was a wound that hadn't had the time to scab over yet. She was now fully invested in helping to solve his murder, and the idea that there were people out there who still thought she might have something to do with it was insulting. It made her want to be around people who had known her for her entire life, who knew her heart and her intentions were good.

She guessed the feeling was her first touch of homesickness.

"I'm trying not to let it bother me. As long as you, your team, and Jo know I had nothing to do with what happened to Garrett," Grace lamented as she held back tears. It would be embarrassing to cry before she even sipped her first Bellini. Crying was some fourth Bellini shit.

It felt like slow motion as Sean reached across the table and put his hand on Grace's, for a moment, then pulled it back. "Of course not," he said. She knew he meant it.

The tender moment was interrupted by their waitress dropping off their meals, a busboy following with their drinks. The sandwich in front of Grace was massive, and she contemplated asking for a takeaway box upfront, there was no way she could finish it. Before she could ask, the waitress was on to another table.

Sean held up his beer. "Cheers," he chimed.

Grace tilted her head and held her drink up as well. "To?"

"Uh," Sean said, clearly flustered. "To… solving Garrett's murder."

"Oh! Yes! Solving the murder!" It occurred to Grace that she had more information for Sean. She sat her drink down in a hurry and a swig of it sloshed onto the tablecloth. "I talked to my contact at the temp agency Garrett used to hire me this morning. She told me someone emailed her saying Garrett would no longer need their services."

Sean furrowed his brow. "She got this email recently?"

Grace gave him a nod. "Within the last two weeks. That was the last time she and I spoke. And she said that all her communication with Garrett had been through a Gmail account, one I'd never heard of."

"Do you remember what this email address was? And can you give me your contact's number? I'd like to follow up with her directly."

Grace picked up her phone and went into her notes app. She held the screen up to Sean and he copied the email addresses into his tablet. Then, she went to pull up Hannah's contact information.

"Her name is Hannah. She can be a little bit erratic. She's young, I think. But she's nice enough." Grace held the phone back up to Sean.

He typed Hannah's number, double checked he got it right, then looked up at Grace, grinning. "You know, you are really coming in handy here."

Grace felt the blood rush to her face. "Well, I try," she said coyly. She turned her head to look out to the street, hoping the break in eye contact would tone down the redness in her face. She couldn't help but look in the direction of the studio.

When Grace got back to her apartment, she pulled out her laptop to update Maya.

M –

You're a genius! I had lunch with the police officer in charge of Garrett's case today. They knew about the painting and the subreddit (because, unlike me, they know what they are doing), but they didn't know it was public knowledge now that the painting was listed on the dark web.

He noted a few other things they learned from the subreddit, and in general:

- Garrett had dated some artist named Kate before he met Jo and it turns out she was loosely involved in an art trafficking scheme. The police spoke to her and she has a solid alibi for the night of the murder, and insists she and Garrett hadn't spoken since their breakup.
- A former classmate of Garrett's reached out about a guy who used to bully Garrett in high school. Apparently, they'd run into each other relatively recently and the guy took to social media to vent about what a snob Garrett had been. He got pretty heated in the comments, which led the police to reach out to him too, but again, an alibi.

From everything he's seen, Sean (the cop) thinks the murderer has to be someone who has a good number of connections OR multiple people were involved. From the camera being cut while the crime happened, the listing on the dark web, and the poison, it seems like either the guy is a jack-of-all-trades or has friends in low places.

There were a few other things they looked into, but they all turned out to be duds.

I don't think I'm going to tell Jo about the subreddit. Did you see the posts about me and her? Ugh.

Anyway, love and miss you. Kiss that baby for me.

– G

Within ten minutes, she had another text from Maya:

Lunch with a police officer, huh? What does he look like?

Chapter 15

Jo held the phone so close to Grace's face, she went slightly cross-eyed.

On the screen was an ad featuring Wyatt, including a photo that was surprisingly low res for someone with his art connections. Didn't he know a single photographer? It looked like he asked his mom to take it on her 1999 Blackberry. He stood facing the camera, one arm pointing out straight like Uncle Sam or Smokey Bear.

"Is he about to tell me how I can prevent forest fires?"

Jo rolled her eyes. "Just read!"

Don't miss your opportunity to model for hot young artist Wyatt Randall, master of mixed media art. Randall is looking for women aged twenty to forty to pose for a large-scale exhibit, which will blend audio, video, paint, and sculpture for a full sensory experience. Email allie@randallart.com with headshots and contact information.

Grace could feel Jo watching her read. Her excitement bubbled when Grace finished and looked at her. "It's the *perfect* opportunity. Wyatt rents an office space downtown, and I guarantee it's where he'll hold casting calls."

She'd told Jo about her conversation with Hannah, about the shady email address, and Jo had written it on the crime board. She'd kept her meeting with Sean a secret.

Grace scrunched her nose, unconvinced. "But... Wyatt knows you. You can't show up to his casting call without him being suspicious."

"Duh," said Jo, flopping down on one of her velvet couches. "Which is why *you* are going to the casting call."

Grace waited for the laughter and the "kidding" to come after Jo's comment, but she seemed sincere. This stunning woman looking at her and making the suggestion she could be believed as a professional model made her feel like she was staring into her mother's face again when she told her, "Yes, you would make a great veterinarian!" knowing her daughter was incredibly allergic to almost all animals.

"You cannot be serious."

"I am completely serious," said Jo. "I've already picked out the outfit you'll wear, and I called my glam squad. I told them my friend had a date after a brutal breakup, and we needed to boost her confidence."

Grace snorted. Breakups require a relationship.

"I mean, Wyatt probably saw me with you at the funeral. Wouldn't he know something was up?"

Jo had confirmed Wyatt was at the funeral, somewhere in the crowd of nondescript men with expensive art school degrees.

Jo snorted back. "I don't want to hurt your feelings, Grace, but Garrett's funeral was nothing other than a networking opportunity for Wyatt. He was gone before the service even started. He wasn't paying attention to anyone who wasn't going to boost his career."

Grace hadn't noticed Wyatt's early departure because she hadn't noticed him at all. Another reason why she wasn't qualified to investigate him for murder.

"I cannot do the casting call, Jo. I am not a model."

Jo tilted her head, confused. "You're literally gorgeous."

Jo was the embodiment of the ideal woman in Grace's eyes. She was waiflike and petite, but also had an ass and boobs. Her hair was shiny and her skin was clear. She walked like she had a pole running from her tailbone to her skull. And then there was Grace, with her untamable curls and visible blackheads and flat butt, destined never to inspire a rap song.

It baffled Grace that Jo could think she was gorgeous.

Jo got up from the couch and kneeled in front of Grace. "Seriously, do you know what I would give for those curls? For those freckles?! Look at me, this cookie cutter human. You are so unique. You're so truly… *Grace*."

They probably could have gone on like this for hours, two women raised on media that told them the "ideal" was whatever they were lacking. So able to see the beauty in other people but also able to point out their own flaws and magnify them until they couldn't look at anything else. She thought back to all the drunken conversations she'd had with other women she didn't know (or even more dramatic, ones she did know and *hated*) in bar bathrooms, basically just an exchange of loud compliments.

"HE DOESN'T DESERVE YOU."

"YOU'RE SO PRETTY I'M GOING TO CRY."

"YOUR OUTFIT IS SO CUTE YOU CAN'T EVEN TELL YOU PEED YOUR PANTS."

Jo was on a mission, and she believed in Grace, even without a bar bathroom in sight.

"You're going to keep Wyatt's attention, and we are going to use that attention to get information."

Grace thought back to her conversation with Sean and the promise she made about not being alone with any suspects. However, her prior education in the modeling industry, aka having consumed the bulk of all *America's Next Top Model* episodes, told her casting calls were typically filled with gorgeous hopefuls and a panel of people ready to tear them to shreds. The whole point was that these were *public* humiliations.

Grace closed her eyes, breathed in deeply, then breathed out.

"When are we doing this?"

"You're on his schedule for next Monday, October 14th."

The part of the investigation requiring her to get a prom-queen makeover and dress head-to-toe in designer clothing was, Grace could admit, not terrible. They even cut her long hair to her shoulders, something she'd wanted to do for a while.

"Do you have lash extensions?" one of the girls asked, her face only inches from Grace's as she applied eyeshadow.

"Uh, no?"

"Ugh," the girl said. "I hate you bitches and your thick eyelashes."

It was one of the more aggressive compliments Grace had ever gotten.

By the time they were done with her, and she got a glimpse of herself in the mirror, Grace was starting to feel like she could pull off this whole thing with Wyatt.

Wyatt's office was in an old warehouse downtown. Jo had driven Grace, grilling her for the scripted answers Grace had memorized this week. They'd even gone over her "model walk." *Eat your heart out, Tyra.*

Jo dropped Grace off a few blocks away so she wouldn't be spotted. While Wyatt had probably glossed over Grace at the funeral, he knew exactly who Jo was. Jo was going to park in a nearby garage, throw on a hoodie and sunglasses, and sit outside of a restaurant near the warehouse, in case Grace needed her.

As Grace walked briskly down the street, she noted the shift in temperature. Another cold day. She was shivering and cursing herself for not bringing a jacket.

Through the tall glass doors at the entrance of the building was a reception desk. Next to it was a large freight elevator. The lobby was sparse, with only a few fake plants and several large paintings Grace assumed were Wyatt's. They weren't Grace's style. Everything else was concrete and metal, though there were plenty of windows to bring in light. She wondered if they had paid some consultant a million dollars to come in and tell them to leave the walls unpainted and add a plastic ficus.

Grace walked confidently (she hoped) toward the reception desk, where a woman who looked to be about sixty had her head down, immersed in her work. Grace slapped her hands down on the raised counter in front of the woman's desk, and the woman's head shot up. At closer range, Grace realized the woman was probably younger than she'd thought, but she'd gotten an immense amount of plastic surgery done, and it had done the opposite of what Grace assumed she intended. Her name tag said "Inez."

"Hi, Inez. I'm Daphne Drew. I'm here to see Wyatt Randall."

Inez's smile was sweet, and Grace felt awful for noticing all her plastic surgery. If Grace was just slightly more self-conscious, she'd probably keep the Botox business running herself, as she'd started to develop crow's feet and that mid-brow eleven before she even turned twenty-eight.

"Sure. I'll make a call up to his secretary, and you can take the elevator up to the third floor." She pointed to the freight elevator, which Grace knew was meant to add to the chic industrial feel of the building, but in reality looked like it had more than an average chance of failing and crashing, burying its unlucky inhabitants in the basement. As Inez dialed up to Wyatt's office, Grace reluctantly went inside, closed the gate, and pressed the "3."

She'd texted Sean last night, wanting to know if he'd dug up any information on Wyatt that would help her in her quest, or possibly render it unneeded. Sean said he'd spoken with Wyatt, who said he'd been meeting with possible models the night of the murder. *It's been weeks,* Grace thought, *why is he still looking for models?*

Wyatt's secretary had vouched for him, but when Sean had asked to speak with the model Wyatt had been with that night, Wyatt told him it was confidential. He also refused to show Sean his calendar, security footage, or any emails confirming where he was. Still, with the secretary's backing, it seemed Wyatt wasn't the murderer.

Grace still felt uneasy about it, but she knew if Jo got hold of this information, she'd want to continue with their plan. So, she'd kept it to herself.

As she pulled the gate to the elevator open, Grace started to panic. Based on the building's size, there had to be a ton of space on this floor, and yet it seemed mostly empty. A row of all-glass conference rooms to the right contained only tables and chairs. In front of Grace, about fifty feet ahead, was a makeshift waiting room in front of a normal office desk, where a woman sat. There were no other models here. She told herself the woman's presence meant this wasn't a private meeting, but she had a sinking feeling in her gut. The sign next to the door behind the woman had Wyatt's name on it.

She approached the desk, and the woman looked up, staring at her through thick lenses rimmed in gold. She didn't smile.

"Hi, Daphne Drew, here to see Wyatt."

"Welcome." She sounded bored, or maybe like she'd been dissociating from her body and felt Grace was rude for interrupting her. She had no nametag, and didn't offer her name. What was the name on the ad? Was this Allie? "Please take a seat, I'll let Wyatt know you're here."

Grace sat on a plush leather chair as the woman went into Wyatt's office and closed the door behind her. For a second, Grace felt like she might be able to accomplish her goal without even facing Wyatt. Jo wanted a photo or file of his calendar, so they could see who Wyatt was meeting the night Garrett was murdered. And here was his secretary's desk, left unattended. She could stand up, open the calendar app, snap a photo, and run to the elevator. If they caught her, she could say she had IBS and needed to get to a toilet. It was better to cry diarrhea than to be caught stealing information from a possible murderer. But as she went to get out of her chair, the woman emerged, and she had to pretend she was adjusting her position.

The woman moved to the side of the door and motioned for Grace to go in. "He's ready to see you."

Grace smiled and walked into the office, carefully engaging her "model walk." Jo had told her to seem confident and flirty. That was the type of woman Wyatt went for. Like he was vetting the other half of a power couple. Jo had also told her Wyatt was a functioning alcoholic and would most likely offer her wine. She'd told her to take it and suggested she go for a red. "In case you need to dump it on him and leave a mark," Jo had joked, pleased with herself.

There was already an uncorked bottle of white wine on the desk next to an empty glass. Wyatt stood there behind his desk, beaming, holding another, half-drunk glass of wine.

"Daphne!" He spoke as if they were old friends. "Come in, come in. Care for a glass of wine?"

Grace's ears were ringing as she sashayed to his desk to shake his hand. "Wyatt, what an honor. Uh… I'm not much for a white. Got any red?"

She couldn't read Wyatt's expression exactly, but he seemed to be impressed she'd sauntered into his office and immediately made a command. He licked his lips, she noticed. "Absolutely. Love a woman who knows what she wants." He corked the white and took it to a small wine fridge next to a large bookcase. Like Garrett's, the bookcase was filled with art books. Unlike Garrett's, there were no books that weren't composed mostly of pictures. He uncorked a bottle of red and poured her a healthy serving, then slid the glass across the table. He motioned for her to sit down and started to sit in his own chair.

She tried to sit as gracefully as possible in the tight skirt Jo had picked for her.

"Daphne, I like to get to know my models a little bit before we get into all the nuts and bolts."

"Sure," Grace said, trying to keep up her confident and sexy persona. Her cheeks were already starting to ache from smiling so hard.

"Tell me, what's your story?"

Grace gave a short summary of Daphne's life story. She was from Virginia, graduated top of her class, but realized there was more money in exotic dancing and dropped out of college. She had a great thing going at a top gentlemen's club but decided to go "mainstream" and get into modeling.

If the story sounded overly dramatic, it was because it was a retelling of a story Jo kept seeing pop up on BookTok. In the book, the main character was also an orphan, but Grace had shot this part of the story down. She wanted information, not a Golden Globe.

"Surely dancing had to be lucrative," Wyatt said, one eyebrow raised. "What made you leave the biz?"

People who constantly sought to shorten words to sound laid-back and trendy deserved a special place in hell, in Grace's opinion. It was not a shock Wyatt fell into this category.

"Oh, well, you know, I'm thirty now. These..." She surveyed her body, trying to decide which part of her to blame for her retirement from the stage. "...ankles aren't what they used to be." She stuck one leg out, showing proof of said weak ankles.

Wyatt chuckled. "Ah, well, I'm thirty-four and I know exactly what you mean."

He moved his hands near his face in a prayer position, thinking. "If you wanted to get into modeling, why not New York or LA? Why Philly?"

She'd established herself as a stripper, so it was time to humbly reveal her heart of gold. "I had the flight booked to New York, then my grandmother had a stroke. I was the only one who had the flexibility to take care of her, so I moved here to keep an eye on her while I looked for one-off shoots."

This cover story sounded ridiculous to Grace, but she felt like she delivered it well. She could picture her poor, sick grandmother sitting at home, wrapped in a Philadelphia Eagles blanket, complaining about how all drivers from New Jersey were tailgaters.

Wyatt's face was still scrunched in thought, then it relaxed. He brought his hands down and placed them on his desk. "What a woman," he said. Something about the phrase gave Grace chills. The bad kind.

Wyatt stood up from his chair and adjusted his belt. "I'm sure you did your research on me if you didn't already know about my career."

Grace held back a snort over his idea that he was a household name, like Banksy.

"I'll save you all that." He gave her a sly grin, and she had to admit he was probably one of the most handsome men she'd ever seen. The pictures didn't do him justice. His sandy blond hair had a wavy texture, a certain ruggedness added with a matching five-o'clock shadow. He looked more like a frat boy than a creative, but you could never judge a book by its cover. He walked around the desk and leaned back on it. Her knee was about a foot away from his, and she could now tell he had striking hazel eyes.

"Let's get started," he said.

He grabbed her hand, which sent a jolt through her, again, of the scary variety. Less *Ghost*, more *Poltergeist*. She tried not to react as she stood up and let him guide her to a raised platform in the middle of the room. She'd walked around it to get to Wyatt's desk, but she hadn't thought too hard about it or its purpose. Wyatt led her onto it. She stood on a literal pedestal while he walked around her in a circle, taking in every inch of what he was looking at.

She had no idea if this was normal, what he was looking for, or if she had it. She felt like a piece of meat, like he'd walked in on her taking a shower and pulled the curtain aside like it was nothing; his for the taking.

It felt like hours had passed when Wyatt spoke. "The project I'm working on is a mixed-media project about the female body."

She cringed at the word "female," a word she thought should be reserved for use by incels and nature photographers.

"I'll be capturing the natural form in paint, charcoal, video, and sculpture." He paused like she should say something. She didn't. "You probably know sculpture isn't a regular medium for me, but the more I've done it, I've realized I have a true talent for it."

Grace was still holding the glass of wine, she realized, her crossbody bag still slung across her shoulders.

Wyatt approached the platform and placed his hand on Grace's hip. She tried not to squirm out of his reach, locking in her smile and pretending like this was a completely normal, possibly sexy experience for her.

"Your body would lend well to sculpture," he said, sliding his hand up to her waist. He kept it there and started to circle her again. She assumed he was looking at her butt when he said, "I may make a few artistic choices, but you're a fine place to start." And then she felt his hand slide down onto her ass and squeeze.

She didn't react right away, like she wanted to. Instead, she did some quick math. There was no bathroom attached to this office. Her wine + his crisp white shirt would = him leaving the room, most likely. He didn't seem like the type to risk a stain on organic cotton, probably imported from Italy. She had to act like it was an accident. She spun slowly toward him in a way that once again said she was feeling flirty and not ready to run. He was smiling up at her, a glint of something in his eyes that made her wish she was invisible. He leaned slowly toward her, and she mirrored his movement. His mouth slowly moved toward hers until the wine reached the edge of her glass and dripped down the front of him.

"Shit!" he yelled, stepping back.

She made a grand display of bringing her hand to her mouth in shock. "Oh my gosh, I am *so sorry,* what a klutz!"

He looked furious as he glanced up at her, but then he seemed to realize a meltdown would halt what the two of them had going on, and he collected himself.

"It happens, Daphne. Don't worry about it." His scowl turned into a sickeningly sweet smile. "I'm going to go freshen up, this shirt is custom."

Grace was twisting her hair around her finger, smiling down at him. *Of course it's custom.*

He walked across the room, holding his shirt away from his skin, then slipped out the door as it closed behind him.

Grace acted immediately. She climbed down from the pedestal, heading toward his desk. She pressed the spacebar on Wyatt's computer and groaned to see it required a password. She had no time and no intel to guess it. She started to walk away from the desk, thinking she could sneak out while he was in the bathroom, then she noticed the leatherbound book. She opened it. A planner.

She thought about taking it, but her bag wasn't large enough, and surely he'd notice, so instead she flipped to September's monthly layout. On the date of Garrett's murder was a name: Olivia Olsen. She snapped a photo of the full spread, in case the rest of his schedule turned out to be helpful, then slammed the book shut, shoving her phone back into her purse and walking toward the door.

The knob turned.

Wyatt walked into the room, fussing with his soaked and still stained shirt, and looked up at Grace in surprise.

"What are you doing?"

One hand was still in the bag, and even she was surprised at how quickly she came up with the lie. "I thought I had a Tide pen in here, I was bringing it to you."

The scary-sweet smile returned as he leaned back to close the door. The soft click of the door latching gave Grace chills. She could hear her heartbeat in her ears, its pace quickening. She'd been so anxious to find out if Wyatt was a murderer, she hadn't stopped to consider all the other shades of evil he might be.

"Aren't you thoughtful?" he said, lurching toward her. One hand settled on the back of her neck, the other cupping her behind. He smelled like white wine and menthol cigarettes, the combination enough to turn Grace's stomach. The moisture from his shirt seeped into her blouse.

She thought about playing coy, staying in her role of the hometown sexpot, but she was terrified. Her brain was shuffling through ideas to get her out of there. Maybe she could grab something off the desk and hit him with it. She'd taken a self-defense class in college, but was she supposed to step on his foot or knee him in the crotch first?

Then she remembered the bag slung around her body and the insistence of her mother that she never leave the house without pepper spray.

"Wyatt, I–" Grace didn't actually have anything to say, but she needed him to look at her, and not down at the bag she was unlatching then carefully rummaging through.

"Yes, Daphne?" Their faces were mere inches apart when she finally wrapped her hand around the canister of pepper spray. Before either of them could say another word, she pulled it out, held it near his face, and sprayed.

Wyatt's screams were immediate. He stumbled back awkwardly, red-faced with his palms pressed against each eye. "YOU BITCH!" he yelled, and Grace sped toward the door. She pulled it open, ran out, then slammed it shut. Wyatt's secretary was still seated but whipped her head around, mouth ajar.

"Wyatt's hurt!" Grace said. "Going for help!"

The woman looked confused and didn't move right away, then she ran into Wyatt's office as Grace sped toward the elevator. She shut the gate with precision and mashed the button for the first floor. It seemed to be moving in slow motion, but eventually it jolted to a stop and Grace flung the door open again, sprinting toward the front door. The phone at the front desk was ringing and she knew it would be about her. She had her hand on the metal door handle and flung it open in a fury to run out into the street.

She ran a block and ducked into an alley, pulling out her phone and texting Jo to get the SUV ready, then continued in Jo's direction for the remaining blocks. She was ready to crumble into a pile on the ground when she saw Jo's headlights, but rallied enough to get to the door, violently pull on the handle, and throw herself inside.

"Drive!" she said to Jo, who pressed the gas with so much power Grace was sure they'd left tire marks.

Jo navigated through the city with relative ease, and eventually they were getting onto an off-ramp, the city shrinking in the rearview mirror. Grace was still breathing hard, and Jo had the good sense not to ask her any questions until she could form sentences again.

"I don't think..." Grace took a sharp intake of air. "...Wyatt is the murderer."

She coughed, clearing out the mucus coming loose due to her surprise cardio.

"But he's assaulting women."

Chapter 16

Jo wouldn't stop apologizing. She was sitting outside of the ensuite in her master bedroom, the door opened a crack so Grace could hear her from inside. It was Jo who insisted she come back to her house and take a hot bath.

"I never would have sent you in there if I knew that was going to happen," Jo said regretfully through the crack in the door.

Grace was sitting up in the tub. The water hit above her chest, and she tried to enjoy the warmth, but couldn't get her muscles to relax. She looked out the window next to her. It framed the lawn, trimmed in trees beginning to change color.

Men are more likely to be the victims of a homicide than women. But women are more likely to be victims of an intimate partner, Grace thought, as she slid her head beneath the water. It had been so long since she'd needed to hold her breath. How long could she go?

She held for twenty-eight seconds, then came up, gasping for air. Jo didn't seem to notice in her fog of guilt.

Jo continued to check in on Grace as she soaked, and it was doing nothing to relax her, so she eventually crawled out, toweled off, and pulled on the robe Jo had left out for her. She opened the door and looked down to see Jo hugging her knees to her cheek, face splotchy.

Jo faintly shook her head, then raised it to make eye contact with Grace.

"I need you to know why I don't trust the police."

Jo got up and walked over to her bed, pulling one leg underneath her as she sat. Grace followed, pulling the robe tight so she would be fully covered. Jo looked shattered, and for a brief moment, Grace contemplated telling her she didn't need to give her story. At the same time, she felt like she needed to hear it.

"When I was younger, when all my friends were in college," she said quietly, "I went with them to this house party. I was pretty bitter about missing the whole college experience, but at least I could drink with them. There were a bunch of people I trusted there, but I wandered off drunk and met this guy out back. Apparently, he was the school golden boy. Lacrosse player, three-point-nine GPA, every parent's dream, unlike me."

Grace could feel every muscle in her body tighten. Even without the experience she'd had with Wyatt that day, she had other, less extreme examples. Of being touched without her permission. Of an inappropriate comment that made her look around the room for someone safe. The details always differed. Sometimes it was daytime, most of the time it was night. There was usually alcohol involved; occasionally, everyone was sober. From what Grace had discovered during sleepovers with friends and articles about strangers, the universal thing was the guilt. Of not putting themselves in the situation, of not punching the guy in the face, of failing to realize it was assault when it was happening, of not reporting it… or of reporting it.

"He did, you know, what he wanted to me. I put up a fight but the drinks and – I was tired, too. I had barely slept the night before then didn't nap during the day and I don't know why I even went out, but I did. And he assaulted me."

Grace felt like she should grab onto Jo's hand or give her a hug. She didn't know if that was how Jo wanted to be comforted.

Jo was crying harder now. "I went right to the police. I found my friends and went back to their apartment to sleep it off, then I went right there. I should have gone to the hospital, but I thought if I went to the police first, they would send me in the right direction or know what to do, you know?"

Jo reached up to wipe a tear away. Her hands were shaking.

"As it turns out, the golden boy's dad was in local politics. And he was best friends with the sheriff. He'd gone right home to Daddy to tell him what he did. The sheriff may have even known before I got back to my friend's place that night. By the time I went to the station to report it, he was ready. They sat me down in a room and asked if I was sure it was him. They told me I smelled like booze. They asked me if the outfit I was wearing was the one I was in the night before. Then they started to ask if I remembered anything happening at all."

Grace grabbed Jo's hand, to remind her she wasn't alone. "I was probably there for an hour. And by the time I left, I was questioning everything. They didn't even make an official report. Said if I wasn't sure, there was nothing to record." Jo was now speaking calmly and evenly. She'd probably played this memory thousands of times since it happened. "I never ended up going to the hospital because I was so confused. I didn't want to have my dad get the bill and ask me what I was doing there."

She sat up straight.

"I went back to my friend's apartment. I got through the day, and then the month, the year. And the whole time, the golden boy went on living his life. He never got a single consequence." She sniffed. "So, I don't trust the police."

Grace hadn't realized she'd been holding her breath until she blurted out, "My dad is a police officer. Well, was. He retired." She was already kicking herself as it came out of her mouth. What if Jo took it to mean she thought she was being unfair or didn't believe her, or maybe Jo thought she was a complete nut for taking Jo's deep-seated story and making it about herself?

But Jo seemed to understand.

"I know there are good ones out there. I'm sure your dad is one. I mean, I know they're brave, and most of them devote their lives to justice, but… it's never sat right with me that if you've got the right credentials, you can make a crime disappear. My biggest fear is that we never find out what happened to Garrett. I've been a victim and seen the justice system fail me, and I can't let it fail him too."

A comfortable moment of silence passed between them, each of them seemingly processing Jo's story being out in the open.

"Listen," said Grace as she slipped closer to Jo, still holding her hand. "What happened to you is not your fault, and nothing you did was wrong. It wasn't wrong not to fight back, it wasn't wrong you ended up not reporting it, the only wrongs were your assault and the way you were manipulated after." She took a deep breath, not sure of how Jo was going to react to the next part. "But I hope you understand that for myself, today, I need to tell the police about this."

Jo's mouth tightened. "Yeah, of course. Definitely."

Grace let her shoulders fall in relief and pulled Jo into a hug. It had to be triggering for Jo, the topic of assault bringing her own experience to the surface. But she also didn't feel as if she should have to explain to Jo why she needed to report it.

They pulled away from their hug, each staring down at Jo's floral bedspread. Grace felt shaken, vulnerable, and honestly, so stupid. Why didn't she make up an excuse when she realized she'd be in Wyatt's office alone with him?

"We also need to find a way to keep ourselves safe."

Jo looked confused. "Safe from what?"

"Safe from whoever else makes it onto your crime board that you make us investigate." Grace smiled to show Jo she didn't consider anything with Wyatt to be her fault either.

Jo heaved a gigantic breath, and tears formed in her eyes again. "Wait, you're not quitting? I can't believe you still want to help me."

A part of Grace didn't want to help anymore. She'd signed on for this job with the idea that she'd support Jo through her grief and pass around theories about what happened to Garrett while the police did the heavy lifting; but today she'd taken things too far. She felt fortunate she'd been able to get away, and was forbidding her mind to play out what could have happened if she hadn't thought on her feet.

A past version of Grace would have called her parents already and asked them to come help her pack up the apartment. She'd be booking them flights, grateful she never got around to truly unpacking. But she realized two things in the aftermath of Wyatt's attack: that she now considered Jo a friend, and she absolutely needed closure about what happened to Garrett.

The woman in front of her was still a shell of her former self, the one with the talented husband and the false safety she felt interacting with her friends and acquaintances, never suspecting one of them of plotting her downfall. And just hours ago, Grace herself had escaped a locked room with a man who'd made it clear he was going to get what he wanted no matter what it did to her.

And yet here they both sat, planning their next moves. They'd been robbed of their autonomy, had their sense of safety destroyed, and felt guilty about what they did in the aftermath of trauma; however, they still believed in truth and justice, even if they were the ones who had to bring everything to light.

Grace felt strong at this moment, and she couldn't remember the last time she'd been able to say that.

She needed to make sure Wyatt Randall paid for what he did. And she needed to find out who killed Garrett. Not only for Jo, for herself. She couldn't leave Philadelphia before she knew what happened to him.

Jo excused herself, and Grace took a few moments to recalibrate before she joined her downstairs.

When Grace stepped into the kitchen, Jo was holding up a measuring cup, squinting at its tiny numbers. There was flour everywhere; enough that Grace wondered if Jo had gotten any in the bowl.

Grace pulled out her phone and started to pull up Sean's contact information. She hesitated a moment as she stared at his name, then looked up at Jo.

"I don't know if I'm going to press charges. If they ask."

Jo looked toward her, shocked. She set the measuring cup down on the counter. "Why the hell not?"

Grace had run the story through her head a dozen times at this point. Wyatt had been unwilling to give his computer to the police or share the name of the woman he'd been with the night Garrett was murdered. And because Grace had now experienced Wyatt's version of a "casting call," she had a feeling Wyatt had treated this woman the same way, and he was nervous she would tell the police. All she needed to do was give Sean the woman's name as a tip, and she hoped Olivia would incriminate Wyatt without Grace having to do anything else.

But Jo had no idea Grace was in regular contact with Sean. She would have to choose her answer carefully.

"I don't want to be wrapped up even tighter in this. I think it's enough to give them Olivia's name and hope, if something happened to her, she feels comfortable telling them."

Jo's face revealed conflicting emotions, but she nodded.

Grace gestured to the phone and started walking to the front door. "Be right back," she said.

Once the door was closed behind her and Grace was pretty sure Jo couldn't hear, she called Sean.

When he picked up, he sounded happy.

"Hey there!"

Grace's heart was pounding. What if Olivia wasn't a victim and simply supported Wyatt's alibi? Was she fine with that? With the idea that he'd touched her without her permission, and was going to get away with it?

She wasn't speaking, and she could tell she was making Sean nervous.

"Grace, is everything OK?"

No, she was not fine with it.

"Wyatt Randall assaulted me, and I think he's done it to other women."

"He *what*?" Sean wasn't yelling, though his voice wasn't calm. It sounded like he was trying to put a lid on his rage, hoping it wouldn't bubble over.

"We went to go figure out what he was hiding about the woman he was with the night Garrett died and–"

"What did I say about not putting yourself in danger?!"

Grace felt like she was being reprimanded, which was frustrating, even though she *had* told him she wouldn't be alone with any of the suspects.

"It wasn't danger until it was!" she said.

"What did he do?"

She didn't want to say it, give all the details she was hoping time would bleach from her mind. It had only been a few hours and she was desperate to stop thinking about it.

"He grabbed me. My neck, my butt." She could almost smell the cigarettes when she spoke about it. She felt hot bile rising in her throat.

Sean's heavy breathing came through the phone.

"Otherwise I'm good. I sprayed him with pepper spray and… he can't come after me, we gave him a fake name, Daphne."

She wished she could see Sean's face, to know whether his silence was due to a calm settling over him, or the murmurs of a volcano erupting.

"I am OK. I promise," she said, trying to get him to add more to the conversation.

Eventually she heard a deep sigh and he said, "Is this you reporting the assault? And… did whatever you were in there to find give you any hint he's our murderer?"

She wanted Wyatt to pay for what he did, but she didn't want him to know who she was.

"No, I don't want to report it. I'm nervous it *could* lead to him figuring out who I am. But I don't think he killed Garrett."

"I mean, I told you we had no good reason to believe it was him. But why do you say that?" asked Sean.

"Because I took a picture of his calendar. I'll send it to you. There was a name on it, Olivia Olsen, and I'm pretty sure he was with her the night of the murder like he and the secretary said."

She thought about the unsmiling secretary. Did she know what Wyatt was up to behind closed doors? Was she disgusted? And if she was, why wasn't she telling anyone? Was he hurting her, too?

"I think he might have done something to Olivia, like he did to me. Maybe worse. I think that's why he wouldn't give you her information."

Sean took a few seconds to process this. "Send over the picture and I'll find this Olivia, see what she has to say."

"Thank you," said Grace.

"Are you sure you don't want to report this, though? If Olivia says Wyatt never touched her, he's off the hook."

"Yeah, I don't want to be even more involved in this than I already am. I wanted you to know, I guess."

Sean made a sound like he was sucking air through his teeth. "Well, I'm sorry this happened to you. And I'm begging you guys to stop with the freelance cop thing. It's not worth risking your safety for this information. Officers go into dangerous situations with training and bulletproof vests and weapons and some of them still don't come out."

He was right, of course, and Grace was upset with herself for getting so deep into Jo's investigation that she threw common sense out the window to get a name.

"Yeah, it's not going to happen again. We don't even have any other suspects," she said.

A noise came from the other end of the line, one Grace couldn't decipher. "Not to add to our pile of bad news, but the email address you got from your temp agency contact was a dead end."

Grace felt the air leave her body. She hadn't thought about the email address since her lunch with Sean. It felt like it could have led to some real evidence.

"I went to see Hannah, asked her some questions, and she gave me access to all the emails between her and 'Garrett.' Unfortunately, the IP address I was able to uncover was in Australia. So either Garrett pissed off some Aussie, or our murderer is using a VPN."

"OK." It would have been too easy for the murderer to be sloppy, she supposed.

"It was still a good lead, though, Grace."

Good isn't good enough when you're trying to solve someone's murder, she thought.

Chapter 17

"I don't think I can do this."

Jo was standing in her walk-in closet, a chic black cocktail dress hanging from her shoulders, still unzipped in the back. The cloud of her perfume hung in the air.

Tonight was the exhibit featuring Garrett's final work – minus one piece, obviously. It was official now, that they were looking for a killer. Garrett's autopsy had come back and stated he'd been poisoned with strychnine, a pesticide. Jo stayed in bed for two days after they'd found out.

Grace was already dressed in an Egyptian blue midi dress. She'd found it secondhand online and was captivated by the unique arch shape separating the top and bottom of the garment, as well as the knot detail at the bust. She'd never seen a dress quite like it.

"Why do you feel like you can't do this?" she near whispered, taking a few steps closer to Jo.

For a few moments, Jo stared at herself in the mirror. She didn't look away as she tried to explain.

"There is the death of someone, right? The soul leaving the body, the final breaths and all of that. Then, for all the people left behind, there are hundreds of little deaths that follow."

She looked at Grace, who didn't reply, then walked out of the closet and took a seat on her bed. Grace followed.

"Tonight is an event marking the death of Garrett's career. And it's not like he was obsessed with his work, but he loved it, and now that's officially over. No one will ever see new work from Garrett Baros."

Jo's eyes were beginning to haze over. "I've silently accepted many tiny deaths over the past few weeks. I realized right away that Garrett and I would never have kids. It's not like we were set on it, but now it's not an option. And I'm thirty-seven years old. I don't have time to mourn my husband, date, fall in love, and have a baby. That future possibility died with Garrett. And the trip we planned to Japan. Maybe I'll still get there, but never with him, never in the way we envisioned."

Grace fought the instinct to tell Jo she could adopt and they could get on a plane to fly to Japan the next day (though she didn't have her passport, so this was literally impossible). Instead, she tried to listen. She knew well enough that sometimes you don't need an immediate answer. Sometimes you need to tell someone how bad it sucks right now, even if it's not going to suck forever. This conscious listening felt like a muscle Grace needed to work.

She placed her hand on Jo's on the bed.

"Tonight can happen without you, if you need to stay here. But it's not going to be what it could be, without you. And I think you might be wrong. I don't think this is the end of Garrett's career, not really. I think you'll find ways to honor him and to carry on his work, even if it doesn't involve him standing in front of an easel. You said he wanted to spend his life making something beautiful, and he did that. The only way he can keep doing that is through you. Think of Van Gogh. He didn't become famous until after his death."

Jo smirked. "Where did you learn that?"

Grace felt a prick of embarrassment. "Don't be too impressed. I read a Buzzfeed article about the most interesting art facts. It took me five minutes."

Jo was staring at Grace with affection. Grace wondered if Jo was going to give her a hug as suffocating as the one she'd given her on her first day on the job. Instead, Jo pulled her hand away and stood, aiming her back toward Grace.

"Zip me up?" she whispered.

The lobby of the Institute of Contemporary Art was packed. In addition to Garrett's exhibit, there were two additional exhibits by local artists, though each was better known and more experienced. As Grace and Jo pushed open the glass doors leading to the stifling lobby, all eyes seemed to fall on Jo. Except for Grace's. Hers fell on the largest charcuterie board she'd ever seen. Seriously, there had to be four dozen types of cheeses on display, an exhibit within itself.

She heard someone address Jo to her left, and pulled herself from the sultry moment she was having with a large chunk of gouda. It was Hilda.

She was wearing all black, like most of the crowd, which made Grace feel self-conscious. Her intention was always to fit in, not stand out. In her thrifted dress, she was a shock of blue in a black sea.

Hilda kissed Jo on each cheek before taking her hands. "Jo. I'm so glad you could make it. It wouldn't be right to honor Garrett without you."

Jo smiled cordially. "I wouldn't have missed it."

Hilda's attention turned to Grace as she dropped Jo's hands. "And Grace, is it? I'm excited for you to see the completed exhibit. I've seen many of them enter and leave the museum, but this has to be one of my favorites. Shall I show the both of you?"

Grace and Jo nodded and let Hilda guide them toward the back of the museum, past the welcome desk. As they weaved through the crowd, several people greeted Jo by name. Others gave a polite nod in her direction. It was clear that without Garrett here, Jo was the star of the evening.

They walked through a short and dim hallway, which opened into a spacious gallery. The floors were poured concrete, white walls made even brighter by spotlights highlighting Garrett's work: five portraits of influential artists from Philadelphia and one empty frame showcasing the lack of a sixth.

Hilda and Jo silently walked toward the rightmost painting, so Grace decided to go to the left and allow them time to speak privately.

The first painting was a woman with glowing red hair. From the label next to it, the woman in the piece was Hellen Torr (1886–1967), a friend of Georgia O'Keefe known for her modernist paintings. There were a few examples of her work, though not the originals. Grace stared for a while at the print of an oil painting called "Evening Sounds" that looked to her to be a pile of rocks. She hoped no one approached her expecting to have an insightful conversation about art, only for her to reply, "I like how she stacked these rocks."

She moved on to the next painting, of George Biddle (1885–1973), best known for his five-panel mural in the Robert F. Kennedy Department of Justice Building. His accompanying work was easier for her to wrap her head around. There was a cow that looked like a cow, a hillside that looked like a hillside, and people who looked like people.

Grace Gemberling (1903–1997) filled the next frame, and Grace identified this one as her favorite, and not just because the subject shared her name. Garrett had based the painting on a photograph of dead Grace (this is immediately what alive Grace called the woman in her head) in which she wore a beret and a striped dress. Her expression seemed almost annoyed, as if someone had made her pose for a photograph when she'd been desperate to get back to a puzzle or a radio show or a lobotomy… whatever women did in 1923.

The sound of women's heels clacked against the gallery floor and echoed off the mostly barren walls. Garrett's paintings were so warm and vibrant, placed in this cold room. The murmur of conversation hissed around Grace, but she felt so detached from the people standing around her. Maybe her lack of knowledge on art was showing, but she felt like the white walls weren't doing Garrett's work justice. She pictured them in a room decked out in jewel tones, a roaring fire adding to the ambiance. Again, maybe this was just her classless opinion, one to keep to herself.

As alive Grace walked away from dead Grace toward the next painting, Hilda and Jo passed next to her, Jo giving Grace a nod of acknowledgment as Hilda talked her ear off about the "essence" of the paintings.

Grace was surprised to see the woman in the next painting was still alive and well. Arden Bendler Browning (1975–) was a mixed media artist whose work was both physical and virtual, Grace read. Arden's art was abstract, which was intimidating to Grace. If she had trouble explaining why she liked a painting of a tree that looked like a tree, she certainly didn't have the language to explain why she liked the explosions of color that made up Arden's work. She did like it, and so she lingered there for longer than the others.

The last painting of Garrett's was of Jane Piper (1916–1991). Jane was beautiful, round cheeks and plump lips set below a flapper-era bob with finger waves. Her abstract still lifes were vibrant, but Grace couldn't decipher what she was looking at. Clearly, she should have done her homework before showing up to an art museum surrounded by actual artists and art enthusiasts. Something with more substance than a Buzzfeed article.

Grace approached the empty frame and a sickly feeling rose up in the pit of her stomach. She felt a bite of unease at the knowledge she was looking at a subtle reminder of Garrett's death. Grace peeked at the label next to the frame. It gave a name to the mystery man, the one she'd looked for as she and Sean walked through the gallery the day after the murder: David Bustill Bowser. He was one of only two males featured in the exhibit, and the only Black man. Was he chosen on purpose?

She hadn't noticed Jo standing beside her.

"Ah!" Grace let out a yell of surprise and everyone in the room turned to scrutinize them while Jo laughed.

"Sorry," Jo said, trying to catch her breath, "I didn't mean to scare you."

Grace placed a hand over her heart. "It's fine. The empty frame already has me on edge."

Jo pursed her lips. "I know. I see what they were going for – showing where the painting belonged. It's very Isabella Stuart Gardener Museum."

Grace had no idea what that meant, and Jo must have sensed this.

"Geez," Jo huffed while sporting a smile. "It's only the largest American art heist in history. Read a book or something, Grace."

They laughed at this together, a light moment in a heavy evening, and Grace wouldn't have minded leaving right then and there. They'd seen Garrett's work. It was out there for the world to admire, critique. But Jo groaned. "I have to do the required elbow rubbing now, until I make my way through the crowd."

Grace nodded and they headed back out to the lobby, passing Hilda whispering to another museum guest, still blubbering about "essence."

As Jo headed into the crowd, Grace turned directly toward the refreshment table. She hadn't even noticed there was an open bar on her way in, so she stopped there first. The bartender gave her a heavy pour, so she shoved enough bills in the tip jar to cover the drink's cost at an actual bar. Well, maybe not a *nice* bar. Definitely a bar at a mid-level chain restaurant.

After piling a plate with twelve kinds of salami and enough cheese to make even the most lactose-tolerant person stick close to the bathroom, she found a hightop table far from the action and proceeded to stuff her face.

As she people-watched, she wondered what the professional makeup of this crowd was. Mainly artists? A strong sprinkling of financial planners, as Garrett's funeral had been? She had fought panic the entire drive, wondering if Wyatt Randall planned to show his face here tonight, maybe to take some of the spotlight away from Garrett's memory. As if she knew Grace was worried, Jo had put her hand on Grace's knee as they'd pulled up to the building. "He's not coming. I checked," she'd whispered.

Grace did notice a few other familiar faces in the crowd. Jo's mother Molly was blatantly being hit on by a man who could have been her son. The friend who had spoken at Garrett's funeral was chatting with an older couple while holding his wife up with one arm. She'd hit the open bar hard, her champagne sloshing onto the patrons around her, scoring her more than a few dirty looks.

Grace briefly flirted with the idea of heading upstairs to look at the other exhibits, but the further she got away from her table in the corner, the stronger the odds someone would try to engage her in polite conversation and realize she had the intellectual depth of a fishbowl, at least when it came to art.

No, she had her cheese, her wine, her salami, and her solitude, the four main requirements for happiness, and she was dedicated to waiting it out in the exact spot where she stood. After a second helping of charcuterie, this time with more of a fruit focus, Grace pretended to be looking at something important on her phone while she played *Candy Crush*.

She heard her name and turned away from her phone to see Ava, Jo's friend and financial guru. "Hey, Grace!" she said. "Did you need a little break, as well?"

Grace didn't want to admit to Ava that there wasn't much to take a break from, as she'd socialized very little since arriving. Ava leaned against the table, and even that, the smallest movement, looked confident. She wore a swank but understated dress, in black of course. It had long sleeves, a high neckline, and tasteful cutouts above the hip. Ava looked toward where Jo was standing in the crowd, then back to Grace.

"She seems to be doing well." She gave Grace a wholesome smile, which Grace returned.

"She is," Grace said, bringing her hand up to check for crumbs around her mouth. "Every day, it seems like she gets a little bit better."

Ava sighed. "I've been there. I mean, not with a spouse… I lost my little brother a few years ago."

"I'm so sorry," Grace said, as one does.

"Yeah, it was hard." Ava shook her head. "He and I were close, and right after it happened, I wasn't sure I would ever recover from it." She took a sip of the cocktail in her hand, a maroon potion with swirls of edible glitter. Rich people were truly so over the top. "I mean, you never *fully* get over it. Once you lose someone, you're different. You can get back to your regular routine, you can go out to dinner and laugh with someone at a party, but you're not the same person you were."

Ava made eye contact with Grace. "I relied on my community, and Jo was a part of that. She brought me soup. She sent Gloria over to clean my house. Community is so important, their support." She looked around the room, disgust written on her face.

"These people are *not* my community," she said, as Grace's head tilted with curiosity. "And it has nothing to do with money or gender or race or, I don't know, *hobbies*."

Ava picked at a piece of glitter on the black tablecloth, probably fallen from someone's expensive cocktail dress. Probably not edible.

"I've always had this innate ability to see someone and sense their bullshit." She looked out at the crowd again. "So many of these people are fake. I only interact with them because places like these are a great opportunity to find new clients. And because I want to support Jo and help honor Garrett."

She looked at Grace again. "Even interacting with Jo's parents is hard. They don't think I have a clue about what I do for a living because I've never dealt with *old money*. Really, it's their excuse to be racist, sexist, homophobic... a whole list of things they'll never bother to correct." Her eyes grew glossy. "But Jo and Garrett? They are and were real, authentic. And I get that from you, too. You are who you are, and you don't feel the need to perform."

Grace felt stripped bare. She'd been worried she wasn't meshing in with this elite crowd, but here was Ava, a goddess among men, who seemed to think that was a good thing. Furthermore, she seemed to think she and Jo didn't fit here either. She hoped she was blending in as well as they were, though this couldn't possibly be true. She had never seen either of *them* consume the amount of dried meat she'd taken down in a single sitting.

Someone near the rock chair at the museum's entrance was calling to Ava, and she put a finger up to show them she'd be there in a moment.

"Anyway," she said, "I wanted you to know that. It's good that Jo has you." She gave one more smile, then glided toward her companion.

Grace felt honored that Ava had stopped to speak with her. It felt meaningful, as short as the conversation had been.

She was about to text Jo and ask her how much longer she planned for them to stay when she spotted Jo's beet-red and crestfallen face heading toward her from across the room. Grace threw her plate(s) away in the trash can behind her, then turned as Jo reached the table. Jo grabbed

Grace's arm with force, her eyes wild with an emotion Grace couldn't name.

"We have to go. I missed a suspect."

From the back of the SUV, Jo leaned up to speak to Andre.

"Hey, Andre. Would you mind popping in those AirPods I got you? I need to discuss something sensitive with Grace."

Andre reached across the car and opened the glove box, from which he pulled out a small, white case. "Sure thing, Jojo," he said, popping each device into his ear.

"Thank you! You're my favorite driver!"

Grace saw Andre roll his eyes in the rearview mirror, and as he put his turn signal on, Jo pulled out her phone to show Grace a photo.

It looked like a professional headshot, a smiling man with a receding hairline flashing artificially white teeth while giving a thumbs up. The combination was very "used car dealer."

"This is Mark King. A year or two ago, his wife contacted Garrett saying she wanted to pose for a portrait to surprise Mark. Mark was a low-level politician at the time. On some sort of council? I guess he had big ambitions. His fortieth birthday was coming up, and his wife Val wanted to surprise him with a semi-scandalous painting."

Ah, a politician. Used car salesman had been close.

"Garrett was more into traditional portraiture, but he never wanted to turn down the opportunity to try something new. Because of the nature of the portrait, he asked if I could sit in on her sessions. Once a week, for three weeks, she came to the studio and we drank wine and chatted while Garrett painted her nude from the back."

It didn't surprise Grace that Jo had the confidence to chat with a naked woman while her husband painted her. When they'd first met, Jo was drowning in grief and terrified Garrett's killer might come after her next. Grace had mistaken that fear for meekness. She'd thought they were similar in that sense, two women who had their guard up, afraid to take too many steps outside of the box. As the weeks went on, it was clear this was how Jo had appeared when she was in fight-or-flight mode. While that had been a phase for Jo, the result of Garrett's death, it made Grace wonder if she was living her own life like this, choosing between fighting or retreating every day.

Jo put her phone away, but she continued her story.

"When the portrait was finished, Val was thrilled. She paid way over what he quoted her. And we thought it was the end of the story, until a few weeks later when Mark showed up at the studio. We didn't know, but Val had been having an affair, and when Mark saw the painting, he assumed Garrett was the other man. Val tried to tell him I was there the whole time, but he blew up. He got in his car, went to the studio, and ended up punching Garrett in the face. A Good Samaritan saw what was happening from the sidewalk and came in to break it up, and someone else called the police. He was arrested and taken to the station. Garrett didn't press charges. Even so, Mark's political career came to an abrupt end, and Val left him for the guy she'd been seeing behind his back."

"Ouch," said Grace. "But most of those things were Val's fault, really. Do you think he felt like Garrett caused it?"

Jo looked out the window as a sleepy Philadelphia flew by them. "Mark shared photos of him burning the painting on social media, and he's become sort of a social pariah in the years after, barely leaving his house. Obviously, none of this was Garrett's fault, but I wouldn't be surprised if Mark saw the painting as the beginning of the end for his marriage and career."

Andre hadn't turned off the radio; it was still playing a soft rock station, and Grace found herself tapping along to the beat while she thought about Mark and his possible motive to kill Garrett.

"If all this happened a few years ago, why would he kill Garrett now?" *And why would he take the painting? To make another video of him burning it? Is there an OnlyFans site for arson?*

Grace watched Jo turn toward her in the dark, the right side of her face illuminated by the glow of the console.

"I have no idea, but it's time to do some serious internet stalking."

If the police ask, Jo was the one who used the word "stalking."

RESEARCH

Tips for finding information about someone online:

1. ***Start with social media. Note usernames so you can see if they are using them across multiple sites.***
2. ***Next, search public records. Use any version of their name you can think of, like maiden names, middle names, and nicknames.***
3. ***Start low, in local courts, when looking for criminal records.***
4. ***Do an image search of their photo to see if anything comes up.***

Chapter 18

With just under two weeks left until Halloween, Grace would rather have been focused on finding a costume that was the perfect mix of sexy and smart, or deciding whether this was the year she splurged and bought full-size candy bars to hand out on the stoop of her apartment building.

Instead, she and Jo were planning their investigation into Mark King.

When November hit, it would be two months since Garrett's death. While it wasn't enough time to consider this a cold case, the police still hadn't publicly named anyone of interest or made an arrest. Grace checked in with Sean and knew they hadn't gotten many tips, and the ones they did get led nowhere.

So the only logical step was to stalk Mark King. Digitally, of course.

While finding information about Mark on the internet felt like the easiest part of the job so far, Grace took it upon herself to add some stalking hacks to the RESEARCH document. She'd watched dozens of YouTube videos about open-source intelligence and the best people-finding sites, but their best bet still seemed to be scouring social media.

They sat on the floor of Jo's living room, fire roaring and an impressive snack selection spread out on the coffee table.

Each woman sat cross-legged in front of a laptop, ready to make groundbreaking discoveries. Grace brought up Val's social media profiles, while Jo started with Mark.

Mark was on almost every site, but his profile pictures were all from his political days, and his security was tight enough they couldn't see anything beyond that. Val was remarried, her profile picture of her, her husband, and their adorable but cross-eyed newborn.

"She moved to Arizona," Grace pointed out. "And she's not friends with Mark. It looks like she scrubbed him from her profile."

Jo leaned over to see for herself. She frowned. "It's probably a waste of time to look too closely at her. I doubt they've communicated since the divorce."

Jo had moved on to Mark's LinkedIn profile, using her premium account so he wouldn't see she'd looked at it.

"It looks like he just started working for the mayor's office. Before that, he had 'entrepreneur' as his job title. And we all know that could mean anything in between being the CEO of a thriving startup and unemployment." Jo smirked at her screen.

Grace turned her attention to Google, where she was sifting through every piece of information she could find about Mark. Most were old interviews from his campaigning days. One was a link to a Pinterest account with two boards including design inspiration for man caves, tips for brewing an IPA at home, and quotes by dead military officers. It didn't seem like he had any sort of criminal record. The only bad press he'd gotten was over his dispute with Garrett.

Do an image search of their photo to see if anything comes up.

Grace took Mark's LinkedIn profile photo, airdropped from Jo, and did a reverse image search. More professional photos popped up, but then a photo of a couple caught her eye. The man did look an *awful* lot like Mark King. She clicked, and wasn't taken to one of Mark's pages, but a Facebook page for a woman named Delilah Jones. The photo featured a sunburnt and sweaty Delilah kissing Mark King on the cheek. Delilah's page wasn't nearly as locked down as Mark's. As they scrolled, they saw a photo of her German shepherd (named "Apple Pie"), her daughter's high school graduation with the caption "a few months late with this!" and a recent trip to Baltimore that had coincided with Garrett's murder.

Jo opened Delilah's vacation album and she and Grace started to go through each picture one by one.

Delilah with her arms raised in front of the National Aquarium; Delilah attempting to jump for joy in front of the Inner Harbor; Delilah wearing a shocked face as she held a massive plate of crab legs. Over and over, Delilah, but no Mark.

"Well, someone needs to be holding the camera, right?" Grace noted. "She could have set up a tripod, but I don't get the idea that Delilah is technically savvy."

In fact, Delilah's profile picture of her and Mark was so poorly cropped, she'd barely included their faces.

Grace continued to scroll as Jo turned to her own computer. Most of Delilah's posts over the past year were travel photos featuring her and Mark. Hawaii, Alaska, Tennessee, Nebraska; they'd certainly been cashing in on airline miles. Grace got to the first picture of Delilah and Mark, the one where they became Facebook official. They wore matching T-shirts and posed on the deck of a cruise ship.

I'm in a RELATION-SHIP, said the caption.

Grace went to show the picture to Jo, but she looked up as Jo's eyes went wide.

"Oh my gosh, this is it!"

"What's it?"

Jo turned the laptop screen toward Grace so she could read the post Jo had highlighted. It was from a neighborhood group and was posted by Mark four days ago.

"Anyone know of a good cleaning service? Just got a new job and won't be around as much."

Jo was beaming. "This is how we get to Mark King!"

Grace sighed. At least this wouldn't require her to wear a bird mask. But she was *not* going to clean this man's bathroom.

Mark lived in a modest Cape Cod house close to Garrett's studio. Jo heard his McMansion had sold as part of the divorce settlement, the profit split two ways. "They'd just put in a massive pool the summer before," she'd remarked.

They decided to take Grace's truck, a much more reasonable vehicle for any working-class citizen than anything in Jo's garage. They parked two houses down, Mark's house hidden by a wall of mature trees while they reviewed the plan.

They were a local cleaning company offering a free one-room clean to drum up business. They'd bought matching navy polos for the occasion, and even though Grace suggested some basic Ajax and Windex, Jo ordered every cleaning supply they carried at the Container Store.

"I'll give them to Gloria when we're done with them. It'll be like Christmas for her."

Their goal was to try to find anything that might implicate Mark in Garrett's murder, or anything that proved he'd been traveling with Delilah when it happened. They weren't expecting something as clear as a Garrett voodoo doll or a secret stash of clearly marked poison, but maybe a photo of the Baltimore trip that placed Mark there, or a parking ticket that could prove he was elbow-deep in Maryland crab cakes when Garrett died.

Grace pulled her hair into a ponytail and watched Jo get ready. She'd never met Mark, but Jo was something of a local celebrity, which meant she couldn't just show her face. She put on a navy ballcap and pulled a medical mask around her ears, giving Grace pandemic flashbacks.

Jo turned to her. "You've got this. We just need to get into the house."

Grace nodded and climbed out of the driver's seat. She wore a zip-up sweatshirt over her polo and reached into her pocket to feel for the fake business card she and Jo had created from a Canva template.

As Grace approached the house, she felt anxiety prick at the back of her neck. She took two deep breaths. This was different than the situation with Wyatt. Jo was with her this time, and she'd dropped a pin to alert Ava to their location, lying and telling her they were going to pick something up from Facebook Marketplace.

"Really? You're rich as hell. You couldn't buy a new chaise, Jo?" Ava replied.

"It's vintage," Jo responded. And Ava, a devotee of authentic mid-century modern furniture, made no further argument.

Grace gave three quick knocks on the door. The window to her right was open, the curtains swaying faintly from the light kiss of the wind. At first, there was no sound. But when she heard the shuffle of lazy feet, a light groan indicated she may have woken Mark up, or at least interrupted him.

A second later, the door opened.

Mark was taller than she expected, probably over six feet. His hairline had receded significantly from where it had been in his social media photo, a healthy salt-and-pepper blend covering the rest of his head. If she'd inconvenienced him, he didn't show it. He gave her a megawatt smile like the one in his campaign ads. If he'd let himself go, he was at least still prioritizing dental hygiene.

"Hello there. How can I help you?"

"Hello, sir. My name is Elle Croft."

Grace had wanted to come into the situation with some confidence, so she and Jo came up with a name that honored two of their most confident fictional idols: Lara Croft and Elle Woods.

"I launched a cleaning company recently, and I'm focused on growing my client list." She reached in her pocket then handed him the business card for her fabricated venture, *Cleaned by Croft*. (She had suggested *Elle Croft, Room Raider*, but Jo promptly shut it down.) "I have a team member with me in the car and we're offering free one-room cleanings in exchange for a good review online."

Mark examined the card closely, flipping it over.

"No catch here? Just a free room cleaning?"

"Yes, sir! We'd love to show off what we can do."

Mark nodded, then pocketed the business card. "This is good timing. I've been hunting for someone to come in and keep the place looking presentable." He was wearing flannel pajama pants and an old campaign T-shirt. "I just got a new consulting job and I'm out of the house a lot more." He pointed at the logo on his chest. "I used to be well known in local politics. It's good to be back in the game."

He flashed his smile again, and Grace knew this was the perfect opportunity to butter him up. "I *knew* you looked familiar!"

Mark placed a hand on his chest and bowed his head in fake humility. "I'm just your average citizen now, no need to be nervous."

I'm only nervous because I'm about to poke through all your junk drawers, Grace thought.

Mark clapped his hands together. "So how does this work? You go get your guy out of the car and – do I get to pick the room?"

Grace nodded. *Please not the bathroom. Please not the bathroom. Please not–*

"The master bathroom would be great, actually."

Gut punch.

"You bring your own supplies?" he continued.

Grace nodded. "Yep! You just need to show us where to go. I'll be right back." She pointed in the direction of the truck before walking off. Once she had Jo in her sightline, she started to nod, and Jo climbed out of the truck, walking back to the bed and lowering the tailgate to grab their tote of cleaning supplies.

"It's the bathroom," Grace groaned.

Jo cringed, then looked to the sky. "You're lucky I love you, Garrett."

It's hard to learn much based on first impressions, but one thing was perfectly clear once you passed through the threshold of Mark's home: he was a swinger.

The man appreciated a good pineapple, especially if that pineapple was upside down. They were featured on canvases, pillows, a tote bag hanging on a doorknob, and when Grace and Jo walked into the master bathroom they realized they'd also walked into Mark's tropical refuge. Etched into the glass shower door was a pineapple accent that, in another setting, far away from Mark's bright yellow pineapple wallpaper, towels, and bathroom accessories, would have looked subtly chic.

Above the tub was a bronze pineapple chandelier that, again, Grace would have been able to appreciate anywhere else.

"I love a theme," Mark said behind them, which made both Jo and Grace jump. Jo held a hand over her heart, her breathing audible through her mask.

"I see that!" Grace said, before turning to him. "We'll get right to work then! You'll be… around?"

Mark nodded. "Yep! Getting some stuff done in my office. You can yell if you need me!"

With that, he left and went downstairs.

On the side of the soaking tub, nestled between a few candles and draped in a Hawaiian lei, was a photo of Mark and Delilah, kissing in front of a roasted pig, presumably at a luau. Grace pointed it out to Jo. "Nothing settles me into a relaxing bath more than roast pork."

Jo snorted, then turned with her hands on her hips. "Let's get started. Once we're in a groove, one of us can start looking through the bedroom." They hadn't noticed any cameras as they walked through the house, but Jo still kept her voice down. It was a small space, they'd heard the smack of Mark's office door against the jamb. Hopefully they'd be able to hear just as clearly if he came back out.

Grace decided to start with the bathroom vanity, which was sprinkled with facial hair from Mark's last shave. At least, she told herself it was facial hair, so that she could get the job done and not walk out immediately. She took a paper towel, wet it, and ran it along the counter to try to collect as much of it as she could. When she turned to throw it away, she realized Jo was still standing in the same position, surveying the room with her hands on her hips.

"Uh, hello?"

Jo's head shot toward her. "Yeah?"

It hit Grace suddenly that Jo grew up with a housekeeper, then hired her own in adulthood. "Do you know how to clean a bathroom?"

Jo scowled. "How hard can it be?"

Grace smiled. There were few situations they'd been in where she had more experience than Jo. "It's not hard, honestly, but you do need to start somewhere."

Jo spun slowly in a circle and ended facing Grace. "And where is the best place to start?"

Grace was tempted to have Jo start with the toilet, because it was her least favorite task, but it seemed a little cruel. Although, who knew what Mark, Delilah, and their pineapple-loving friends had gotten into in the tub. Maybe it was the dirtiest thing in the room. "Start with the shower." Grace walked over to the etched door and opened it to peek in. "There is a removable showerhead in there, so once you scrub the walls, you can rinse them off easily."

Jo seemed grateful for the direction and went to grab her supplies.

Fortunately, the bathroom was not a complete disaster. Grace had lived with a boyfriend for a while, right out of college, so she knew the more important places to look. Mark was guilty of being a messy shaver, but he seemed to pee into the bowl more than on it, and the ring around his tub was more unsightly than horrifying. It wouldn't take them too long to clean the whole thing, which meant they could prioritize snooping.

Grace just about had the bathroom vanity looking like a model home, even folding the tissue popping out of the box like origami, when Jo stepped out of the shower.

"I did it!"

"You did it!" Grace said, throwing her hands in the air in mock celebration. She took a few steps toward Jo.

"Do you want to start looking in the bedroom?"

Jo peeled off her rubber gloves with a sharp *snap*.

"Yes."

Grace turned her attention to the tub, trying not to imagine how luxurious it could be, filled to the brim with a bubble bath, pineapple-shaped novelty candles the only light in the room. Maybe throw in a pineapple bath bomb to really set the mood. She removed everything from the edge of the tub, including the photo of Mark and Delilah. She dipped a rag in a bucket full of cleaner and scrubbed around the tub, making sure to pay close attention to the grout. The bougie cleaner smelled amazing, like sandalwood, and Grace planned to use as little as possible so she had some left to take home. *Sorry, Gloria.* Happy with the edge of the tub, she turned her attention to the inside.

She shoved a sponge into the pale pink container of cleaning paste and started to work at the ring. It was no match for whatever the heck she was using, and Grace smiled at herself as she saw the efforts of her labor show themselves in real time. She almost didn't hear Jo come in.

"Graaaaaaace," she whispered. She was laughing, struggling to keep it under control. She was wearing a new pair of rubber gloves and held out boxers covered in cartoon pineapples.

"We need to talk about it," Jo spit out. "We need to acknowledge the pineapple in the room. They're swingers, right?" She seemed to catch herself acting out of character and tried to self-correct. "Not that there's anything wrong with that, obviously. Not for me, but hey, we're encouraged all our lives to share."

Grace was laughing now, too. "Stop! Put the underwear away. You're supposed to be looking for *photographs*."

"Well, I thought maybe he was keeping some photos in his underwear drawer," Jo replied as she started to propel the boxers above her head like a helicopter. "But you should know, they *all* look like this."

"He really does love a theme," Grace said, turning back to the tub ring.

She managed to get the tub looking spotless, placed Mark's decor back in its designated spot, and even scrubbed the toilet in record time. Her final task was the easy job of mopping the floor, and when she finished and stepped back to admire her work, she felt a warm sense of accomplishment. She packed up the supplies and walked into the bedroom, where Jo sat, flipping through a photo album.

"All done!" Grace said, and when Jo turned her head to look at her, she caught the glint of tears under her eyes. The top of the mask was wet.

"What's the matter?" Grace rushed to Jo's side.

Jo flipped a few pages and pointed to a specific picture. "Nothing. I found exactly what we were looking for. Mark's alibi. There are pictures of the two of them together, which means he was in Baltimore with Delilah, and nowhere near Garrett when he was murdered."

In the photo, Mark and Delilah stood in front of a multicolor sign that said: "Visit Baltimore." Mark's nose was covered in bandages, and there were deep bruises under his eyes.

"Why are you crying? This is a good thing. You did it."

Jo slammed the album shut. "Because I'm out of ideas! All our loose ends being tied up means we don't get any damn answers and–"

"What are the two of you doing?" Mark's deep voice startled them, and both women jumped to stand.

He was pointing at the photo album in Jo's hand. "What are you doing with that?"

Jo immediately started to apologize, tripping over her words, a sure sign she didn't think before opening her mouth. Grace's eyes darted over to the album, at the photo of Mark and Delilah on the cover.

"She just went through a terrible breakup!"

Both Mark and Jo went silent and looked at her, so Grace had to think quickly. "Her boyfriend just broke up with her, and I thought a few cleaning jobs would help keep her mind off it. But she saw this beautiful photo and she couldn't help but grab it. The two of you look so in love."

Jo was nodding. She turned to Mark. "You seem like such a nice couple."

Grace was trying to concentrate on Mark, but it had just clicked that even his bedspread had pineapples on it, and now she was wondering where someone even buys something like that.

Mark's face softened at the mention of the photograph, but he crossed his arms sternly. "That's my little lady, Delilah."

Grace cringed internally at the phrase "little lady," and she felt Jo send her a telepathic message that she felt the same way.

"It looks like you've figured out the key to a happy relationship," Jo said.

Mark scoffed. "Tell my ex-wife that."

Jo held the album open to one of the pictures of Mark and Delilah. "I don't mean to be rude. Well, more rude than I'm already being. But why do you have bandages on your face in these photos?"

Mark ran a hand down his face. "It's embarrassing, actually, but..." He crossed his arms. "I got hit hard at the batting cages a few years ago. Broke my nose, messed up my breathing and all that. I let it heal kind of wonky and I was living with it, but a few weeks before that trip I was tossing the old pigskin around with a friend and got one to the face again." He shook his head. "The little lady insisted I take the opportunity to have the thing set right, finally. So I had a, you know. Nose job." He hung his head in shame.

"I felt good enough to go on the trip, but I made Delilah promise not to take any pictures of me. The guys would never let me hear the end of it if they heard I had plastic surgery. They'd be asking if I was getting fillers next."

He looked up. "I let her print them out for the album as long as we kept it hidden." He raised an eyebrow. "Not hidden enough, obviously."

Jo placed the album gently on the bed. "I'm so sorry for invading your privacy like that. I just... I need a little hope sometimes, you know."

Mark mulled it over, giving a quick scan of the room, then he pulled his eyes back to Jo. "Yeah, I get it. I've been there. Broken hearts make people do crazy shit."

Like burning paintings. Or punching someone in the face.

Mark took a few steps toward the bathroom. "You guys done in there?"

"Yep!" Grace said, fingers crossed that her work was up to his standards. The three of them walked inside and he took stock of what he saw. "Looks great," Mark said. He turned to them. "You know, this was such perfect timing, with my new job and all."

Grace grinned. "Yes! The consulting job! Are you getting back into politics?"

Mark held up his hands and shook his head. "Ahh, no, I'm afraid those days are behind me. I've learned I enjoy life more if I can keep a low profile, you know?"

Jo was nodding. "Absolutely," Grace agreed. "It would be so hard to have everything out there in the open for everyone to know."

Mark started to walk away from them.

"You probably know this," he said, running a hand along the top of the shower, making sure they'd hit every surface, "but if you want to go into politics, you can't have any skeletons in your closet."

The left side of his mouth lifted and he turned to them, leaning in as his voice lowered to a whisper. "But that doesn't mean you can't hide a femur or two in the back." He winked.

Or maybe a pineapple.

Chapter 19

The dead end wasn't good for morale, especially given that the weather had taken a turn for the dark and bleak. October quietly bowed out, and as Grace flipped her calendar to November, she hoped that something – like a new lead, significant update from Sean, or sunshine – was waiting around the corner. Grace kept up with the subreddit she'd gotten from Maya, but, like most public forums on the internet, it had mostly boiled down to a bunch of people arguing the same point over and over. Any new theories were instantly shut down by inside knowledge Grace had from Jo, or so out in left field it wasn't even worth looking into.

Many people seemed to think, in the absence of someone to pin everything on, that Jo was guilty.

While Grace was happy not to put herself into harm's way to get information about the murder, she also hated seeing Jo struggling with what to do next. She was more withdrawn, back to crying fits like she'd had when Garrett's death was still fresh. Every day, Grace woke up hoping this would be the day Sean called to tell her it was all over.

Grace had even mentioned the suspects Sean had told her about at the cafe, Garrett's ex, Kate, and his high school bully. The police had already looked into them, but the police had spoken to all their other suspects too.

"Kate was the one to break it off," Jo said calmly without even looking at Grace. "I highly doubt she's been harboring homicidal feelings since then. And Garrett's ex-bully was in jail, sobering up in a drunk tank, when Garrett was killed."

Something positive to come from the case cooling was that Grace found herself doing normal assistant tasks. The nonprofit Jo ran was a well-oiled machine without her. Her team worked remotely, though three lived in Philadelphia, and they were in regular communication with Jo. But their annual fundraiser was a big deal, and it required Jo's input.

It wouldn't take place until July, but the theme and big picture ideas would need to be decided before the year ended. The topic was coming up more and more, and Jo and Grace were spending more time around the kitchen island discussing fundraising than they were in front of the whiteboard discussing suspects.

Grace had pitched an idea to Jo that Jo had loved: a charity concert followed by a silent auction. They could sell tickets to the Philadelphia Orchestra, a set minimum with no cap on donations, then raffle off other concert experiences, music lessons, even signed instruments. Jo encouraged her to think big, so they'd been brainstorming musicians from Philly who might donate a guitar or piano.

Grace loved the work around the nonprofit. She liked the idea that she was contributing to something much larger than herself. And she was good at it! Jo herself said multiple times that Grace seemed to have a knack for business and marketing.

When Jo suggested the idea of a girls' night out, Grace jumped on it. Their focus had shifted from the murder as of late. They'd been working hard, publicly trying to make 2025 the biggest donation year yet for the nonprofit, while still trying to collect information about Garrett's murder in the background.

Jo had been purposely vague about what they would be up to, telling Grace to dress for "dinner and a show" and assuring her their night would not involve anything too over-the-top.

Dinner and a show, to Grace, probably meant a cute dress with leggings under a peacoat. It was possible that, to Jo, it meant a ballgown. Grace was having one of those moments where she remembered how different "normal" was between her and Jo. Even in the two months she'd worked for her, she'd gotten used to being surrounded by luxurious things. Seeing expensive cars in Jo's garage was no longer shocking. *This is the car we go to the notary in,* she thought one day as she stared at Jo's Lexus SUV.

Standing in her own closet, Grace was humbled.

She eventually chose a little black dress she'd scored at an outlet sale. There was something magic about the color black, she thought. If a black dress fit you well and was paired with the right accessories, it was hard to tell if it was Dior or discount. Well... from far away. And as long as you didn't touch it.

She paired the fitted dress featuring a modest boat neck with dark tights and a string of fake pearls. Hopefully, no one at the event tonight was a jeweler. She looked at herself in the mirror, admiring the outfit and also making a list of all the ways she might embarrass herself if anyone asked who she was "wearing." Or was that something only asked on red carpets? She couldn't rule out a red carpet when it came to Jo.

She'd curled her hair into loose ringlets and doubled the amount of makeup she typically used on a night out. She wandered from room to room with her phone's camera facing her so she could check in every kind of light if she looked like a clown. Convinced she was not circus material, she topped off the look with a dark red lipstick.

She checked her smartwatch for the time and also to note how many steps she'd taken while getting ready. It was 5:58 pm. Perfect. Jo said the car would be getting her at six, so by the time she found a pair of heels at the bottom of her closet and grabbed her purse, she hit the apartment building's lobby just in time to see the car pull up.

Andre came around to open her door for her, and as she slid into the leather seat, she looked over at Jo, who was similarly dressed in a navy frock and smiling. "This is going to be so exciting! First, the show."

On cue (as it was wont to do), Grace's stomach growled loudly. "Oh man, I didn't eat anything for dinner. I was too busy getting ready."

Jo had picked up her phone, mindlessly scrolling then stopping to look at photos in detail. "Well, you look fabulous, and there will be light refreshments at the show. I'm sure it'll get you through to dinner."

Seeing as she didn't have a choice, Grace also settled into her seat as Andre pulled away from the curb. This had happened to her enough times that she was annoyed at herself for not having become one of those women who kept a granola bar in her bag. She pulled open her bedazzled clutch and peered inside like maybe someone had broken into her apartment and thought to leave a snack here. Instead, she was met with one tube of chapstick, a wad of cash, a receipt from 2013, and her trusty pepper spray.

They were forty or so minutes from the city if you were driving there during the day, but on a Friday night, they were going to hit traffic. As they came to a standstill, Jo announced they were still ten minutes from their destination, and it was already 7:02 pm.

Jo looked flustered. Grace wondered if they were meeting donors for her foundation. It seemed like Jo had a lot to lose by being late. Grace looked down and assessed the heels she'd chosen. *I can run in these,* she thought.

"Why don't we have Andre drop us off here, and we can power walk the rest of the way?"

Grace looked up to the rearview mirror, expecting Andre to be nodding in approval, but his brow was furrowed. "Not sure you ladies should be out by yourselves on a Friday night here."

Jo looked between Andre and Grace. Grace could see her doing the math as to whether a jog through a scary part of town was worth it. She shrugged. "I have a taser."

Grace smiled and caught Andre's eyes in the mirror. "And I have pepper spray, and can confirm it works."

Andre pulled over and let them out onto the sidewalk, yelling that he'd pick them up after, but Jo was already shuffling toward their destination. "This way!" she yelled.

Grace probably should have asked how many blocks they were running to get a better idea of what "ten minutes away" meant to Jo. It turned out to be pretty accurate, and after a ten-block race through downtown Philadelphia and zero broken heels, by the grace of God, they stopped.

In front of an elementary school.

For being so thin, Jo was shockingly out of breath, folded in half, and sounding like she might need an inhaler. "We (huff) are (wheeze) here!"

Grace looked up at the giant brick building. Someone with the initials GFC had tagged the side.

"I see that, but... *why* are we here?"

Jo stood up, wiping what Grace assumed to be sweat from her forehead as she smiled over at Grace. "It's a chorus concert!"

Jo explained everything to Grace as they stood in line at the auditorium's concession stand, run by the PTO. *Go Bears!*

Fortunately for them, the show had been slightly delayed because a boy dressed as an acorn threw up all over the stage before the curtains opened.

"I started the nonprofit and its scholarship program three years ago," Jo said as they stood shoulder to shoulder with parents dressed in a mix of church clothes and Flyers jerseys. "We had a ton of interest, which was great because that meant there was a need for what I was providing. It also meant there were going to be a ton of disappointed kids because we only had ten scholarships to give out."

Grace frowned. It seemed like an impossible task to choose which kids would get to pursue their dreams and which would have to find another way or move on to something else.

"So, we picked our winners. I got a lot of unhappy emails from parents. I understood they were disappointed. Many of them had few opportunities in life and they wanted better for their kids. However, a few of these parents were downright mean. Because of this, when I got an email from a parent with a subject line about the scholarship, I braced myself." Jo reached into her purse and pulled out her phone. "But it was this."

She handed the phone to Grace. It was open to a PDF of an email from "Mandy White."

Dear Mrs Baros,

I wanted to thank you for the opportunity you've created for kids in our community. I wanted nothing more than to play piano when I was growing up, but we could never afford one of our own so I could practice. Even though Laila didn't get a scholarship this year, I'm grateful there is a chance she might be able to do more than I did. She wanted to write you this note:

Below Mandy's message was a photo of a note, obviously written by a child:

Thank u 4 giving the gift of music!

They got to the front of the concession stand and Grace ordered nachos while Jo asked for a box of candy for each of them. They shuffled out of the way and walked past the door to the auditorium. The curtain was still closed. They moved to stand at a cocktail table set up to the right of the door.

"Anyway, Laila wrote that note in kindergarten." Jo grabbed one of Grace's nachos as she continued the story, excitedly moving her arms around for emphasis. "I showed the email to Garrett and he fell in love with them. Said we needed to do something because there were only so many good people in the world and these two had found us."

"What did you do?" Grace could feel a glob of cheese slip down her chin and onto her dress. Black was a good choice.

Jo started ripping open her candy box. There was no way the candy would make it to their seats. "We got in contact with Mandy and we told her we were going to sponsor Laila personally. Laila wanted to be a singer and we realized we could make two dreams come true if we got them a piano, so Mandy could play while Laila sang."

Grace's heart lurched at this kindness. She'd caught Jo sitting at the piano in her entranceway many times now, playing some classical piece with fluency. The first time, Grace had mistaken her playing for the radio. Jo told her she'd wanted to be a music teacher, but after her dad made it clear he felt college was a waste of time, she shifted her priority to simply enjoying the music, rather than teaching it.

"Jo," Grace said, a teary smile on her face. For a while, that was all they said, until an announcement over the loudspeakers saying the show would start in five minutes reminded her they were at a school.

"Anyway," Jo said, shrugging, "I know we haven't spent the bulk of our time focused on the nonprofit, but I needed you to see what my vision looked like. If you're going to work for me in the future, I wanted you to have a firsthand look at my plans, and what I want to accomplish."

This was the first time Jo had referred to the future. A future where Garrett's murder was solved, and they focused more on marketing than murder.

"I'd love that," Grace said. "I'd love to see the vision. But what does the vision have to do with an elementary school choir performance?"

Jo started a light bounce on her toes, obviously giddy about what she was going to reveal next.

"I wanted you to see Laila and Mandy. They're doing a duet tonight."

* * *

Grace wasn't sure how long she'd been watching the show before Laila came on. She put it in the ballpark of four to six hours. As it turns out, there are few children who come with a mass amount of raw talent. While most of them were cute, only a few of them seemed to even be able to control what was coming out of their mouths. But it was always clear what song they were singing, thanks to the teacher screaming the words to them. The children mainly harmonized with high-pitched squeals and demonic growls.

In between songs were short skits about kindness and gratefulness. In one, a girl looked for the perfect gift to show her mother thanks. In another, a father and son volunteered at a soup kitchen. In a third, a little boy peed his pants. This was unscripted.

The kids finished something resembling Cyndi Lauper's "True Colors," when the principal came to center stage to make the announcement.

"Wow, kids! You can see how hard you've worked to make this show happen!" The principal was grinning wildly, and Grace wasn't sure if she was truly this happy or if the smile was contractually obligated.

"Now, I want you all to give a big round of applause for our next performer, Laila. She's worked so hard on her solo and this performance is *extra* special because she will be accompanied by her sweet mother!"

Mandy entered from the floor below the stage and took a seat at the piano. Grace couldn't see her face, just her long box braids creeping down past the bench when she sat. On the stage, Laila entered from the right, and the crowd went wild. The principal put her arm around Laila and leaned once more into the mic. "Ladies and gentlemen, Laila White!"

The principal helped Laila lower the mic stand, patted her on the shoulder, and then disappeared from where Laila came.

Laila looked nervously down at her mother. They had similar hairstyles, though Laila's was cropped much shorter, with clear beads at the ends. The beads perfectly matched her dress, top covered with glitter, and bottom a puffy explosion of mesh.

Mandy slowly nodded, and Laila nodded back.

Mandy began to play, light and gentle at first. Laila closed her eyes, and for a minute Grace worried she was afraid until she opened her mouth, bold and beautiful melody falling like a fresh blanket of snow.

Laila's voice was rough and jazzy, something Grace didn't even realize someone her age could have. She sounded bigger than her little frame reflected, and Grace found herself clutching her chest in surprise. The song was "Swing Low, Sweet Chariot," which Grace hadn't heard since childhood church mornings with her grandparents.

Grace looked to Jo on her left and saw tears flowing freely down her cheeks. She'd seen Jo cry so often in the past few months, but never like this. Never for joy. Mostly joy, at least. Grace figured there was a large part of Jo thinking, *Garrett should be here for this.*

The auditorium was silent save for a baby crying in the back and the bewitching sounds of Laila's voice. And Grace realized while she had cursed the crawling clock during the rest of the show, she hoped Laila would keep singing forever. The past few months had been so difficult, but in this moment it was hard to see or feel anything beyond this little girl, her mother, their love of music, and their beautiful connection.

And then the pace sped up, and the audience began to clap along with Laila, some of them singing along quietly. A few people rose from their seats, causing a chain reaction until everyone was on their feet, cheering Laila on, dancing, not caring what their neighbor thought about their moves. Grace and Jo jumped in place as they clapped, broad smiles covering both of their faces. As Laila belted out the final note of the song, everyone began to cheer, in awe of the little girl with the big voice.

Jo reached over and grabbed Grace's hand, giving it a small squeeze as Laila's standing ovation erupted. "Thank you for coming." Grace smiled back, then looked to the stage and gave a whistle in Laila's direction. She could see Mandy's shoulders shaking at the piano. She was crying. And Grace didn't need to see her face to know it was a picture of pride.

Grace and Jo met Mandy and Laila in the lobby. Laila spotted Jo first and ran toward her, colliding with her as they embraced. "Jojo! You made it!"

Jo held Laila. "Of *course* I made it! There was nothing more important to me than seeing you sing!" Jo stepped back from the girl and turned her attention to her mother. "Mandy!"

The women embraced, and then Jo stepped back to make introductions. "Grace, this is Laila and Mandy. Laila and Mandy, meet Grace! She's been helping me since…"

The beautiful moment with Laila on stage and Jo crying in the audience had ended, and Jo seemed to remember she came with Grace and not Garrett. Because Garrett was gone. Tears welled in her eyes.

Mandy stepped in to hold her. "It's OK, honey. You go ahead and cry. Even on a night like this, some things need to be cried over."

They huddled together until Jo got her tears under control and moved back. Mandy looked at Grace with a warm smile and stuck her hand out, "Nice to meet you, Grace. And thank you for coming to support our girl on her big night."

Grace smiled down at Laila. "It seemed like it was a team effort, but Laila, I need to tell you, I have never heard anyone sing like that. Not in real life, at least."

Laila put her hands behind her back and twisted her body, looking down shyly. Mandy reached down and squeezed her arm, and it made Grace miss her own mother.

"Ladies," said Jo, suddenly back in a good mood and full of excitement, "can you join us for dinner?!"

"Oh, we'd love to, Jo, but Jerome and Malik are around here somewhere." Mandy stood on her tiptoes and scanned the crowd, searching for her husband and son. She spotted them and waved. "They'll want to say hi, Jojo. They didn't get to see you at the funeral."

Grace didn't realize they'd been at the funeral, which didn't surprise her because she was proving again and again to be a terrible detective, and because the crowd had been so large that day.

Jerome and Malik walked over a few seconds later and the group exchanged introductions, greetings, and hugs. The family was going home to cook their usual "celebration" dinner and Jo was still tight-lipped on where they were going to dinner. The bunch parted so everyone could move on with their night.

The air was colder than it had been earlier as Grace and Jo emerged from the school, and Grace was grateful for Andre, who pulled up at the exact right moment. The women climbed inside the car and Jo leaned forward to tell Andre to "head to the place."

Grace had been expecting a swank art show and dinner with a city view, but sitting through an elementary school holiday pageant had made it clear she should avoid setting any expectations, so instead of questioning Jo any more, she looked out the window and enjoyed the ride, premature Christmas lights twinkling occasionally in storefronts and on street lamps.

After a ten-minute drive, Andre pulled over in front of a strip of businesses in tall brownstone buildings, much like the street housing Garrett's studio.

Grace climbed out and stood on the sidewalk, taking in the restaurant's facade as she waited for Jo to walk around the car. A neon sign glared in the dark of the night, "Tony's" greeting her in bright red. There was a historical sign out front, green with gold letters, stating that this restaurant was more than one hundred years old. There was a sign in the window telling DoorDash drivers to head to the back, and as Grace's eyes went up past the crown molding that separated the first floor from the second, she noticed a second-floor balcony that was too small for any real purpose.

When she felt Jo standing next to her, she finally asked. "Why here?"

Jo sighed. "This is where Garrett and I went on our first date."

Chapter 20

The smell hit first.

There was nothing on earth that smelled better to Grace than the alluring scent of roasted onion and garlic tossed in olive oil. Nothing else, just garlic and onion. Italian restaurants took this to the next level though, adding in roasted peppers and tomato, melted cheese.

The combination of scents sent Grace back to childhood Sunday dinners with her grandparents. Each week, it was spaghetti. Grace's grandmother was even more risk-averse than her, and she considered it a risk to include any herbs or spices in her cooking. There was no need to keep a spice cabinet when you only used salt and pepper, so instead, this area was for anything sugar-filled that could be used to bribe the grandchildren into behaving. At one point, even the salt went away when Grace's grandmother got tired of her doctor talking about her high blood pressure. It may not have been particularly flavorful food, but a whiff of crushed tomatoes still made Grace feel like she was falling asleep in her grandfather's La-Z-Boy, belly full of noodles.

The smell wasn't the only comforting thing about Tony's. The decor, though tasteful, looked as if it hadn't been updated in the restaurant's hundred-year history. This part of the restaurant was busy. She hoped Jo had made reservations.

Jo knew Tony (*of course she did*) and explained that Tony was *really* Tony IV and the restaurant had opened in 1905 under Tony's great-grandfather, Tony I. The OT, if you will.

While they waited at the front of the restaurant for a greeter, Jo boasted about its history. It had hosted presidents, movie stars, pop queens, and sports royalty, many of them featured in large, printed photos on the wall to their left. Jo had pointed it out to Grace, and she seemed most excited about the picture of Adam Sandler. If you didn't know, you'd assume Jo was part of the family who founded Tony's, with the way she stitched such love and pride into her descriptions.

But Grace was getting to know Jo well, so she knew Jo was so passionate about this place because it was easy for her to picture Garrett here. Dinner here with Jo felt like a gift, something Grace had earned by being a shoulder to cry on for the last few months. In return, she was getting something that felt bigger: a peek into a place Jo loved, made even more important because it carried the memories of the person she'd loved. Who she still loved.

And while this thought was beautifully sentimental, it stirred up a darker thought in Grace's mind. *What if Garrett's murder is never solved? What if this dead end, this bump in the road… is permanent?* She could picture Jo, ten years older, still looking into suspects, still on the hunt for any clue that might lead her to the truth. The image almost made her sick. Garrett's death would cut two lives short if Jo never got any sort of closure.

A flustered young man approached Jo and Grace. "Two of you dining with us this evening? Got a reservation?"

Grace blinked a few times successively, staring at him, still fairly lost in her daydream.

Jo nodded to the greeter and gave her name. He scanned his list and made a mark with a ballpoint pen, then motioned for them to follow him. He took them through the room and up a small staircase to their left to another level of the restaurant. The floor was ornately tiled, with floral patterns in white, teal, and red. The walls were made of wooden panels, white in the center with dark wood trim. On each panel was a hand-painted scene, probably five feet wide by three feet tall: the Leaning Tower of Pisa, the Colosseum, and more. There was something so *authentic* about this place.

Once they were seated, the waiter handed them each a menu and then left to grab glasses of still water and freshly baked bread. They were one of three groups seated in this area, though it was eight pm now. Elderly couples and families with little kids would already be asleep. This was the dinner time of the childless and the troublesome, Grace's mom always said when they rolled up to a late dinner.

Though the only trouble Grace was planning on getting into tonight was some serious carb abuse. *So many pastabilities. Don't gnoch it till you try it.* She kept these quips to herself.

The menu featured your traditional Italian fare of lasagna, spaghetti, alfredo, etc, including a selection of seafood, beef, chicken, and pork dishes. As everyone knows, the true star of any Italian restaurant is its tiramisu, so Grace was prepared to order light to make room for it. She debated getting a salad, but it seemed like a waste to go to a place known for its pasta and choose lettuce. Instead, she went with a half portion of the chicken piccata, pretending like the sauce was not essentially straight butter someone squeezed a lemon into.

When the waiter returned with their water and a basket of bread, they told him they were ready to order. Jo went with the half portion of fettuccine alfredo, and Grace looked forward to seeing if her choice, too, was to make room for dessert.

As the waiter shuffled through the doorway, he passed a large bald man with a goatee. The man was wearing all black save for a little white apron tucked around his waist. His shirt was covered in flour, so Grace wondered if the apron was more of a stylistic choice.

"Tony!" Jo exclaimed, rising from her seat. She met him in the center of the room in a vigorous embrace. Tony lifted Jo off the floor, her feet dangling above the ceramic tiles as she let out a cheerful groan.

As he set her back down, Tony smiled at Jo. "It's been too long, way too long!" Then, his face turned somber. "I was real sorry to hear about Garrett, Jo. He was a good guy. Good guy *and* a good tipper, and it doesn't get better than that."

Tony took Jo's hands in his and lowered his head as if he were scared to make eye contact.

"I wanted to come to the funeral, but half the staff was out that week with some bug. Did Marie give you the flowers?"

"She did, Tony. They were beautiful. Thank you."

Forgiven, Tony let go of Jo's hands and formed his mouth back to a smile. "It was the least we could do. The two of you have been good customers and good friends."

Jo grinned and placed a hand on Tony's arm, turning him toward Grace. "Speaking of good friends, Tony, this is Grace. She's been helping me out since Garrett's passing. She worked for him first."

She never would have told you it would mean so much to have Jo call her a friend, but the title made Grace blush. It had been a long time since she made a new friend, and she was glad it still elicited an emotional response in her like it had in elementary school, when everyone was desperate to be someone else's best friend.

Tony presented his hand and Grace shook it. He was startlingly strong, knocking her off balance, but his face was friendly and open. "Nice to meet you, Grace! Is this your first time here? You don't look familiar."

It was impressive that Tony seemed to know many of his customers, but one hundred years was a long time to accrue regulars. "It is! I'm from Florida originally. Moved here a few months ago."

"Ah, well I hope you're surviving the Pennsylvania fall alright. And that you like it here enough to stay."

Grace nodded. "I'll test your tiramisu and let you know!"

The three of them laughed like old friends, then Tony turned to Jo, speaking more quietly, his voice deeper.

"Did that asshole little brother of Garrett's end up showing his face at the funeral?"

Jo's eyebrows raised. She looked from Grace to Tony twice, like either of them might be able to give her the information her face was asking for. "You mean his brother Alex?"

"Yeah, Alex was his name. I assume you know about the fight they had the last time Garrett was here?" Tony crossed his arms, his face a scowl. Clearly, it had been memorable for him. Jo seemed clueless.

"Garrett didn't say anything about arguing with Alex. When was this?"

Tony thought for a moment. "A few weeks before Garrett died? They came in with their mom. They ordered dinner, and it was going well enough, then that Alex kid started screaming in Garrett's face, calling him a piece of crap and, you know, other things I'm not going to say in polite company."

Jo took a seat back at their table, so Grace followed. "Garrett didn't tell me he and Alex got into it."

"Well, I think he was a little embarrassed his brother made such a scene. I grabbed Alex and pushed him out the door. I told him to take a walk around the block and not come back to my restaurant again. I'm not running that kind of establishment." Tony leaned over the table and propped himself up with his hands. He shook his head. "The mom followed him out the door, but Garrett came over to settle his check and everything. Told me the brother wanted money for something, but Garrett told him no since he'd already paid for school and it didn't pan out. Seemed pretty reasonable to me."

Jo was nodding along to show she was listening, but she was staring at the paper placemat in front of her, which featured a sketch of a dancing cannolo.

"Jo, you OK?" he asked.

"Yeah, I… I didn't realize they'd had a falling out so close to when Garrett died. That's… that's awful."

"Your mother-in-law never said anything? She was real distraught about it all."

Jo rubbed her hands along the tops of her thighs. "Honestly, I haven't talked to her much. I told her about Garrett, and then when I didn't feel like I got enough time with her at the funeral, I tried to call her. I got her voicemail. I guess I'm just realizing she never called me back."

"Was Alex at the funeral?" Grace asked. She had no recollection, though she hadn't noticed Laila and Mandy at the funeral either.

"No. Which was shitty, but not necessarily a red flag. Alex has social anxiety, and will do anything to get away from a crowd."

Jo was biting her lip and mindlessly tapping her thumb on the table. "I did sort of feel like Amy was avoiding me at the funeral. More than usual."

"She usually avoids you?" asked Grace, Tony asking the same question with his facial expression.

Jo shrugged. "To be honest, they never got comfortable with me. I mean, they were kind and everything, but Garrett and I had different childhoods. Outside of both sets of parents getting divorced, there wasn't much in common. Amy was uncomfortable that I came from money. I think she compared her situation to my parents', and in terms of wealth, came up short. Amy would never have asked us for a dime, but Alex acted as though he was entitled to whatever we had. When he asked Garrett for the money for school, we were happy to pay. He flunked out the next semester. We put him up in an apartment until he found a job, but he trashed the place and got evicted."

Tony was shaking his head, also looking pretty proud that a guy he'd deemed an asshole was indeed asshole-y.

Jo bit her lip and looked nervously toward the windows in the front of the building. "For Amy to come with Alex when he asked for money… Alex is probably in something deep."

Jo and Grace locked eyes. Was it something deep enough to lead to Garrett's death?

A server slid past a confused Tony, a plate in each hand. "I have a chicken piccata?"

Grace raised her hand and the man sat the plate in front of her gently. He smiled at Jo. "Then that makes this your fettuccini alfredo!" He handed Jo her food, then asked them if they wanted fresh parmesan. They each shook their head, so the man gave a bow, a slight nod to Tony, and went on his way.

As Grace grabbed her fork, she saw Tony shift. He shook his head, bringing his hand up to rub the bald spot on top. "Well, ladies, I know it's bad timing, but I've got to get back to the kitchen." He leaned toward their table and placed his hand on Jo's. "You need anything, you tell me. Got it?"

Jo smiled, and she and Grace watched Tony head back to work.

Grace started to swirl her pasta around her fork, the zesty and buttery scent making her stomach growl. But as she took that first bite, as delicious as it was, she realized that she'd lost her appetite at some point in the last few minutes. Suddenly the idea of eating any more was enough to trigger a gag, and she instinctively pushed her plate away from her.

She looked across the table, where Jo was swirling her pasta as well, but not taking any bites. Jo looked up and there was a moment of understanding between the women.

The server was unloading a tray next to their table, and as he finished grating cheese over four different pasta dishes, Jo tapped him on the shoulder.

"Sorry to bother you. I think we're going to have to take our order to go. I remembered we have work to do at home."

Chapter 21

Grace wasn't sure if Amy would cooperate – but the weather certainly wasn't going to.

Jo had asked Grace to spend the night and come with her to confront Amy in the morning. After Andre dropped them off, they stood eating leftovers and Tony's nearly perfect tiramisu (he was going to get a great Yelp rating) over Jo's kitchen counter.

It didn't feel like Grace's place to discuss whether Alex and Amy had something to do with Garrett's murder. The other suspects were acquaintances of Garrett's at best. This was *family*. His family, but also Jo's. It seemed like something Jo should handle on her own.

But it was clear Jo was also spiraling, repeating statements stuck in her head like a turntable, like, "She wouldn't protect one son if he's hurt the other… right?"

She needed backup.

Jo's ranting didn't stop until the early morning. Eventually, they both fell asleep on the couch.

They left Jo's house at seven am. With a one-hour drive ahead of them and a quick stop for coffee and pastries, Jo figured they'd get to Amy's house around 8:30. Andre offered to drive, but Jo had politely declined. She told Grace this was a unique situation, a family issue, and she didn't want Andre to hear anything he'd feel he had to pass along to Gloria, since she was a close friend of Amy's.

It was raining lightly when they left, an unseasonal drop in temperature threatening to turn it to snow, but as they headed north it grew harder, taking the visibility down to about twenty feet in front of them. The radio was playing Top Forty music, turned down so low Grace couldn't tell what any of the songs were. Her muscles clenched as she watched Jo navigate through a sheet of fat raindrops, sliding occasionally but never scaring them enough to stop.

At 9:17, they pulled in front of a humble two-bedroom house. Its picket fence was broken in several places, and the drapes were pulled shut. Despite the tattered flag hanging from a post on the front porch, which said "Welcome" above a graphic of a butterfly, it did not feel welcoming.

Jo exhaled. "From terrifying driving conditions to a terrifying conversation, I guess," she said, her nervous fingers playing a little song on the steering wheel.

Grace could see Jo's jaw muscles tighten. Her cheeks were dramatically drained of color, something she wasn't sure she could blame on the temperature.

"You good?" she said.

Jo brought her mittened hands to her face for a moment, taking slow, deliberate breaths, then removed them. "Yes. I'm good."

They got out of the SUV and Grace's foot landed in a deep puddle. She wasn't wearing boots. She'd never gotten around to buying a pair. Instead, she'd borrowed a pair of Gloria's sneakers. She felt the cold, dirty water creep down her sock and briefly wondered if she'd be able to survive winter if fall was already this bone-chilling. Since she hadn't expected to stay over, Grace also had to borrow some of

Jo's clothes. Jo had handed her a pair of cashmere-blend leggings and an Anine Bing sweatshirt that the internet said retailed for two hundred dollars, which was covered up with a wool trench coat that couldn't button the whole way. Grace felt like a toddler in a ballgown, terrified to tear or stain Jo's designer goods. But she had to admit, the clothes were *insanely* cozy.

One of the hinges on the front gate was off, so Jo opened and closed it carefully. While the walkway leading to the porch was slick, they made it to the door without incident.

Jo didn't waste a moment second-guessing her decision, opening the creaky screen door and giving three confident knocks on the solid wooden door behind it. A woman's voice yelled, "One minute!" as at least two dogs barked like they'd cornered the most wanted man in America.

Oh God, dogs, thought Grace. *I didn't bring my allergy meds.*

The metal scrape of a lock coming undone was the last noise before the door opened and a stunned Amy looked at her only daughter-in-law.

"Uhh. Hi. Jo? I–wuh… I wasn't expecting you. Everything alright?"

Jo's face was stoic, showing no hint of familial care but also not a clear show of anger.

"You lied to me, Amy."

For a moment, Amy stared at Jo. Then her eyes crept over to Grace, which made Grace nervous enough to introduce herself.

"Uh, hi, Mrs Kline. I'm Grace. I worked for Garrett. Now I work for Jo."

Amy didn't react right away. Then she took a step back and gestured for the women to come into the house. "You're welcome to come in."

Jo and Grace stomped their feet to try to get the bulk of the snow off, then took a step inside to remove their shoes completely. Instantly, Grace was struck by how... well... *normal* the house was. For months, she'd been going back and forth between her still barren apartment and Jo's dated yet luxurious home. There was something wholesome about the way this place looked, and even how it smelled: a long-forgotten Bath and Body Works scent mixed with wet dog and dust. This was a place where people *lived.*

None of the wood in the house matched, and frames filled the living room walls with candid photos. The couch was old and lumpy and a cabinet full of knickknacks sat in the corner, clean, but crowded. Amy had a fire going, and Grace was fighting the urge to curl up in front of it and nap on the lumpy couch, which looked to be the perfect amount of *worn* to make it a truly great nap.

One picture in particular caught Grace's eye. It was a group of children, ages ranging from around two to thirteen. One of the older boys was clearly Garrett. And his cousins, maybe? They were all sitting around a coffee table with four large Domino's pizza boxes on it. The floor was covered in a green shag carpet, and the couch Garrett was leaning back on was scratched in the corner, like a cat had found it to be the best spot for destruction.

How stark the difference was between the Garrett she knew and the Garrett in this photo. You'd never know, looking at this kid, that he'd grow up and be featured in magazine spreads, his paintings selling for tens of thousands of dollars at auction. You'd also never guess how his life would end. That someone would ever want to hurt this little boy, excited to be having a sleepover at his grandparents' house with all his cousins. A toddler was sitting on Garrett's lap in the picture. Grace guessed this was Alex.

Amy motioned for Jo and Grace to sit on the couch, while she took a chair next to the fire. The dogs, which Grace hadn't gotten a look at, were scratching at the back door, eager to greet them. Grace's nose started to run.

"What is this about me lying to you?"

Jo was taking off her coat and unwrapping a red knit scarf from around her neck. Amy shifted uncomfortably in her seat.

"Why didn't you tell me Garrett and Alex fought a few weeks before Garrett died?"

Amy's eyes darted to the ceiling, then toward the fire.

"I figured Garrett would have told you."

"Well, he didn't. And now he can't. So I want you to explain it to me."

Amy was wringing her hands, looking everywhere except Jo.

"I don't know what to tell you, Jo. That's the whole story. They fought. It was bad timing, and now they will never get to apologize to one another."

Amy's eyes were filling up with tears. So were Grace's, as she tried to will away her dog allergy. Her brain told her she shouldn't have come along, because she was crashing an intimate conversation between two grieving women *and* because she was only minutes away from needing to ask for an entire box of tissues. She tried to suck in her snot as quietly as possible. *Famed mystery writer Jessica Fletcher would never forget her allergy meds on the scene,* Grace thought.

"That is *not* the whole story, Amy. What were they fighting about? Why were you even there to begin with?

The restaurant owner is a close friend and said he told Alex not to come back, ever. It couldn't have been as small an incident as you're making it out to be."

A tear rolled down Amy's face, and she brought up a hand to wipe it off. "This is hard for me."

"I know, Amy." Jo's tone was a mix of empathy and frustration. "It's hard for me too. I can't stand not knowing what happened to Garrett."

Amy looked startled. "Wait. What does their fight have to do with Garrett's death?"

"That's what I'm here to find out."

"You can't think Alex had anything to do with Garrett's death? That was his big brother. He loved him." Amy's voice was getting louder as she defended her youngest child.

"I know he loved him, Amy, but you can't tell me you didn't notice Alex flying off the handle all the time? He was always coming to us for money. His temper went from zero to a hundred in a matter of seconds! I figure Garrett didn't tell me about the fight because I'd witnessed him trying to bring Alex back to earth over and over. You can't blame me for questioning him when he publicly screamed at my husband, who was dead two weeks later!"

Both women were crying now, and Grace wanted to walk outside and shove her face into a cold puddle for relief. Her eyes darted around the room, looking for a box of Kleenex. She was too afraid to interrupt and ask for one, though. She used her sleeve to wipe below her nose.

"Well, it wasn't Alex," Amy said, smacking her palms onto her thighs at her son's name.

"How do you know?!"

Amy looked like she was going to explode; from rage, from grief, from sadness, Grace couldn't tell. She didn't know Amy well enough, and also her eyes were watering now, she could barely see.

"Because he was in rehab, Jo!" Amy's eyes shot wide, keeping harsh eye contact with Jo, now clearly frustrated.

Jo shut her mouth and stared directly at Amy. Grace knew Jo needed more than this. She needed the entire story.

After a beat, Amy's posture slackened, and she leaned on the arm of her chair as she told them everything.

"Alex had a business idea. He was so excited about it. I hadn't seen him put so much hard work into anything, well, ever." Amy chuckled as she said this, her grin deepening her smile lines. "He'd come downstairs and spewed statistics at me and my husband, Tom, about success rates and returns on investments. I didn't understand a word of it, of course, but I was thrilled to see him passionate about something other than video games."

Amy's hand found one of the buttons on her shirt and she began to fidget with it as her face morphed from pride to anxiety. "He dropped out of college and has been working minimum wage jobs ever since. He didn't have enough money to make these dreams come to life. When he mentioned going to Garrett for money, I told him to try another avenue first. I've never asked anyone for money in my life, though God knows there were times I desperately needed it. But Alex insisted this was an investment opportunity for Garrett, and they would both come out winners in the end. When they set up a meeting, I decided to come along, to make sure Garrett understood how serious Alex was about this."

There was some sort of ticking coming from the kitchen, and the pressure in Grace's sinuses was becoming downright painful. Still, she was trying to stay focused on Amy's story.

As was Jo, who stared at her mother-in-law intently, her eyes softer than when they'd arrived.

Amy cleared her throat before continuing. "We got to the restaurant at the same time as Garrett, and Alex was ready. He'd spent the entire ride up practicing his pitch – he even had notecards!" She huffed a laugh, then looked at Grace. "If you knew him, you'd know how out of character it was. Anyway, as soon as we'd ordered drinks, Alex went into his business pitch. I watched Garrett's posture, and even though he was nodding and smiling in all the right places, I knew my boy. I knew he would say no before Alex even got to the ROI." She shook her head.

"Alex did so well, worked so hard. But when he asked Garrett what he thought, Garrett told him that while he could see how much thought Alex had put into it, there was still more work to be done to fully build out his idea." Amy made a small "tsk" noise and clutched at her chest.

"I'll never forget the way Alex's face fell. Garrett went on to say that he'd need to see some profit, some proof, before he put his money in Alex's hands. I think that really shook Alex's confidence."

Amy went off on a tangent, telling the women about how Garrett had been her easier child. That through her divorce from his father, he'd remained happy and well-adjusted. He was never too into sports or monster trucks or other things boys his age seemed to like, but he loved movies and art and math, not a subject that often came easily for a creative kid. He was likable, agreeable, and talented at what he did. She didn't realize how easy he had been until she had Alex, who spent the first six months screaming his head off, then much of the next ten years doing the same.

Where Garrett had maintained a small group of close friends, Alex seemed to know everyone and connect with no one. Garrett's A and B test scores towered over Alex's Cs and Ds. Everything was harder for Alex, and Amy found it difficult sometimes to treat her boys the same. Everything seemed to go Garrett's way, and nothing seemed to go Alex's.

"I know that the paths their lives took were mostly due to their decisions. Garrett was responsible and thought through each decision, while Alex's life motto seemed to be, 'It's all gonna work out!' Though it so often didn't. It just seemed like Alex had to work twice as hard to get half as far."

Jo interrupted Amy's train of thought.

"Alex asked Garrett for money when he was about eighteen. Garrett and I were already married, and Alex knew I came from a wealthy family." Jo looked to Grace, then back to Amy, who was nodding shyly. "Alex said the money was for tuition and Garrett – and I – were happy to give it to him. But nine months later, he dropped out, and needed more money for rent. Garrett helped him out again, but warned him it would be the last time. Alex was kicked out of the apartment within weeks."

Jo looked toward the floor.

"It was a difficult balance to know when to support him and when to cut him off." She looked back to Amy, her eyes mournful. "I can't imagine what that balance would have felt like as a mother."

Amy's eyebrows came closer, her mouth tight, and you could see she was fighting off tears. The last few months had taken a toll on her.

"A–anyway," she said, sputtering a bit, "Garrett said no to Alex's business pitch, and Alex was furious. He told Garrett he was a – excuse my language, but – a selfish piece of shit. That it was disgusting he was living the life of a celebrity while his brother was struggling to make ends meet and the roof of his mom and stepdad's house was leaking."

Amy held up a hand toward the other women.

"For the record, I hadn't let Garrett know, about the roof. My problems are not mine to pass on to my children. But Garrett would have helped if I asked. I know he would have. It wasn't fair of Alex to throw that in his face."

Jo was leaning as far in Amy's direction as she could.

"I tried to calm Alex down," Amy continued, "but Tony had already noticed and I saw him heading in our direction. As he got to the table, Alex yelled, 'I guess you like to enjoy watching other people suffer!' Which led to Tony grabbing Alex by the shirt collar and heaving him out the door, adding a warning to not come back."

Amy bit her lip and stared over at the fire, which needed a log or two tossed on.

"I should have stayed. I should have comforted Garrett. I didn't realize then how little time I had left with him. But I gave him a quick apology, gathered my things, and scrambled out the door to find Alex. I eventually spotted him a few blocks away, fist bleeding because he'd punched a brick wall."

The light from the window seemed to dim, or maybe it was Grace's imagination, synthesizing the dark details of the story.

"Garrett was calling me, but Alex wanted to leave, so I sent him a text to let him know I'd call him later. It took a minute or two to convince Alex that I should drive, but he eventually gave in and… we went home."

The closer Amy had gotten to the end of her story, the more emotional she became. By the time she got to the word "home," she was what many would describe as "blubbering." It was hard to understand what she was saying over shuddering sobs, and adding to the intense awkwardness in this moment, Grace could no longer handle the discomfort of her symptoms.

"I am sorry to interrupt this, honestly. Amy, do you have any allergy medication?" Grace barely recognized her own voice, nasally and lacking enunciation. "I apologize, I'm allergic to dogs."

Amy nodded and Jo asked her where she kept her medication. Jo left the room briefly and came back with a glass of water and a pill for Grace. Grace swallowed the pill and apologized profusely before chugging the rest of the water.

The small break had given Amy a moment to calm down, which eased Grace's embarrassment.

Jo took her seat again.

"And what happened? After you got home?"

Amy was fanning her face; whether she was hot or trying to dry her cheeks, Grace was unsure. "Alex stayed in his room for a few days. My husband said he heard him leave a few times in the middle of the night; he's always had insomnia. Sometimes he'd run out or go meet a friend late at night. He's twenty-five, so we can't exactly tail his every move."

She put her face in her hands for a moment, then sat up with fresh tears.

"A few days later we got a call. Police had gotten a report of someone overdosing in a bar bathroom, and it turned out to be Alex."

Grace felt empathetic toward Amy. It was clear she loved both Alex and Garrett deeply. She'd already lost one of them. To see the other struggle must have been crippling for her.

"We didn't even know he was using. We assumed he was regularly smoking weed, maybe experimenting with harder drugs, but..." She trailed off.

And then she looked directly at Jo.

"I am a terrible mother. I might be a terrible person. I thought I had done a good job, but I didn't protect Garrett from the person who wanted to hurt him. And I didn't protect Alex, either. He became an addict living under my roof and I thought he was, you know, smoking a joint sometimes. Like it wasn't a big deal. What kind of mother allows that to happen?"

Amy was fully breaking down, her face a deep maroon and shirt soaked with tears. Jo slid off the couch and went to kneel next to her, for a moment just holding her. When they'd arrived, Jo was convinced she'd need to play hardball with Amy. She was angry and felt lied to. But hearing all this, it seemed she'd realized Amy was only trying to survive this season of her life. The one that took one of her sons and came close to taking the other. Alex didn't have anything to do with Garrett's death and Amy knew this, so she hadn't told Jo about their fight.

"I am so sorry, Amy. I'm so sorry, I didn't know. And I'm sorry about Garrett. We didn't get a chance to talk at the funeral, and I know I'm his wife, but the loss of a child is a level of pain I'm not even sure I can comprehend. And to be experiencing everything with Alex as it happened..."

Jo was crying now too. She reached up to stroke Amy's cheek. Grace wondered if this was the closest they'd ever been to one another, what their interactions were like before tragedy gave them a reason to be here, broken, staring into one another's eyes.

"You are not an awful mother, nor are you an awful person." Jo wiped her nose with the back of her hand and Grace ran over to the tissue box she'd finally spotted to get two for each woman, also pulling two for herself.

"I couldn't save Garrett, either. And I don't even have a clue as to who would want to hurt him. I'm terrified months will pass and we still won't know what happened, and eventually, everyone else will stop caring."

Amy was nodding, still allowing Jo to touch her cheek, still crying.

"I want you to know I will never stop caring. I will never stop caring about what happened to Garrett, and I will never stop caring for you and Alex."

Amy sucked in hard. "Oh, Jo. I should have taken more time to tell both of you how important you are to me."

Jo stood up, then leaned her forehead down to rest it on Amy's. "You raised a good boy, Amy. And I'm going keep telling people about him for the rest of my life."

Grace had seen dozens of wedding day kisses, baby announcements, engagements, and stories of perseverance, but she was pretty sure this was the most pure moment she'd ever been a witness to. Because of how ugly it truly was. A mother had lost her son, a wife had lost her husband, and both women were feeling like they'd failed on a catastrophic level. Yet they sat in this average living room filled with dog hair and high school prom photos and promised one another they would not fail again. They would not fail each other.

* * *

At lunch, Amy made sandwiches for everyone and they took turns asking questions.

"Where is Alex now?" Jo asked Amy.

It took about three days to convince him to go to rehab after his overdose, but he agreed before the hospital released him. Amy and her husband drove their son overnight to a facility outside Chicago. It was the closest place with immediate availability. The program was six weeks, and then he had the option to move to a halfway house close to home.

"They do regular drug testing, have people come to speak to them, counselors, enforce a curfew," Amy said. "All important things for him. He hasn't relapsed yet, though they tell us he will. They said almost all of them do. He can come visit us, usually he shows up a few days a week."

Jo was rearranging her sandwich more than eating it.

"When did you tell him about Garrett?"

Amy sighed and stared at the ceiling.

"Only a few weeks ago." Amy dropped her chin. "It felt as if something like that would be the perfect excuse for him to go on a bender, so we put it off. We spoke with the halfway house and they got a room set up for us to tell him in person with a therapist present." The tears started flowing again. "He took it badly, of course. Especially with the way things had ended with them. He asked to have extra eyes on him at the facility because he didn't trust himself. It was a few weeks before he felt like he could try to get back to normal. Somehow, he hasn't relapsed. Yet."

Grace could barely imagine the weight Amy was carrying on her shoulders. No one would have blamed her for falling apart after Garrett's death, and yet she'd still shown up for Alex. Still thought about her son's feelings more than her own.

"For what it's worth," Grace interrupted, overcome with emotion, "you are a good mother. You're the mother Garrett deserved. And the mother Alex deserves." She sniffed. "And I'm sure one day, he'll tell you himself."

Amy reached across the table with both hands, one grabbing Jo and one grabbing Grace. "Thank you, girls. When you came in here guns blazing, I didn't think we'd have a moment like this."

They sat there hand in hand for a while, until Jo brought up the cost of rehab after insurance and insisted she pay for it. Amy resisted, but Jo said if Garrett knew what his brother was going through, he'd be his first priority.

"We're going to talk about that roof, too," Jo told Amy, her eyebrows raised.

Amy hugged both Jo and Grace when they left, promising them she'd come and visit soon. Jo wanted her to look through some of Garrett's personal items and choose a few for herself, but there was no rush.

On the drive home, the conditions were much improved, and it made for a more relaxing experience. And yet, they barely spoke in the hour drive back to Grace's apartment. Grace imagined Jo was thinking the same thing she was, the same thing she texted Maya when prompted for an update about today's investigation.

We're back to square one.

Chapter 22

"You just have to get a little creative, ya know?" This time Maya's phone was propped on her floor, aimed up so Grace could see her face as she paired ten thousand tiny socks from a laundry basket. She did her best work at nap time these days, whether it was laundry or crime investigation.

Grace stood in her kitchen, arms aching from lugging all her groceries up the stairs in one trip and putting them away. She had a new goal to make it to her grocery store, Wegmans, at least once a week to stock up on moderately healthy foods. The takeout was showing its impact, in both her bank account and her love handles. Step one was trying to buy more leafy greens and chicken to grill. Step two would be actually making the salads and not watching the greens wither into a sad, slimy pile until she just threw the container away, unopened. It was at least a step in the right direction.

"I'm not sure I can get very creative. I only have so much information about Garrett, I don't know every person he's ever had a conflict with."

Maya was whipping her head back and forth, trying to find the match to a teensy blue sock with a duck embroidered on the side. "I mean, from the sound of it, he didn't really have any conflicts, right? He seemed to be a Zen kind of guy." She released an "ugh" and tossed the lone sock aside. "Something I would know nothing about."

Grace leaned her phone against the coffee pot that she'd filled this morning, now sitting cold and half-empty. "He definitely avoided conflict. And didn't seem to make many enemies."

"I still can't believe the killer wasn't that Wyatt dude. He sounded shady. And, I mean..." Maya looked toward Grace sympathetically. Grace had told her everything about what happened with Wyatt. "...obviously he was extremely shady, but he had a lot of the red flags we see with killers."

"We" here meant people who considered true crime a hobby, not a career. So Grace took the comment with more than a few grains of salt.

Grace tried to picture the crime board in her head. Kelly's, Wyatt's, and Mark's photos still hung toward the top, little red strings leading to notes about the men's work, personal lives, and motives. But all of them had a thick red X over them now. The board itself felt like art; a commentary on what life had been like since Garrett's murder. Maybe Hilda would display it in an exhibit one day. Unfortunately, Grace and Jo couldn't get much use out of it without another suspect.

Grace shrugged. "Hopefully he gets some harsh consequences for his actions and decides to turn his life around. And hopefully he turns it around somewhere other than here."

I hear Antarctica is nice.

Maya let out a little groan. She held up the duck sock. "Was this the one I had, or is this the one I was looking for? Oh!" She leaned out of the camera's frame, then returned, beaming triumphantly. "We have a match!"

She folded one sock over the other to keep them together, then turned to throw them into the pile on the floor next to her, but stopped. She sat still for a moment. So still that Grace wondered if the feed was frozen. But then she brought the socks in front of her again, unfolded them, and held them up.

"Your job really does give you a big motive to kill your boss."

Grace's mouth went a little dry. *What is this?*

"What are you talking about? I'm pretty sure we can rule me out as a suspect, Maya."

Those postpartum hormones really do a number on you, I guess.

"No, not *you* you, but someone in your position. Garrett was always working, was trying to make a name for himself with the new exhibit, and who's to say that he wasn't a little testy because of it? While murder seems extreme, any employee would be rightfully pissed after getting snapped at for the hundredth time, right?"

Garrett had seemed stressed to Grace, but he never took it out on her. However… she was new. If he wanted to keep her on as an employee and not have to hire someone again after doing it once already, he'd probably be on his best behavior. She knew how Jo felt about Garrett's old assistant, Vivian, but she had no idea what the relationship between Vivian and Garrett looked like.

"You're talking about his old assistant? Vivian?"

Maya let her hands fall into her lap. "Yep."

"I don't know anything about her."

Maya rolled her eyes playfully. "Isn't figuring this shit out what Jo is paying you for?"

Chapter 23

Jo *really* didn't like Vivian.

The only thing resembling contact Grace had with Vivian herself was through the extensive notes Vivian had written, printed, and sorted into a tabbed binder at the studio. The notes left nothing out, as far as Grace could see. They went over her average schedule, daily duties, phone numbers for businesses they regularly worked with, and even scripts for answering the phone.

Clearly, Vivian was type A. Grace put herself at more of a type L.

But unless she'd missed a remarkable scientific study, having above average organizational skills wasn't a gateway to murder, and Jo had never given Grace any hint they had a reason to look at Vivian further. She'd even gone so far as to say she didn't think Vivian was capable of such an act.

The women sat in Jo's living room, the afternoon sun enveloping them in a cozy warmth. But the mention of Vivian's name had made Jo visibly uncomfortable. And as Grace went over her conversation with Maya, Jo's discomfort seemed to shift to frustration. At first, Grace was worried Jo's frustration was because she was bringing up a suspect they'd already talked about, until Jo groaned, "I can't believe I didn't think to look closer at her."

Jo told Grace she knew only a handful of things about Vivian (few of which she liked), but one of them happened to be her address. She'd attended a housewarming party there right after Vivian moved in. She'd insisted they pick Vivian up a bouquet of flowers even though Garrett felt a wine in a good vintage would be enough.

"I told Garrett that a house isn't a home without flowers, and he'd given me a little laugh and kissed me on the cheek. Vivian seemed grateful for the gift, but we only ended up staying an hour. That's how long I could stand listening to Vivian talk about the new art and furniture she'd purchased for the house, tastelessly disclosing the cost of every item to get the stunned reactions of her party guests. I knew how much Garrett was paying Vivian, and while it was a good wage for the area, I also knew Vivian had to have racked up some serious credit card debt. She was focused on *things*, never ideas or connection," Jo said to Grace. Then she sighed, shrugged, and followed that up with, "But anyway. I know the address. Which should make it easy for us to wait for her outside her house."

Days later, freshly armed with information that Vivian was only in the office three days a week, Grace arrived at Jo's house before the sun crept over the horizon. No time to waste when it comes to covert stalking missions. The porch light was still on as she pushed her key into the lock and turned. She'd been honored when Jo gifted her a set of keys. Not only did it make the job easier, giving her full access to the house whenever she needed it, but it was physical proof of the trust she'd built with Jo.

She hung her coat in the front closet and began to unlace her shoes when the sound of quiet voices caused her to pause. Jo's voice and… a man's? Grace placed her shoes quietly and carefully by the entrance, and followed the muffled conversation. While the lights were off in the living room, it was illuminated by the kitchen lighting. Just as Grace approached a good vantage point to peek, she stepped on a squeaky floorboard, which was enough to catch the attention of Jo and her guest.

"Grace?" Jo called out.

I need to perfect this sneaking thing before we get to Vivian's.

"Yeah! Hey!" Grace said, sashaying into the kitchen with false confidence and her best *I didn't hear anything* face.

Jo sat at the kitchen island, her back to Grace, both her and her father, Malcolm, looking over their shoulders.

"Hello, Ms Anderson!" Malcolm said, rising off the stool. "So nice to see you again!"

Once in a full standing position, he offered Grace his hand.

"You too, Mr Smith. Sorry to interrupt. Am I… am I early?" She looked at her watch, but it was just after 6:30. Technically she was a few minutes late.

"Oh, no. You're good," Jo said, standing and stretching her arms above her head. "Daddy is an early riser, so this is the best time to nab him for a meeting."

Malcom shrugged and let out a little chuckle. "Can't sleep past 4:30 am. I've always been like this."

"Anyway," Jo said, annoyance dripping from her words, "Daddy's company is sponsoring an upcoming event for the nonprofit, and I just wanted to get his signoff on the design of the ad." She handed him a piece of paper. "It's been a pleasure, as always, but Grace and I have a meeting to get to."

Meeting was a generous word for what they were about to do, Grace thought.

Malcolm started to take a few steps toward the front of the house, but stopped and turned to Jo again. "You'll let me know if you change your mind, about Jack?"

Jo rolled her eyes. "I don't need Jack to be involved in my finances, Daddy. I have Ava, remember? Why do I have to remind you of her existence so often?"

Malcolm let out a groan. "Oh, I know she exists, my dear. But Jack has loads more experience than her. You can never be too careful."

Jo leaned up to kiss her father on the cheek. "Sure, Daddy. Whatever you say. Let me walk you out."

Malcolm and Grace exchanged a curt goodbye, and he and Jo disappeared toward the front door. Grace went to the fridge to check out Jo's selection of flavored seltzers, and as she made her selection, she heard Jo re-enter the room with a sigh.

"He's exhausting sometimes," she said, sitting down at the island in front of her closed laptop. She grabbed a pen sitting next to the computer and began to doodle, her hand resting on her head.

Grace walked to the other side of the island and opened her seltzer with a *pop*. As she brought the drink to her mouth, she could smell its light lemon scent, feel the bubbles against her nose. She took too large of a gulp and nearly choked over the volume and carbonation. She let out a little cough and wiped her mouth against her arm before allowing silence to push Jo to say more.

"You'd think with how much he plugs Jack as a financial advisor, he'd be getting royalties." She shook her head. "At least I was able to grab him for a quick morning meeting and didn't have to subject myself to one of his four-hour-long 'business' lunches. 'Legacy' this and 'inflation' that." This realization genuinely seemed to improve Jo's mood.

"Anyway. I don't want to talk about him anymore," Jo proclaimed as she grabbed a tube of chapstick from the counter and applied a liberal layer to her lips, finishing the move with a loud *smack*.

"Today is all about Vivian."

RESEARCH

Grace's notes from the blog post "The Idiot's Guide to Following a Subject".

1. ***Use a rented car so you aren't spotted.***
2. ***Have an understanding of the location you'll be in.***
3. ***Keep enough distance.***
4. ***Have an escape plan in case you are compromised.***

(The blogger also said to make sure to have snacks, in case it takes a while. I'll be packing Cheez-its. I'll share if you ask nicely.)

Chapter 24

An hour and a half later, a balloon of guilt – no, a *balloon ARCH* of guilt – was filling in Grace's stomach. She'd told Sean she'd stay out of trouble and *specifically* told Maya she wouldn't take part in any stakeouts. She was a rule follower, and the lies she'd told over the past few months were starting to weigh on her. It wasn't that she considered Jo a rule breaker, more that someone with the reputation and bank account of Jo Baros simply had fewer rules to follow.

But this wasn't a stakeout, right? Stakeouts happened in cars, hidden by the blanket of night. Sure, Jo was waiting in a car. But Grace was on foot, pretending to scroll Instagram while she waited to get a glimpse of Vivian. It was broad daylight, the kind of crisp and clear November morning that almost generated enough dopamine to get you through dinner. *Almost.* It was a cold day, but at least Grace's socks were dry for this investigation.

The plan was this: Grace would lean against a tree until Vivian left her house, then she would follow her, keeping enough distance to go unnoticed. If Vivian happened to get into a car, that was fine. Jo was waiting up the street in a Lexus she'd rented from Turo.

Use a rented car so you aren't spotted.

Grace would just hop in, hugged tightly by luxury leather, and they'd tail Vivian that way. If she took public transit, Grace would follow, updating Jo on her whereabouts so she could stay one step behind, ultimately meeting her wherever Vivian's office ended up being so they could interrupt her workday.

Grace had suggested simply calling Vivian and asking her to meet somewhere, but Jo was insistent they should catch Vivian off guard. "She's so polished. I don't think it would be difficult for her to lie to someone's face, but specifically if she had time to rehearse the lie. I don't exactly have a motive for her, but... she could be hiding something."

It was possible Jo simply didn't *like* Garrett's former assistant, but Grace kept that to herself.

Grace was sweating in her coat, which was layered over a sweater, a long-sleeved shirt, and then a camisole. She was still adjusting to the cold weather. Over-adjusting, actually. She pulled off the wool beanie that had fallen out of Jo's coat closet this morning. Grace had picked it up and complimented it, and Jo urged her to keep it. "Everyone needs a standard wool hat to wear in the winter here," she'd said, which Grace felt was an overexaggeration since most hats she'd seen so far featured sports logos in a low-quality polyester.

She shoved the beanie in her coat pocket and went back to her phone. She thought about texting Maya to give her an update on their latest escapade, but she was actively trying to avoid her. All Maya seemed to want to discuss on their calls, beyond Garrett's murder and Miles's latest milestones, was Sean.

"Is he hot? Does he have tattoos? Did he talk about his 401k?"

Grace rolled her eyes at each of these questions. "It would be wildly inappropriate for me to be wondering these things about an officer who is investigating a case I'm involved in."

"Why? He's a cop, not a monk."

Grace had left the conversation at that.

She was just about to dive into the task of unsubscribing from email lists she'd only joined for a discount when she heard the slamming of a door and looked up to see a woman who was undoubtedly Vivian.

Vivian wore a peacoat over a tweed blazer that matched her knee-length skirt. Her blouse was made from cream silk, and the outfit was finished off with gold jewelry and the kind of heels Grace couldn't even look at without her ankles hurting.

So, Grace thought, *she values appearance over comfort.* She looked down at her pants – the same pair of sweatpants disguised as trousers she'd worn the day she found Garrett's body. She didn't expect to have much in common with the woman she replaced.

Though her heels were high, Vivian was walking at a swift pace, and before she knew it, Grace was practically running to stay a solid thirty feet behind her. Once they had made it a block, Grace figured Vivian was taking some sort of public transit. She tried to pull out her phone and text Jo, but Vivian was walking so quickly, and Grace couldn't afford to stop, so she ended up sending something along the lines of: *Shed taking the bus I guess.*

Close enough.

Grace continued her chase for another block until Vivian stopped at a corner bus stop and checked her watch. Grace was wheezing, and took the opportunity to grab a seat on a nearby bench that still gave her a clear view of Vivian.

She pulled out her phone to see that Jo had texted back, *I will translate this to say she's taking the bus. Give me details when you can.*

Grace dropped a pin and snapped a photo of the sign.

She said a silent thank-you to Jo for checking the schedule and getting a bus pass ahead of time. Grace mostly drove in Florida, and public transit was something of a mystery to her. If she had to come up with money on the spot or sign up for something on her phone while other riders stared at her judgmentally, there was a good chance she'd chicken out.

She felt in her pocket for the tiny card and kept a close eye on Vivian, who was typing furiously on her phone.

A few minutes later, the bus pulled up, and Grace sent the number and destination to Jo. She let Vivian board, waited a few extra paces for others to get on, then climbed up the stairs and scanned her pass without issue.

Vivian was seated at the middle of the bus, face still in her phone. There were no open seats left, so Grace grabbed onto a pole on her left and prepared to stand for the ride, but then a hand tapped her on the shoulder. She turned to find a teenage boy, Jansport backpack slung over one arm, coat nowhere to be seen – because, teenage boy – in shorts and slides with socks. It was like he woke up in a completely different climate than Grace did.

"You can have my seat, ma'am."

Grace could feel her eyes bulge over the idea that this boy identified her as a frail older woman who needed his seat more than he did, but she didn't want to insult good manners and, quite frankly, didn't want to stand either.

She thanked him and sat down in his seat, humbled and seething.

It had been a while since Grace had been on a bus, and she found it more nauseating than she remembered. She tried to turn her head toward the driver, to focus on a still piece of landscape, but she could feel the slow but vicious headache that went along with motion sickness creeping in. She couldn't turn around and watch Vivian, she'd have to wait until the bus stopped moving. It felt like hours went by as she practiced breathing slowly, her already sweaty body now on fire thanks to her panic. She looked around to see what she could throw up in an emergency, and had to settle for the least expensive looking handbag in her line of sight.

Maybe, if she puked in some woman's Kate Spade bucket bag, Jo would offer up a bag from her personal collection to replace it. Not the Birkin, but maybe a classic Chloe. Grace would feel a lot better if someone got an upgrade out of it.

As they approached the city, the bus started to stop. Each time, Grace glanced back at Vivian, who never took her eyes off her phone, then slowly turned her head forward to avoid jostling her aching brain any further. Finally, on the fourth stop, she looked back to see Vivian tossing her phone into her bag and standing to hold onto the leather strap above her. Grace stood as well, adrenaline mostly taking over from the nausea, and when she saw Vivian head toward the door in the center of the bus, she made her way to the front.

It wasn't an immediate removal of symptoms as Grace stepped onto solid ground, but she was thankful to be rid of the gentle sway of the partially electric city bus. She sent another quick text to Jo as she watched the direction Vivian was headed. She followed, a quick waft of coffee smacking her in the face as she struggled to keep up, a reminder that she needed to load up on caffeine when her schedule and her stomach would allow it.

Vivian power walked three blocks before she angled toward a tall building with European-style gargoyles staring down. Grace watched as Vivian disappeared through a revolving door, then hurried up the few steps in the front to take a turn herself. She momentarily lost sight of Vivian, but then caught a glance of her bun in line at a small coffee cart. Once Vivian got her order, she stopped at a separate counter to pour some half and half into her cup, then sped off toward an elevator. Grace pushed through the crowd as she saw Vivian press the button – she couldn't miss this elevator. Vivian stepped in and Grace made a leap toward the doors as they started to close, getting a solid arm against them to keep it from happening.

Vivian looked at Grace judgmentally.

"So late," Grace offered with a smile. Vivian ignored her and pressed the button for floor eight. Grace pressed ten at random, then looked at the directory posted on the wall of the elevator.

Floor number eight: Brennan, Brennan, and Doyle, Attorneys at Law.

Chapter 25

Jo said she'd be there in ten minutes, which gave Grace enough time to scrape her shoe along the curb, trying to dislodge some fresh gum, and for her to do a little digging on Brennan, Brennan, and Doyle.

Their website loaded slowly, and at first Grace could only make out some perfectly coiffed heads of hair in the main image. Grace knew what was coming, because it was an industry standard for attorney billboards, websites, and other promotional materials to include a lineup of confident lawyers, their faces sharp and cold like you'd just said "Reputation" was an overrated album without realizing you'd been speaking to the board of directors of the Taylor Swift Fan Club. Eventually the image loaded, predictably, to reveal two intimidating men in suits flanking an even more intimidating woman in an even better suit.

A quick skim of the about page told Grace that Louise Brennan, her brother Trent Brennan, and the unrelated Richard Doyle were the city's most formidable criminal defense attorneys.

Criminal defense.

They had a great track record of getting clients' sentences thrown out or reduced, and worked on cases on a huge range of topics, from tax evasion to assault to… murder.

Grace had only started reading the attorneys' individual bios when she heard heavy breathing behind her and spun around to see Jo clutching her chest. *Seriously, how is someone so trim also so out of shape?* They really needed to join Kelly at her bootcamps.

"OK, so what's up?" Jo said before sucking in another huge breath.

Instead of trying to explain, Grace handed over her phone. Jo took a few minutes to browse, which seemed to help get her heart rate back to a normal level, and eventually her head snapped up, anger flaring from behind her eyes. "*This* is where she's working?"

Grace nodded.

"OK, well, you have to admit that this is shady as shit."

Technically, there was a decent chance this was all a big coincidence. Vivian stopped working for Garrett and took this job weeks before Grace arrived and Garrett was murdered. Not to mention that the process of finding, interviewing for, and having an employer pick you for a job is a complicated one.

But it was also hard to see the word *criminal* and not jump to Vivian having something to hide. She'd worked for Garrett for years and then all of a sudden put in her two weeks with no warning. What if she did have some reason to kill Garrett, and she knew she'd need to have friends in the right places in case she didn't get away with it?

"It might be shady. It might not. We don't know until we talk to her."

Jo nodded and handed the phone back to Grace, then started to walk toward the revolving door. Once inside, Grace led her to the elevator and pressed the button for the eighth floor as people squeezed in around them. Jo had her arms crossed. She looked slightly annoyed and frighteningly determined. Vivian had no idea what was coming for her.

The elevator stopped on nearly every floor, so it felt like an hour before they reached number eight. They maneuvered around the rest of the riders when the door opened, and without looking too closely at her surroundings, Jo marched toward the glass doors leading to the reception desk. They were still a few feet away when she addressed the woman sitting there.

"I need to speak with Vivian Haywood."

The receptionist seemed to think this greeting was rude, probably because it was. She scrunched her face in contempt. "And who am I speaking to?"

Jo kept an unsympathetic face. "Jo Baros. She worked for my husband, Garrett Baros. But he was murdered two months ago, and I'd like to talk to her about it."

It was a risky move, bringing up her husband's murder, but Jo succeeded in confounding the unsuspecting receptionist, whose face suddenly softened as she reached for her phone. Grace couldn't tell if Jo's name rang a bell to this woman, or if she was so uncomfortable talking about murder that she would do anything to hand them off to someone else.

She pressed a few buttons on the keypad and waited until someone answered. "Can you please send Vivian Haywood to the reception desk? She has someone here to see her."

She hung up, placed her hands gently in her lap, and looked at Jo. "She'll be right out."

Jo nodded and turned to sit in a chair across from the desk. Grace followed, buzzing with anxiety over how the interaction with Vivian would go. She'd never seen Jo act like this around anyone. Clearly, these women were incompatible.

Typical office babble sounded around them. Someone stood at a scanner, trying to figure out its buttons. The phone rang once and you could hear from her voice that the receptionist was still shaken from her interaction with Jo, who sat staring directly ahead, not bothering to look around or pass time on her phone.

The distinct click of heels on a marble floor began to grow louder, and after a few seconds, Jo stood as Vivian came around the corner to the reception area. The flush of Vivian's face was instantaneous as she spotted Jo. Grace could have sworn she read the word "shit" on her lips. She paused in place for only a second and then plastered a fake smile on her face as she approached them.

"Jo! What an unexpected surprise! Shall we chat in the hallway?"

Vivian took a quick look at Grace and pointed to the hallway where she came from.

"There are some sensitive things I'd like to discuss with you. Maybe your office would be better."

Vivian pursed her lips. "I don't have an office."

It seemed like Vivian was looking to Jo to make an alternate suggestion, but Jo just stood there, keeping eye contact. Vivian crossed her arms, looking like an animal in crosshairs. "Let me go get my jacket. There's a spot nearby where we can talk in private."

Grace and Jo followed Vivian to a cafe up the street. No one spoke.

The restaurant seemed to be at full capacity, but Vivian whispered something to the greeter, who disappeared into the restaurant, and reappeared seconds later to take them to a table in the back.

They wove through the crowd and were led to a small table in the back corner, a single lilac in a mason jar at the center. The three of them sat down and started to unwrap their napkins as the greeter placed menus in front of them and took her leave. The table was secluded enough that other diners wouldn't be able to overhear any private information.

"How did you manage to pull that off?" Jo asked, pointing back to the entrance of the cafe.

Vivian smiled at her. It was strained. "Oh, I've been seeing the head chef here for a few months. He has them save this table for me, just in case."

Grace stifled an "aww," because as romantic as that sounded, she felt legally obligated to dislike Vivian. You didn't swoon on the behalf of women you didn't like, but you also didn't cross your fingers that they lived a miserable existence. You simply wished them a lifetime of mediocre Tinder dates.

"What a guy," Jo said, her smile somehow even less natural than Vivian's. "Why is it so crowded here so early on a Tuesday?"

The dimples in Vivian's cheeks popped when she smiled. "They've built up a good brunch reputation. It's hard to get a table here at this time on any day of the week." Vivian did have a pretentious attitude about her, like Jo described. She looked as if she wanted Grace and Jo to thank her for getting them the best possible table to conduct their inquisition.

Vivian stared at Jo for a moment, the dimpled smile dropped. Then she got down to business, folding her fingers together on the table. "What did you want to talk about? I was so sorry to hear about Garrett. He was really, truly a good man." She seemed to mean this, but Jo didn't seem to care.

"So sorry that you didn't even show up to the funeral?"

Oh. Yeah. Vivian *wasn't* at Garrett's funeral. Not that Grace was great at remembering who was there and who wasn't. But she felt like she would have remembered Vivian and the strained interaction that would have come with her greeting Jo at the church.

Vivian stared down at her lap. "I sent flowers. Unfortunately, being so new to my company, I tend to draw the short straw when it comes to working overtime. I haven't been able to take a lot of time off."

Jo didn't answer. Grace felt awkward and invisible. She hoped they could order soon, or she might need to open her stakeout Cheez-its. She decided to introduce herself, both to break the tension at the table and distract herself from her hunger. "Uh, I'm Grace, by the way. I took over for you once you left." She extended her hand to shake Vivian's, who responded by only grabbing the tips of Grace's fingertips and giving one light shake. It was such an odd move that it made Grace wonder if this was Vivian's first handshake ever.

Vivian brought back the fake smile. "So nice to meet you. It was you, then, who found Garrett's body?"

Grace nodded.

"I'm so sorry that happened. I guess it was better you than me, though. I wasn't built for situations like that."

Grace tried to hide her confusion. Situations like what? Emergencies in general, or specifically finding a dead body?

She went to say she didn't feel like anyone was built for situations like that when she was interrupted by their waiter.

"Hi there, everyone! My name is Marcus and I'll be your server for today." Marcus clearly didn't sense the tension at the table as he filled their water glasses. "Our brunch specials today are an avocado toast topped with a fresh corn salad, and a stack of our *divine* lavender vanilla pancakes. Can I get anyone a cocktail?"

Grace checked her watch. It was just after ten am.

"No," Jo said, smiling up at Marcus. "But thank you."

Marcus gave a polite nod. "Then I'll let you ladies look over the menu and I'll be back in a few!"

Grace wanted to ask Marcus to stay. She needed a friend as she sat as a third wheel to this hate date.

The women each picked up their menus to browse. Grace wasn't paying attention to anything she was reading. She wasn't even sure if she'd be able to eat with her stomach in knots. She'd choose something at random when the waiter showed back up, she wasn't picky.

Her eyes still on the menu, Jo spoke to Vivian. "Obviously we're here because we haven't gotten far with the investigation into Garrett's death."

Vivian cringed a bit at this, like she'd hoped they were here to talk about something else. "We?"

"Well, the police, of course." Jo looked briefly shaken at her slip of the tongue. "But we, Grace and I, were hoping you might be able to share your opinions on it." She looked up to make eye contact with Vivian. "Obviously, you've already talked to the police. I hoped I could talk to you myself, woman to woman."

Vivian's throat bobbed. "I'm sorry there aren't any answers yet. I never expected months would go by without an arrest."

Jo gave a slight nod.

Vivian folded up her menu and carefully set it on the table, then placed her hands in her lap. "And yes, I spoke with the police. I told them everything I knew… which honestly wasn't much. I'd obviously worked for Garrett when he had those run-ins with Kelly Dewitt and Mark King, so I threw their names out. Garrett sometimes complained about a certain contact at a gallery downtown; it didn't seem like a big enough feud to lead to anything."

Jo nearly cut Vivian off. "And what were you doing, the night Garrett was murdered?"

Vivian's eyes bulged. She placed her menu on the table.

"*Like I told the police,* I stayed in that night. We'd finished our day early and I grabbed some takeout and a bottle of wine and rotted on my couch."

Jo raised an eyebrow. "So there was no one to verify this alibi?"

Vivian sat up straighter, which impressed Grace because her posture had already looked close to perfect. "What are you trying to get at here, Jo? I showed the police my receipts. No, there was no one to verify my alibi. I *own* my home, so I have no doorman and no neighbors to pass in the hallway, but I also had no *reason* to kill Garrett, if that's what you're asking me? You know I enjoyed working for him."

Jo also owned her home, so Grace wasn't sure why Vivian put the emphasis on that word. Jo did imply she liked to brag about material things. But Vivian had just stomped all over the motive Maya had come up with for her – she'd liked working for Garrett.

Jo set her own menu down.

"I don't know, Vivian. Don't you think it's a little bit strange that you quit your job with Garrett a few weeks before his death to go work for a criminal defense lawyer and then didn't bother to show up for the funeral? What would you think if you were me?"

Vivian pounded the table with her fists, silverware clinking and water sloshing in her wake. "You think I know what's going on in that conceited little head of yours?!"

Vivian seemed to have a similar impression of Jo to the one Jo had of her.

Jo smiled at the insult. "Did Garrett seem happy to you?" There didn't seem to be any rhyme or reason to her questioning.

The change of subject seemed to throw Vivian off. "Yes," she scoffed. "He seemed happy. He seemed grateful to be doing what he loved, that you were willing to support him. He was excited about the possibility of landing the exhibit downtown." She looked around the restaurant as she spoke, voice dripping with disdain, like she hated to give Jo this good news.

Jo sucked her lips in against her teeth, eyes growing a bit misty. Vivian shifted again.

"Of course, I know he also felt guilt about how much you invested into his career, and he was focused on boosting profits so you wouldn't have to be as involved. Obviously, as the person who managed the finances, I had a front row–"

"Wait, what?"

This was the first time Grace had spoken since her introduction, and it seemed to startle the other women, who whipped their heads in her direction.

"You managed Garrett's finances?"

Vivian looked confused, or maybe like she thought Grace was confused, which *did* confuse Grace.

"Yes, it was a main aspect of my job. Do… did you not manage the money?"

Grace's heart rate doubled. Both Vivian and Jo had creased brows, staring right at her.

"N–no, I didn't even… I never saw a single spreadsheet. Garrett told me he had someone else managing that. He wanted me to focus more on running errands and marketing him. I had nothing to do with paying the bills or anything."

Vivian's mouth dropped open. "That makes no sense. Garrett told me to include everything in the binder I left, there were dozens of pages going over all the financial tasks."

Grace shook her head. "There was nothing about money in the binder."

It felt like a bomb had been dropped in the center of the table. Grace didn't need to ask if this felt significant to anyone else, she could see Jo's breath increasing, the way Vivian was staring down, picking at her almond-shaped nails with a perfect French manicure.

"I met with our lawyer. Everything with the will was normal. His fees were paid. Who…" Jo trailed off as the waiter returned.

"Any questions, ladies?" Marcus reappeared, again unable to read the room.

Yes, Grace thought. *About a billion questions.*

No one said anything for a moment, which seemed to confuse Marcus. "Do you… know what you want?"

Jo ordered eggs, bacon, and wholewheat toast, Vivian chose a spinach omelet, and Grace chose the lavender pancakes. They watched Marcus walk away and for a moment no one spoke until Jo blurted out, loudly and dripping with anger, "Who the hell had access to Garrett's money?"

* * *

The rest of brunch was awkward and silent. The moment Jo finished her plate, she waved her arm and asked for the check. She paid for the three of them and thanked Vivian for her time coldly. No one brought up again that Jo had basically accused Vivian of killing Garrett.

Grace and Jo crawled into Jo's SUV, and Jo cranked up the heat to full blast. She rubbed her hands together, warming them, before she placed her face into them. The cloud of Grace's breath hovered in front of her.

Jo lifted her head and placed her hands on the steering wheel. "Well, I don't suspect her any less after that."

Grace was staring at a piece of frost slowly melting as it was blasted with heat. "Yeah, there are some strange elements there, but she doesn't have a motive for killing Garrett. And the police weren't apprehensive enough to make her a suspect."

Jo bit her lip in thought. "I do believe she was confused, about the finances. I guess I didn't even think about that. How stupid am I? That I was worried about someone killing Garrett for money but was totally unaware of who was even managing his?"

Jo ran her hands through her hair.

"I'd wanted Garrett to use Ava as a financial manager. I told him it would be simpler, to have one person with a full view of all our accounts. He was already uncomfortable having me foot the bill for a lot of his business expenses. I think he wanted to prove he could manage on his own, was worried Ava would keep me too in the loop about how his business was doing. I wish he'd considered it." Jo looked up to the roof of the car, the light *tap tap tap* of her foot on the car mat filling the small space.

She looked at Grace. "Did the police ask you about Garrett's finances?"

Grace tried to think back to her first conversation with Sean. Money had come up. He'd asked her if she noticed anything odd about the business's finances. And then she realized. "He asked me if I noticed anything off, with the money, and I said Garrett hadn't mentioned anything. I meant I had no access and Garrett didn't share anything with me. He may have thought I meant I'd been managing the finances and Garrett had no complaints."

Jo closed her eyes, craned her neck, and sucked in, hard.

"I don't even know where to start, I... do I call the lawyer? Ask him who paid him? Why did I not ask you about this sooner?"

Jo had come undone many times since Garett's death, but she'd never been hard on herself. The stress of trying to put all the pieces together was getting to her.

"We aren't professional investigators, Jo. We're going to miss things. Even obvious things. And there is a good chance we don't solve Garrett's murder."

Grace wondered if Jo let herself think of the possibility their investigation might lead nowhere. Or even that the police investigation might lead nowhere. That they may never get answers to the who and why. That feeling of dread Grace had felt at Tony's restaurant started seeping back in, the panic that they might not solve the case after all. She could hear Gloria's words in her head, as clear as day: "I know she wants to find answers. We all want answers. I just hope she doesn't lose her mind in the process."

"Vivian isn't off the hook," Jo said as she put the car in drive.

Chapter 26

It had been one thing to eat a meal at the cafe across the street, but Grace's stomach was churning over the idea of walking back into the studio.

That morning, Grace and Jo had gone through Grace and Garrett's work laptops, returned by the police, trying to find any clues about who could have access to Garrett's accounts. They were able to log into Garrett's bank and nothing in his transactions seemed out of the ordinary. Money had been coming in and going out as Jo expected. Maybe they were barking up the wrong tree, or there was an easy explanation for all of this. The accounts were frozen now, all money transferred to Jo. If someone had been taking money from Garrett, they couldn't anymore.

Jo had sent Kelly a short email a few weeks ago. In fact, it was only one line:

Are you and the historical society looking for a new project?

The women had been passing ideas back and forth about what to do with the studio space. Jo's business didn't need a brick-and-mortar location. She felt like the studio space had the potential to help the community in a different way. She'd gone to Kelly with an idea for a children's art studio – one that would educate artists of the future and teach them about artists who came before them, like Garrett.

This was the evening they'd finally look over the space and figure out how they could use it to their advantage. Jo's basic idea was to use the lobby as an education center with rotating exhibits on local artists and a permanent exhibit on Garrett. The gallery space would be where the children created, as well as where their work was displayed. Garrett's office would serve as storage, a place to keep all the spare paint, brushes, smocks, clay, etc.

They planned to name it after Garrett as well as Kelly and her family: The Baros-Dewitt Youth Arts Center.

Jo and Grace shared the good news with Kelly over dinner in her favorite restaurant. When their words finally sank in, Kelly burst into tears. "That is… so lovely, Jo. I know my mother and grandmother are smiling down on you."

There was something hopeful about the idea of fresh artists coming to create in the spot where Garrett's easel once sat.

Kelly was already waiting at the studio when Grace and Jo arrived, forever the quintessential professional. She clutched a notebook of ideas in her hand. Grace had to admit she had a soft spot for Kelly. She really *did* look like Grace's aunt, and it was obvious she loved her town and her community. Her enthusiasm was even enough to convince Grace to come to two more bootcamp classes.

This was the first time Jo had returned to the studio since Garrett was killed, and Grace was grateful that someone had removed the caution tape blocking the door at some point in the past few months. Probably another business owner, feeling it was bad for foot traffic. Grace looked at Jo, trying to figure out her feelings, and Jo turned to stare back, showing that she realized she was being closely watched.

The women stepped inside, taking in the studio space that had been splashed on newspaper covers for weeks. The community was desperate for Garrett's murder to be solved so things could feel a little more normal. Grace didn't need to ask Kelly if the murder had been bad for tourism; who wanted to visit a suburb reeling from tragedy between road trip stops in Colonial Williamsburg and Times Square?

Being back at the studio, Grace had to fight her brain from imagining Garrett coming around the corner at every moment. While Jo and Kelly opened Kelly's notebook on Grace's old desk, Grace wandered into Garrett's workspace. She walked to the sink to see paint dried at the bottom of the basin. Remains of the last thing he'd ever painted, leftovers from the portrait of David Bustill Bowser no one got to see. There were no new updates about the listing on the dark web.

Jo and Kelly entered the room, Jo gesticulating passionately, pointing out where she envisioned putting the easels and the pottery wheel. It was nice, seeing her so excited about something other than the investigation. But Grace could feel a creep of panic up her spine, being in this space again. She thought enough time had passed, but the studio still felt like a crime scene. Her skin suddenly felt itchy, and she could feel the sensation crawl down her throat. Since she couldn't very well leave her body, she decided the best thing would be to step outside for some air.

"Hey, I'm going outside for a minute." She interrupted Jo and Kelly discussing whether they wanted to get a professional-grade kiln for the space.

Jo turned to her, one eyebrow arched. "You good?"

Grace gave a grin which she was sure Jo could see right through and paired it with an eager nod. "So good. Just a little stuffy in here, right?" She didn't wait for either woman to agree, but turned and walked brusquely toward the door.

The mid-November air punctuated a much-needed change of scenery. Grace stepped toward the bench in front of the studio, but that, too, had memories tied to the day she found Garrett. Instead, she leaned against the building, crossing her arms in an attempt to stay warm. The now-sparse trees were wrapped in white lights, the city already prepping for the holiday season. Soon, Christmas-themed canvas flags would adorn each streetlight. Storefronts would twinkle with trees so perfect, Martha Stewart herself would have to dole out a monotone but gracious compliment.

Nothing had stopped when Garrett died. The most wonderful time of the year was still scheduled as planned. It might just not be quite as wonderful this time around.

A light sleet was falling from the sky as Grace took it all in. She scanned the rooms above the stores, passing over a few forgotten Halloween decorations, until one specific light caught her eye and made her pause. It wasn't a decoration, but a steady, solitary red light, blinking every few seconds.

Like the light of a camera.

And if it was the light from a camera, it was a camera that directly faced the street, overlooked the studio, and, if it had been on at the time… might have caught a glimpse of Garrett's murderer.

Grace felt her body move instinctively toward the boutique that sat below the blinking light, but when her feet reached the curb, she willed them to stop.

I should let Jo handle this, she thought.

Jo was the bold one, the one who came up with the ridiculous idea that they should investigate in the first place. Jo was the one with the money and the connections.

And yet…

Weren't moments like this the reason Grace stayed in Philadelphia in the first place? She'd been tired of life just happening to her. She wanted to be the one in the driver's seat, calling the shots, no matter the outcome. If fortune favored the bold, maybe it was time for Grace to develop some grit and take control. This seemed like the perfect place to start.

And then her feet were moving again, fueled by an infusion of bravery, anxiety, and perhaps some optimistic stupidity. She barely remembered to look both ways when crossing the street, saved by a particularly slow afternoon. She jogged across, blatantly jaywalking and not caring one bit, making a beeline for the door to the right of the boutique. When she was ten feet away, she heard a baby's cry come from above. She hadn't noticed that the window she'd spotted the light through was open, just a crack. She looked up to see if she could spot someone, but as she did, the window slammed shut.

Which meant someone was home.

She threw open the door, which lead to a thin hallway and narrow staircase. She climbed to the second floor, where another door greeted her. Once she went through it, she realized that she wasn't quite sure which of the three apartments lining the right side of the hallway was the one she was looking for. She took a chance and knocked on the first one. After a minute or two, there was no answer, and she knocked again. Giving up, she moved to the next door, which had a sign taped to it that said, "No knocking. Baby is sleeping."

This is it.

As Grace hesitantly lifted her arm to knock, she thought about Jo, who'd stood on this side of her door, hoping that a stranger might agree to help her. How this one moment of audacity had led to a chain of events: their friendship, an excuse for Grace to message Sean, the ruling out of suspects. All because Jo had the courage to knock.

So Grace knocked. Lightly, so that it could be heard, as knocks were meant to be heard, but not wake the baby if it had happened to fall asleep in the last two minutes. She had no idea how babies worked. A few seconds passed and she heard a chair scoot across a wooden floor. The woman on the other side of the door was muttering to herself, probably cursing Grace for failing to follow simple instructions. And in fact, when the door did open, Grace was staring into the face of a young, pretty, but very annoyed Asian woman holding a baby in cute but stained pajamas.

"Can you not read?" The woman pointed to the sign on the door.

Grace's face burned hot in embarrassment. "I can read. And I'm sorry to bother you. I promise that I wouldn't have knocked unless it was extremely important."

The woman bounced the baby slightly, keeping her eyes on Grace, her face steely. "OK, well. What is so important then?"

Oh shit, I forgot to plan this part.

Grace winced. "At first, this is going to sound insane. But just let me get to the end and I promise it'll all make sense."

The woman's expression didn't change, but since the door wasn't slamming in Grace's face, she continued.

"My friend owns one of the storefronts across the street. It's an art studio. Or, it was, until her husband was found dead there a few months ago."

The woman's demeanor changed. She hugged the baby a little bit tighter, but let her facial expression relax. "Baros was his name. Right?"

Grace nodded, and the woman mirrored her movement. "It was terrible, what happened to him." She looked at the baby, then back to Grace. "As a parent, you hope that you've chosen a safe space to raise your kid. And I felt so confident in my decision until that happened. It's still not solved, right?"

Grace shook her head. "There have been some small leads, but nothing substantial."

The baby let out a little cry, and the woman brought a pacifier to its mouth. "I feel so deeply for your friend. If I lost my husband... I don't know what I would do." The baby settled again, and the woman looked at Grace. "But what does any of this have to do with me?"

Grace was mindlessly playing with a gum wrapper she'd left in her right pocket, ripping it apart with her pointer finger and thumb. "Here's the insane part. I spotted a flashing light from your window, facing out into the street. Any chance it's a camera?"

It was a camera. Or, more specifically, a baby monitor.

The woman had invited Grace into her apartment. "I'm Cara," she said, placing the baby down in a pack and play. She pointed toward it. "This is Lucy."

Grace smiled. "She's adorable. How old?" Grace had enough auntie experience to know this was a question new moms loved to answer, very specifically.

She's two months, five days, seven hours, and twelve minutes old.

"Uhhh," Cara muttered. She looked up, like maybe the answer was written on her ceiling. "Oh shit!" She looked back down to Grace. "She turned five months yesterday, and I totally forgot to post about it!"

Cara was flustered. Grace realized that her shirt was covered in stains. The apartment was unkempt, pillows and blankets tossed on the floor next to empty bottles and stuffed animals. When Grace glanced back to Cara, she recognized the familiar look of embarrassment.

"Sorry, I normally wouldn't have someone over with the apartment in this state, but–"

Grace cut her off before she could say any more. "I hijacked your day. Besides, I only need to take care of myself, and my apartment looks so much worse than this."

This was a lie. Her apartment was actually pretty clean at the moment. But Cara didn't need to know that.

Cara shot Grace a grateful smile, and crossed the room, heading toward a short hallway. "Here, let me show you the camera."

Grace was led into the sweetest, smallest room she'd ever laid eyes on. White wooden furniture filled every corner, including a small bookcase full of children's classics. Across from the crib was a canvas of Cara, Lucy, and Lucy's dad, the proud parents admiring the baby and all their handiwork that went into her.

"We didn't know if she was a boy or a girl," Cara said, pointing to the green paint on the wall.

"I like it. Very calming."

Cara nodded, then pointed up above the door frame. "There's the camera. The room is so small, we were only able to configure everything right if the crib went under the window. So the camera could really only go above the doorway."

Grace was right. The camera looked out into the street, with a perfect view of the studio, where Kelly and Jo must have still been discussing their grand plans.

"Do you have the camera on all the time?"

Cara leaned back against the crib, which creaked slightly as she rested against it. "No. Only at night. The only reason it was on just now is because I'd put Lucy down for a nap. So, I guess it is on during the day sometimes."

"Did the police stop by to question you at all? Would the light have been on then?"

"They did, yes. But I wasn't home, just my husband was. I took Lucy to visit my mother, so there would be no reason for him to use the baby monitor. He told the police everything he knew... which was... pretty much nothing. I hadn't even thought about the camera facing the studio until now."

So, the camera was most likely off when the police were around. They wouldn't have seen the light, and had no reason to search the apartment.

"And does the footage get saved anywhere? Like, if you wanted to go back and look at it later?"

Cara perked up, crossing her arms. "Actually yes. It's much fancier than the camera I'd put on my registry. My mother-in-law is always trying to one-up everyone, so she decided to drop a fortune on the latest video monitor. Really, all I want from her is for her to come over and hold the baby so I can get a damn shower."

Grace desperately wanted Cara to get back on the right subject, but looked to her as a sort of kindred spirit. She wondered if this was how other people felt when they were in a conversation with *her*.

"But anyway, on top of the astronomical cost, they want you to pay for a monthly subscription to save all the video footage." Cara shook her head. "Absolute crooks. I'd never pay that. But it did come with a free one-year subscription."

Grace's pulse jumped.

"Do you know how to access it? If I told you a date, could you see if you have footage from that night?"

Cara stiffened. "I don't see why not. But. Are we looking for… are we trying to see if I have video footage of the murder?"

Grace pulled her top lip into her mouth, bit down. "Yes. I'm sorry. But that's what we're looking for."

As Grace plopped down onto Cara's couch, her phone buzzed in her pocket. *Shit.* She probably should have given Jo and Kelly a heads-up before she went full Miss Marple on the situation. She looked to her left where Lucy lay peacefully snoozing, then pulled out her phone and declined the call, opting instead to text.

Grace: *Sorry, ran across the street for a minute. Will be back soon.*

She looked back at the sleeping baby, who Grace had to admit was *really* adorable. Her cheeks were pink and plump, and her eyelashes were the perfect combination of long and thick. *Those things would cost a fortune at a salon.* She started to miss Maya's baby, Miles. Or maybe it wasn't a missing, or about Miles at all. Maybe it was a sort of longing.

Her phone buzzed with Jo's reply.

Jo: *You've already been gone for like fifteen minutes. We're almost done. Are you shopping???*

Grace: *Not shopping. I'll explain soon.*

Grace turned her phone off vibrate and slipped it back into her pocket as Cara walked into the room with her laptop. She sat next to Grace and already had the camera footage pulled up.

"You said it was September 5th, right?" Cara whispered. Grace nodded.

"OK, well, I paused the footage at about nine pm."

"The police think the window we're looking at is between ten pm and twelve am. Are we able to fast-forward so we can get to that range more easily?"

Cara nodded and pressed a button. The video began to play, quickly. Occasionally, you'd see the baby move, and the camera would focus on her. If someone walked down the sidewalk, the focus would shift to them. All you could make out from passing strangers were their outlines; dark blurs. If this video did happen to show the murderer, Grace wouldn't be able to tell who it was without getting the video cleaned up. She'd need to send it to Sean.

As the video passed the 10:30 pm mark, two blurs appeared and stopped in front of the studio.

Murderer...s?

"Stop!" Grace yelled, and she saw Lucy stir out of the corner of her eye. "Sorry," she whispered, as Cara stopped the video. She pressed a button to rewind the video by fifteen seconds, and together they watched as the blurs came back into the frame. One seemed to knock, and after ten seconds, a blur appeared in the studio. Garrett. They appeared to greet each other pleasantly, or at least neutrally, and the three blurs headed in the direction of Garrett's office.

"Let's try to see when they leave," Grace said, her eardrums pulsing with the beat of her heart.

Cara sped up the video again and then paused when they saw two figures emerge from the studio, one holding a boxy object in their arms. The timestamp read 11:27 pm.

Grace could barely believe her eyes. This could be it. This was the first real clue they'd uncovered, but it was possible that it was a clue so good, it might just solve Garrett's murder. "Can you email this to me? From around ten pm to twelve am?"

Cara tilted her head, considering. "Yes. Just give me a minute to figure it out. Can you write your email down?" Cara grabbed a stack of Post-its and a pen from her coffee table and handed them to Grace, who took her time writing out each letter, not wanting to risk confusion. She handed the Post-it to Cara, who typed into her computer.

Grace pulled her phone out of her pocket and asked Jo to meet her outside the boutique, telling her that she might want to send Kelly home first.

When she looked up, Cara met her eyes. "It should have just sent."

Grace opened her inbox, and there it was, sitting bold and unread. She looked at Cara. "I really can't thank you enough for this."

Cara shut her laptop and smiled. "I want this street to feel safe again. For her." She tipped her chin toward Lucy.

"I want that too," Grace replied.

Another chain of events was beginning, ushered in with a knock.

* * *

Jo was already standing in front of the boutique when Grace appeared on the street.

"What the hell are you doing? Why were you up there?" Jo sounded worried, but also annoyed.

"I have video. Of the murderers."

Jo froze. Her mouth dropped open. "Did you just say 'murderers'? Plural?"

Grace nodded, then explained seeing the flashing red light coming from Cara's apartment. She gave Jo a basic rundown of the past half hour, leaving out how sweet Lucy looked as she slept, and then told her that Cara had sent the video to her email.

Jo's eyes flared wide. "Is your laptop in the car?"

With a nod of confirmation from Grace, the women took off down the street, where Jo's SUV was parked. Grace was so eager to get to her computer, she pulled the door handle before Jo had a chance to unlock it. After a few seconds of Jo fumbling with her keys, Grace heard the doors unlock, and she flung hers open, reaching for the laptop she'd left on the floor of the passenger seat, covered by one of Jo's designer scarves. *Probably not the best cover. Someone would definitely want to steal that, too.* She opened the computer and typed in her password, only then remembering to shut the door.

Grace's laptop was at ten percent. It wasn't enough time to do anything major, and she'd have to charge it later if she wanted to catch up on the latest season of *Love is Blind*, but it was enough to view the video and send it to Sean over Jo's hotspot.

Grace went right to her email, double-clicking on the message from Cara. The file only took a few seconds to download, and in her haste, Grace clicked in the wrong place before correctly selecting the file.

Jo was sitting in the passenger seat of the SUV, watching Grace intently.

The video loaded quickly and played automatically. Grace went to the 10:35 pm mark and waited for everything to unfold. She handed over the laptop to Jo, pointing out how to speed up the video when she wanted to see the figures leave the studio.

It had to only be a few minutes that passed as Jo watched, her expression blank. It felt like hours to Grace. Jo clicked a few buttons, to speed the video along, Grace assumed, and finally she looked straight ahead, through the windshield. Jo smacked the back of her head against her seat. "This doesn't tell us *anything*. It's impossible to make out who those people are."

"No, Jo, *we* can't make out who those people are. *We* don't have the technology for that. Luckily, there are people who train for this kind of thing." Grace tilted her head.

Jo hesitated for a moment, staring at her knuckles, bending them over and over, as if she were checking her fingers still worked. Then she looked up at Grace and nodded. She was ready to go to the police.

Grace forwarded the email, then texted Sean.

Check your inbox.

Chapter 27

When Grace was younger, there was nothing more exciting to her than a school field trip. The location didn't matter; all options guaranteed memories with friends, new experiences, teachers who couldn't possibly keep a watchful eye on everything at once, and a perfectly portioned Lunchable, complete with a Kit Kat. When she got really lucky, her mom let her bring a disposable camera to capture the highlights, though Grace had a habit of putting her finger in front of the lens.

The night before a trip, sleep was always fleeting. Grace would toss around her blankets dramatically, get out of bed to peer in the moonlight at the outfit she'd set out to make sure she still liked it, and daydream about what she'd buy in the gift shop with the ten-dollar bill her mom had slipped into her lunchbox. Often, she'd look at her alarm clock and see that it was the wee hours of the morning, worried that daylight might never come.

At the time, she thought these would be the most difficult waits of her life.

If only she could see herself now.

* * *

It had been three days since Grace had sent Cara's baby monitor video over to Sean. He'd got on his computer right away and watched it.

He'd been so shocked by what he saw that he called Grace immediately.

"How did you get this? We asked the neighbors if they had any information."

Grace rehashed her spotting the red light and her interaction with Cara and Lucy.

"Wow. You really are coming for my job. You're really something, Grace."

It had taken everything in Grace not to giggle like a schoolgirl in reply.

Sean said he didn't have the tools to improve the quality, which meant the video would need to be sent to a specialized team. He didn't have a timeline for when they'd get it back.

Grace texted him every morning, in case he forgot they'd been working together on this case, so he should feel socially obligated to update her with any news. To his credit, he replied to her with endless patience and not a bit of snark each time.

"You know you'll be the first person I call when I know anything."

Grace liked the idea of being the first person Sean would call, about anything.

Jo was too anxious to accomplish anything of much importance. The downtime would be well spent working out more details for the silent auction, or which of Garrett's pieces they would use in the permanent exhibit at the art center, but Jo couldn't concentrate on anything.

So they started a puzzle.

It was a thousand-piece puzzle of the Eiffel Tower, which Jo had casually mentioned she'd seen a dozen times and Grace had no interest in visiting (though she kept this to herself). Jo had dug the puzzle up from the closet of one of her spare bedrooms and plopped it down on the table in the breakfast nook.

Grace had looked at her expectantly, wondering if the Eiffel Tower or puzzles were a clue to help solve Garrett's murder, but when she asked, Jo explained it was just a puzzle. She was tired, she was frustrated, and she simply wanted to do this damn puzzle. So, Grace had poured each of them a glass of white wine, used a knife to cut open the puzzle box, and dumped the pieces onto the table.

Everyone knows the "right" way to put together a puzzle is to start with the outside edges. These pieces are easiest to find because they have at least one flat side. It didn't take them long to do this part, maybe half an hour. The ease and speed with which they completed the puzzle's frame turned out to be nothing beyond a false promise, though. Another hour into it and they'd only laid about two dozen more pieces.

Grace thought about jokingly asking Jo if she'd ever watched a YouTube video on how to solve a puzzle, like she'd done with solving a murder, but it was clear Jo was distraught over their slow progress. Her head was in her hands, fingertips perched near each temple, a scowl resting on her lips. Maybe the puzzle was a metaphor to her, another thing she was missing the pieces of, that she didn't want someone else to do for her, that was taking too long and wearing down too much of her resolve.

Garrett had been dead for three months, and still, they were missing most of the picture, it seemed. By now it was lunchtime, and Grace asked Jo if she wanted her to make them something. She'd given a curt nod and not offered any suggestions of what she was craving, so Grace stood up and browsed the pantry, eventually pulling out pasta and a jar of Alfredo sauce before going to the fridge to find chicken.

It wouldn't be as good as Tony's, but it would feed them. Plus, she would get the chance to use the pot-filler.

Five hours later, Jo screamed as Grace slid the last puzzle piece into place. They had only paused to eat lunch, then had taken two or three short bathroom breaks each as the wine hit. They'd finished the first bottle quickly, only a swig left in the second. Grace felt tipsy and light. She was a puzzle *master*, a devoted friend, and great at drinking wine. She and Jo jumped to their feet, grabbing each other's arms and spinning around in a circle like they were in some sort of upper-fueled session of ring-around-the-rosy. They were so busy celebrating this little win, their own little view of the Eiffel Tower, that Grace didn't even hear her phone go off. Once she'd poured the remainder of the wine down the drain and Jo had excused herself for a nap, Grace grabbed it and saw two missed calls from Sean, along with a text.

Call me. We have our guy.

Grace could hear her heartbeat in her ears as she stared at the screen. She needed to wait until she knew Jo's door was shut. Jo was too fragile right now – she couldn't tell her it was all over until it was a done deal. At the sound of the now familiar *click*, she rushed toward Garrett's office to call Sean back. As she shut the door, she pressed the call button.

It only rang once before Sean's voice was in her ear. She'd expected him to sound elated at being able to give her good news, but his tone was somber.

"Grace, is Jo with you?"

"No, I waited until she went upstairs. I didn't want to give her false hope until I knew everything."

Sean let out a sigh. He sounded exhausted.

"My guys were able to make improvements to the video. To be honest, I don't even know how they do it, it's not my area of expertise. They were able to get a clear enough shot that they're confident they've identified our suspects, so we brought them in this morning. One folded right away. A full confession, mostly because he hadn't been the one calling the shots and was hoping he'd get a lesser sentence if he came out with it."

Grace had waited so long for these words, they didn't feel real. For three months, she'd woken up with the knowledge that Garrett's killer was out there, spending time with friends, enjoying good food, laughing at jokes. All things Garrett would never be able to do again. This would be closure, for her, for Jo, for the whole team working the case. She thought about poor Amy, one son lost to violence and another struggling to keep his head above the surface due to drugs. She needed this, she needed answers.

"Grace..."

Something in the way Sean said her name made her stomach tighten.

"Sean... what's the matter? This is good news, right? We know who killed Garrett, we can move on from this whole thing."

"I don't think Jo is going to be moving on from this for a long time, Grace."

And then he told her who killed Garrett. And for a second she wondered if it would have been better to let this case go unsolved.

Chapter 28

It felt odd, Grace thought, to know something that was going to change someone's life forever; to be at the point in the investigation where there was no turning back. They'd done what they set out to do, and soon Jo and everyone who knew her and Garrett would know who killed him.

Grace had pictured how proud and accomplished she might feel in this moment, yet here in the present, she felt her chest tighten with discomfort.

To keep her hands and her mind busy, Grace got to work cleaning the main floor of Jo's home. There wasn't much to do as Gloria ran a tight ship, but she managed to throw a few expired condiments out of the fridge, organize the pantry, and wipe some fingerprints off the powder room mirror. She had a cloth and Windex in hand when she heard the creak of stairs and froze.

Shit. I should have been practicing what to say to her.

She turned just as Jo entered the room, looking groggy but refreshed. She halted and gave Grace a bemused look as she eyed the cleaner. "What are you doing? Did you forget what I'm paying you for?"

Grace tried to think of what a parent or therapist might say to someone to ease the pain of what Jo was about to learn, but her mind was a blank slate.

"They have him," she stammered.

Jo's confusion deepened for a moment. "You mean they… they have the person who killed Garrett?"

Grace placed the cleaner and cloth down on the breakfast nook table and took a few slow steps toward Jo as she nodded.

"And you know? They told you who it is?"

The overwhelming urge to hug Jo came over Grace, but she stood her ground. "Yes," she answered.

The expression on Jo's face didn't change for a moment. She was shocked, clearly. And then she said, "Don't tell me."

It was Grace's turn to be confused. Was Jo really going to go this far just to sink into a pit of denial?

But then she spoke again. "I'm going to go change, and then we will drive to the police station. I want to see their face for myself." And with that, she turned and left the room.

There was no time to call Andre. Besides, once Andre knew the truth, so would Gloria, and then Amy.

"I cannot process this information with all of them in my ear," Jo said as she shut the passenger door. Grace offered to drive, worried that Jo wasn't in the right head space to operate a motor vehicle. There was a ravenous edge in Jo's voice, like she was starving for information, for closure, for revenge.

Grace drove carefully due to a light snow that had begun to fall, holding steady at five miles below the speed limit. It was the kind of snow that both children and adults could appreciate; it made for a beautiful view out your living room window, but wasn't substantial enough to keep you housebound. Mixed in with the snow were streaks of trees and streetlamps, lights that reminded Grace of unreliable rides at a state fair, strokes of color and nausea. The whole world seemed to be moving in slow motion, blurry and unsettling.

At a stoplight, Grace looked over at Jo. She was staring straight ahead, not bothering to check out the decorations or the snow. She looked defensive yet frail in the sort of way a puppy might look at the pound. Grace thought about Jo's strength and poise and tried to convince herself this was all going to work out fine. But a voice in the back of her mind was whispering, *She'll never be OK again.*

What if she had never moved to Philadelphia? *Maybe then the murder would have gone unsolved. Could that have been a better outcome?*

If the roads had been worse, Grace could have delayed Jo's suffering a little bit longer. Jo had so graciously let Grace into her world, and now Grace would do anything to avoid that world crumbling around her. But in no time, they pulled into the slush-filled lot in front of the station, and as she put the car in park, she heard Jo's seatbelt release.

Will she be glad to know? Will the truth make up for the unimaginable loss?

Grace felt like she might be in a fever dream, her palms and underarms sweaty despite the crisp breeze that smacked her in the face as they climbed out of the car. Jo's walk was aggressive, determined, and Grace struggled to keep up with her as they climbed the short flight of stairs up to the station and stepped into the lobby. Warmth washed over her and she squinted as she went from dreary outdoors to harsh fluorescent lights. It smelled like burnt coffee. She wondered if someone had emptied the pot and been too lazy to brew another one.

Jo was walking toward the front desk, but Grace held back, suddenly feeling as though she were overstepping. She didn't hear what Jo said to the officer over the hum of office chatter and a radio commercial for a local roofing company, but then the woman picked up a phone, and within a minute, several officers were walking down a hallway toward them.

Grace's breathing hitched as she eyed Sean. His hands were clasped near his belt buckle and he had a serious, professional look on his face. When he spotted her, he gave her a small, quick smile, then it was back to business. She wished she could hug him, go to him for comfort. Because in a few minutes she would have to comfort Jo, and she wasn't sure she was cut out for it.

Jo said something to Sean, but Grace didn't hear this either. Another officer motioned for Jo to follow them, and Jo turned toward Grace, her face still stern.

"Come on," she said, and then fell into line behind the man. Sean waited for the women to pass, then followed behind Grace, his hand brushing the small of her back for a moment, a little reminder that he was there. The hallway was crowded, a mess of people coming and going. Grace tried to think of what sort of crime happens most in the winter. She wished Maya was here. Not just for her little facts, but to help Jo. Jo needed someone maternal, soothing. Was Grace really who anyone would want holding their hand through one of the worst moments of their life?

As they stopped in front of a heavy metal door, the thought triggered something in Grace's mind, and without warning she was replaying some of the worst moments in her own life: finding Garrett's body, her first heartbreak, the death of her grandmother with the bland spaghetti, the accident she and her parents were lucky to walk away from.

"You ready?" Sean asked Jo, and she gave him a frenzied nod in return.

And as the door creaked open, Grace realized that this moment, the moment she watched Jo come face to face with Garrett's killer, was going to shoot right to the top of both their lists.

"D–daddy?"

Chapter 29

Malcolm sat at a table across from another officer, two cups of coffee steaming between them.

He looked at Jo with pleading eyes, and Grace felt like she might have to look away. The knowledge that it was Malcolm who betrayed Jo had nearly eaten her alive on the ride to the station. How was he even functioning since Garrett's death? How was he so OK?

"My girl," he said softly.

"Don't call me that," Jo said coldly. "Don't even use my name. Don't call me anything. Just tell me what you did. And why you did it."

It sounded as though there was a small scuffle behind them, and Grace turned to see an officer carrying a few extra chairs. The room was silent, other than the scrape of metal on concrete, and Grace and Sean took two of the seats.

"I'm going to stand for this," Jo said as an officer approached her, her eyes locked on her father.

Malcolm looked at his hands on the table and let out a slow breath.

"I'm not sure where to start but…"

"How about the beginning, you absolute monster?" Jo crossed her arms over her chest. Her legs looked shaky. Grace wished she would sit.

Malcolm gave a slow nod, and started to tell his story.

"I'm afraid that I had fallen on some hard times over the past few years. Jack and I have always been rather old-fashioned when it comes to our business. We like to invest in what we know, what we understand. And that strategy worked for decades, no use fixing what isn't broken. But as technology advanced and it became more and more lucrative to invest in the tech space, I guess we just… fell behind."

"So you made some bad investments. And what about your gambling debts?" Jo's eyes narrowed as she spoke. Grace was astonished that Jo hadn't collapsed yet. The room had started to feel stuffed and uncomfortable, and the smell of cheap coffee and someone's cologne wasn't helping.

Malcolm rolled his shoulders back, avoiding Jo's penetrating gaze. "Yes, that was… that was an unfortunate factor in all of this, too. I'm afraid luck hasn't been on my side lately."

Jo laughed so loud, Grace jumped, and she saw a few of the others do the same.

"Oh, I feel terrible for you," Jo gibed.

Though it mattered very little in the grand scheme of things, the damage Malcolm was suffering at each of Jo's little comments showed on his face.

"Anyway," he continued, head down, "I'd been keeping close tabs on any news of Garrett's success. I'd noted that he'd had some large sales, was catching the eye of a lot of big names. I know you keep a tight watch on your money, Jo, but… your husband is not a careful man. I know his strengths don't lie in the business side of things, and I was hoping that his casual attitude when it came to money would give me a way in."

"Into what?" Jo's words were firm and clipped.

"Into Garrett's bank account. And possibly yours."

Jo didn't react right away, and when she did, her words were not aimed at Malcolm, but toward one of the officers. "I think I will sit, actually. It seems this might take a while."

The man grabbed another chair for Jo, and she took a seat across from Malcolm.

"So. You wanted my money to pay off your debts."

Malcolm finally looked at her, but instead of remorse, he wore opposition, like Jo had gotten him all wrong, like he deserved a chance to defend himself. "No! No, no, it wasn't like that. Not in the long term. There was a deal, a *huge* high-end hotel deal that a colleague presented to me. The issue was that he was on a time crunch, and he needed my answer relatively quickly. I had a few weeks to make it all happen. You and Garrett seemed to be living large, not hurting for cash, so I thought if I could access your accounts, I could take out a small loan, then return it. With interest. So I went to Jack and..."

Jo gasped. "Jack. Jack is involved with this as well?"

Sean cleared his throat and Jo turned to him. "He's currently being questioned a few doors over. We actually found him first, and within seconds, he threw your father under the bus. Let us know it was all his idea."

Jo's head jerked back to Malcolm. "So you're as bad at choosing your friends as you are at choosing your investments." When Malcolm didn't respond, she continued. "Well, go on. Tell me this plan."

Malcolm brought his hands together. "It was never supposed to go as far as it did. We visited Garrett's studio in June, and that's where we met Vivian."

Grace felt her core tighten. Was Vivian involved after all? She saw Jo's eyes flare wide at the mention of Vivian's name.

"We realized that if we wanted access to Garrett's accounts, we'd need to go through her. Or, we needed to get rid of her. She was too involved, too careful. Jack called in a favor to a well-known lawyer in the city. Some might call it blackmail. Now that he'd ratted me out, I might as well explain what kind of man he is as well. Anyway, the lawyer agreed to take Vivian on as her assistant and pay her well above what she was worth. We told Vivian that she'd caught our attention. That she was a valuable asset who could use a strong woman to mentor her in her career. Garrett would never understand what it was like to be a woman trying to climb the corporate ladder, I'd reminded her."

Everyone in the room seemed to be rapt with Malcolm's story. The only thing that tore Grace away, for just a moment, was Sean's arm wrapping around the back of her chair.

"Vivian took the bait just like we'd hoped. She couldn't believe her new salary. She was so eager to get on the payroll, when we told her she'd need to keep her job a secret because of the nature of her boss's clients, she agreed, no questions asked. As soon as Vivian put in her two weeks' notice, we called Garrett, asking him if he'd ever consider Jack taking him on as a client. Told him that as his business grew, he'd need someone more experienced to steer him in the right direction. He told us about Vivian quitting. He couldn't believe the lucky timing."

Malcolm paused, and looked at Jo. "My girl, I promise…"

"No," she said. "No promises, only answers. Tell me how all of this leads to my husband's death."

Malcolm picked up his coffee and took a sip, and Grace felt so odd, facing him in a big group. He was like a gorilla at the zoo, everyone watching to see his next trick. Although, that was insulting to gorillas.

He cleared his throat. "When we got access, two issues were immediately apparent: you and Garrett had separate accounts, and Garrett's were nearly drained. We started to sift through Garrett's transactions and realized he was spending any profits he made on promoting the business, and then some. We could see that you were keeping the business afloat by depositing large chunks each week. It never stayed in the account long, and each month the amounts grew larger. I'd hoped I could avoid dipping into your joint account by accessing Garrett's, or maybe only taking a small enough amount that you didn't notice. But neither of those were an option."

Malcolm leaned into the table and looked to Jo again. "He was draining you, Jojo. And if it continued down the path he was on, he would eventually drain you dry. Everything I'd given you, everything you worked for would be gone. And so, like Vivian, I decided that the best thing would be for him to go."

Grace had expected Jo to lunge over the table, screaming obscenities in Malcolm's face, for her to claw his skin raw. Instead, she sat stone-still.

One of the officers asked the next question.

"And how did you enact this plan you made? To get rid of Garrett?"

Malcolm leaned back in his chair slightly, and Grace said a silent prayer for the legs to come out from under him. When all four legs were back on the ground, she went back to listening.

"I made an email account for Garrett, one we had full access to. I gave the excuse that we'd need some verification codes when we logged in to Garrett's bank account, but the Gmail account allowed me to communicate with Hannah without Garrett seeing. Hiring a replacement for Vivian was the easiest part, because we weren't looking for a particularly exceptional candidate."

That stung, Grace had to admit.

"Jack had to go along with my plan. We've known each other for far too long, know each others' secrets, as we've proven tonight. It was him who had the contact who was able to cut the camera transmissions. But I was the one who was able to get the strychnine."

"The poison," Jo said, her body eerily still.

"Yes. The poison. A few years ago, one of my buildings developed a rat problem. It was an effective rat poison, toxic at small doses, and completely colorless. It was easy to mix into a drink. It had a bitter taste that was less noticeable when mixed with a potent alcohol like scotch. And it was easy to get, just sitting on the shelves in your local home improvement store. We set a date and time with Garrett to get together and discuss the future of his business, to toast to his success."

Malcolm looked at the officer sitting closest to Jo, the one who had been questioning him before everyone else entered the room. "I reminded him that Jo and I don't discuss finances, so to keep it to himself. He was fine with that. He wanted it to be a surprise to Jo, that he didn't need her anymore."

From the corner of her eye, Grace spotted something on Jo's face. A tear.

When we showed up at the studio around 10:30, after we confirmed the security cameras were down, Garrett was happy to see us. I watched him closely. I could tell he didn't taste anything in his drink. Half an hour later, he started to choke and his head flopped onto his desk. When Jack checked for a pulse, he felt nothing. So... we packed up the poison, scotch, and glasses, and left."

His tone was so nonchalant, like he was telling someone the story of how he'd gotten out of a speeding ticket or how his latest vacation went. He spoke like a man who didn't regret his crime, only that he was caught. It made Grace sick to her stomach.

"And what about the painting?" Sean asked.

"Oh, uh, I spotted that on the way out. I knew Jack had some connections in the art world, so we took it. Figured anything we got from selling it would be icing on the cake." Malcolm let out a cough and grabbed his coffee cup to take another sip. Grace saw his hand shake as he sat it back on the table.

"After Garrett died, I thought maybe I could still make the deal happen. I came up with a new plan to have Jo invest in the hotel chain. I was going to tell her she didn't need to lift a finger, Jack could manage the account since I was also investing. In reality, we would simply pull money from Jo's account to invest in my name as well. We could lie to Jo about her returns, until we had good results. She'd never have to know."

Malcolm ran a hand through his white hair. "Only Jo wouldn't even have a conversation with me about it. I hadn't even had the chance to bring it up with her when my contact got in touch to let me know the deal was off."

By then, Jo was so upset following Garrett's death that she didn't want to have a conversation with Malcolm that went any deeper than the weather. When Malcolm reached out to the hotel developer to ask him for more time, he told him he was rescinding his offer.

It was the loudest silence Grace had ever heard. Everyone sat, their eyes going between Jo and her father, the revelation that Garrett's death hadn't even worked in Malcolm's favor hanging in the room like a toxic fog.

"So you killed my husband for NOTHING," Jo screamed as she stood. An officer put a hand on her arm gently, just in case. But she didn't lurch toward Malcolm.

"He was DRAINING YOU DRY!" Malcolm yelled back, cheeks red. His white hair making him look like a deranged Santa Claus.

"Guess what, Daddy? I'm *rich*. I'm so fucking rich that if you had just come to me and asked for the money, I would have given it to you. And I wouldn't have needed you to pay me back. That's how rich I am!"

Malcolm's eyes went wide and his face started to move from red to white.

"You had so little faith in me, in Ava, that you couldn't comprehend that we had surpassed you and your skills. You didn't think a woman could do what you did. And you're right. We did more. And we did all of it better. You've been rambling on about your legacy for decades, but your head was so far up your ass that you didn't see that *I am your legacy*. I am all of your best parts and none of this… this poison that you have in you."

Jo spat the last words out, then wiped her mouth with her sleeve. Finally, the tears flowed. They streamed down her face as she gasped for air. Between breaths, she continued.

"Only now this will be your legacy, Daddy. You'll be the man who invested his son-in-law's life only to get cut out of the deal. You'll be the man who took the one thing your daughter loved most so you could get your hands on money you can't even take with you when you're gone."

Jo let out a scream, and Grace leapt to her feet, grabbing the arm of the officer opposite.

And then, Jo was falling, and Grace and the officer were supporting all of her weight. Sean stepped in to help, grabbing around her waist.

"Let's find a place for her to lie down," one of the men said.

And as Jo was gently dragged out of the room, she used the rest of her strength to yell, "Hell is filled with rich men like you!"

Chapter 30

They say there is no cure for grief, only the mild balm of the passing of time.

The case wrapped up just before Thanksgiving. Grace had plans to go home for the holiday and gorge herself on her mom's pumpkin pie, maybe work on her winter tan. But when days passed by without Jo getting out of bed, she called her parents to say she wasn't going to make it. Jo needed Grace more than Grace needed pie.

Her parents booked their flights to Philly right away.

Grace had climbed into bed with Jo, who had the curtains drawn, to tell her she was staying.

"My parents decided to make the trip," she whispered. "Isn't that exciting?"

Jo, whose head had been covered with her comforter, threw the blanket off with a huff. "You're not having them stay in that tiny little apartment? Absolutely not. You'll all stay here."

When Grace picked up her parents at the airport, they'd hugged her so hard she was worried something was dislocated. She'd never been so grateful for their selfless love.

Molly also stayed at Jo's for Thanksgiving and, as it turned out, she was an amazing cook and gracious host.

Grace's parents mentioned over and over that they'd never stayed in a hotel as nice as Jo's house. Jo spent most of her time in her room, but came out for Thanksgiving dinner, and Grace even caught her laughing at one of Grace's dad's corny jokes.

They each took turns going around the table to say what they were thankful for. Molly said her dog and her daughter and tousled Jo's (now clean) hair. Grace's dad said his family and his trivia buddies, which her mom echoed, subbing her book club buddies for trivia. It was too early for Grace to say she was thankful for Sean, so instead she said she was thankful for family, friends, and fresh starts.

She was just about to tell Jo that she didn't have to participate when Jo lifted her glass in the air. "To beauty," she said, "and the people who find it in the darkest places."

Chapter 31

Seven Months Later

Grace and Jo stood in the lobby of Garrett's studio, staring down at a table, another mystery begging to be solved.

"Where the hell are the big scissors?!" Jo yelled, throwing her hands in the air.

"Shhh, calm down," Kelly said. She pushed between them, holding out a comically large pair of scissors. "I've got them! I just wanted to get a selfie!" She set the scissors down on the table and wrapped an arm around each of her friends.

"Everything is great. Our day is finally here."

It was the grand opening of the Baros-Dewitt Art Center, and the three of them had spent the last seven months since Garrett's murder was solved creating a space for the community to be proud of.

It was their time to celebrate – and not just about the opening.

For starters, Malcolm and Jack were each looking at life in prison for their role in Garrett's murder.

Molly had also sold her house and moved in with Jo. It only made sense, as Malcolm *hadn't* been able to make his alimony payments. Jo and Grace's basement detective agency was remodeled into a private suite, the whiteboard moved into storage.

The model, Olivia Olsen, was able to get two more women to come forward against Wyatt Randall, and thanks to their testimonies Wyatt was sentenced to a year in jail, required to register as a sex offender, fined, and ostracized by the art community.

Jo still didn't fully trust law enforcement. It would take time to change a mindset so intertwined with her life experiences, but she'd started seeing a therapist at Grace's suggestion, and she was making progress. The week before the Arts Center's grand opening, Sean had received his invitation, along with a bouquet of wildflowers with a note attached.

Thanks for being one of the good ones. xo, Jo.

He took a photo of them and sent it to Grace. *Don't be too jealous or anything. A woman sent me flowers.*

After a minute or so, his phone vibrated.

And she did that HERSELF. She said it would be weird to ask me to send flowers to my own boyfriend. Much more normal to have my best friend send them.

Grace walked around the Arts Center, looking for anything that might be out of place. She wanted this day to be perfect for Jo after the last year. Who would have thought that solving your husband's murder could be as painful as finding out he was dead?

Grace thought often about what Maya had said when she'd told her they'd caught Garrett's killer.

"You did it! You actually did it! Did you know that around 42.2 percent of murders actually go unsolved?"

As painful as the truth had been, Grace was glad that Garrett didn't end up another cold case. His parents, his brother, his friends, and Jo were no longer keeping themselves awake at night, wondering what happened. There was something peaceful about that. It gave everyone the permission to carry on with their lives, even if, in fleeting moments each day, they still felt the sharp pain of Garrett's loss.

Grace thought that when Garrett's murder was solved, she'd go back to Florida. At first, it was Jo and her mental state that kept her in Philadelphia. But as the life flickered back into Jo's eyes, Grace realized that she'd actually accomplished most of what she'd hoped when she decided to move. She had independence, friends, a purpose. She had a hand to hold and stories to tell. Give all of it up to climb back into her comfort zone, or stay and see what else she can do? The choice was obvious.

Grace felt something on her shoulder, and a moment later, Jo whispered in her ear, "It's not too late to turn this place into a detective agency. We could call it 'The Temp Agency' as a throwback to your roots."

Grace rolled her eyes as she turned to face Jo. "Absolutely not. We've put too much work into this. Besides, I never want to get into a mascot costume again."

"LADIESSSSS!" Kelly called out from the front door. "It's time!"

The ribbon cutting was scheduled for noon, and Kelly always stayed on schedule.

Grace was shocked and honored at how many people showed up. Sean's entire team was there, one of them deep into a conversation with Hilda that Grace could only assume was about the "essence" of the building.

Gloria and Andre's grandchildren were playing with Pete the landlord's kids, while he and his wife asked Ava about the difference between term and whole life insurance. Laila, Mandy, and the boys were walking through the studio space. Laila had come in for a tour a few weeks ago, and her art was already hanging on the walls. As it turned out, she was a well-rounded child prodigy, almost as good an artist as she was a singer.

Molly and Amy were fussing over the giggly baby in Molly's arms. It was his first trip to the United States, but Jo's brother said the plane ride went smoothly. Alex wasn't able to be there because he'd started a new job, but he had sent flowers that sat at the front desk.

Sean was holding Grace's phone so he could get her parents and Maya on video for the ribbon cutting.

Grace grabbed for Jo's hand and gave it a squeeze. Jo squeezed back, and her head dropped to rest on Grace's shoulder. They had met one another in the worst circumstance, but they'd brought out the best in each other.

The crowd let out a cheer for the women, and Jo, Grace, and Kelly waved at everyone who'd come out to support them. Kelly stepped forward, giant scissors in hand, as the countdown began.

"5 – 4 – 3 – 2 – 1!"

Snip.

Ten months ago, Grace would have let Kelly and Jo take the spotlight. She would have found a place in the back of the crowd and hoped no one took much notice of her, unsure if she even deserved to take up space. Since then, she'd made a home out of her little apartment, met the kind of best friend who never forgets to check in, fallen for a man in uniform, posed as a stripper, started a cleaning company, got over her fear of the gym, sent several men to jail, and broken her lifelong streak of never having solved a murder.

Each of these things would become part of the story she'd tell about her life; a story filled with lessons on love and friendship, grief and forgiveness.

And those lessons? Those are the most important legacy anyone can leave.

Acknowledgements

It takes so many people to bring a book to life. And it takes so many moments for a writer to be brave enough to share their work with the world.

The moment that started it all for me was when Ms. Colgan read my essay on my grandmother's funeral out loud to my 7th-grade English class. I'm sure she's read plenty of essays out loud since then, but it was the first time someone told me I was a good writer. My skills were further tested in class by Mrs Dupnock/Gilbert. and Mrs Janisko, may she rest in peace.

After high school, I headed to Indiana University of Pennsylvania's (now defunct) journalism department, where a full crew of amazing staff and faculty put my skills to the test. None of these faculty members challenged me more than Randy Jesick, and I'm forever thankful. (If there is a mistake on a proper noun in this book, please don't give me a 0.)

And while these educators made a lasting impact on me, I've been equally changed by the people who support me daily.

To Mike, who is the first person to read all of my work, thank you for being my partner in all things. [Insert graphic of a corgi with a knife here]. And to Max and Charlotte, my two hopeful authors/YouTubers/graphic designers/teachers/video game programmers: Your passion and creativity inspire me every day. I am so lucky to be your mom. I love the three of you more than can fit on this page. (And more pages would be expensive to print.)

While I'd like to thank my dad, Roger, and my sister, Lilac, I especially need to thank my mother, Bonnie, for her love and devotion to the show *Murder, She Wrote*. Not every child was familiar with Jessica Fletcher, and it served me well as an adult.

I'd be lost without my friends Jordan, Katrina, Laura, and Nicole, who are always willing to read my latest project and give feedback. I'm excited that you can now add one of my books on Goodreads. You deserve it.

I've been blessed with a huge group of women who cheer me on in every phase of life, so I also need to mention Ashley, Brittany, Sam, Victoria, Liz, Heidi, Elyse, Jana, Raphaela, Kuchanda, Alex, Blake, the IUP girls, the gym buddies, Lauren, Janina, and our favorite neighbors, the Bookish in the Burgh ladies, and my sister-in-law Stef.

My oldest friend, Andria, also took my author photos. Thank you for supporting me from literal infancy.

While unconventional, I need to thank my therapist, Laurie, for talking me through this whole process, like she talked me through many other big life changes. I hope there isn't some odd reverse-HIPAA rule against saying her name. Mental health matters.

My agent, James, deserves a gold medal for the number of emails I send him about things that won't happen for months. Thank you for seeing my potential. And to the team at JABberwocky who have helped with various things behind the scenes, I'm so grateful.

Gemma, thank you for picking me out of the slush pile and for passing me to Ella, who has been a dream editor. The team at Datura made my debut experience such a positive one, and I'm sure some people had a hand in my book's creation and promotion that I don't even know. But to Caroline, April, Hayley, Raeesa, Dan (x2), Christiana, and El, thank you for using your unique gifts to help bring *Grace & Jo* to life.

And finally, to you. Whoever you are, wherever you are, I hope that you know your dreams are worth pursuing. If you're looking for a sign to do the thing, this is it.

(Just know that if you belonged here and I forgot you, I'll feel bad about it for the rest of my life. I'm going to blame the ADHD.)

About the Author

Jess Mey is a writer and member of the late-ADHD-diagnosis club. She has a degree in journalism and public relations from Indiana University of Pennsylvania. Jess left her job as a marketing copywriter in 2017 to be a stay-at-home mom, freelancing in her spare time (when she had a break from reading *The Little Blue Truck* to her son for the 238th time). When she's not writing or reading, you can find her at the thrift store, planning a vacation, or playing *The Sims 4*, all while drinking iced coffee, no matter the season. Jess lives in the Pittsburgh suburbs with her husband, two children, and their corgi, Clementine.